A TALE OF TWO DUKES

EMMA ORCHARD

B

Boldwood

First published in Great Britain in 2025 by Boldwood Books Ltd.

Copyright © Emma Orchard, 2025

Cover Design by Rachel Lawston

Cover Images: Rachel Lawston

The moral right of Emma Orchard to be identified as the author of this work has been asserted in accordance with the Copyright, Designs and Patents Act 1988.

All rights reserved. No part of this book may be reproduced in any form or by any electronic or mechanical means, including information storage and retrieval systems, without written permission from the author, except for the use of brief quotations in a book review. This book is a work of fiction and, except in the case of historical fact, any resemblance to actual persons, living or dead, is purely coincidental.

Every effort has been made to obtain the necessary permissions with reference to copyright material, both illustrative and quoted. We apologise for any omissions in this respect and will be pleased to make the appropriate acknowledgements in any future edition.

A CIP catalogue record for this book is available from the British Library.

Paperback ISBN 978-1-83633-862-8

Large Print ISBN 978-1-83633-863-5

Hardback ISBN 978-1-83633-861-1

Trade Paperback ISBN 978-1-80635-291-3

Ebook ISBN 978-1-83633-864-2

Kindle ISBN 978-1-83633-865-9

Audio CD ISBN 978-1-83633-856-7

MP3 CD ISBN 978-1-83633-857-4

Digital audio download ISBN 978-1-83633-858-1

This book is printed on certified sustainable paper. Boldwood Books is dedicated to putting sustainability at the heart of our business. For more information please visit https://www.boldwoodbooks.com/about-us/sustainability/

Boldwood Books Ltd, 23 Bowerdean Street, London, SW6 3TN

www.boldwoodbooks.com

For my wonderful editor, Rachel Faulkner-Willcocks.

PROLOGUE
AUTUMN 1813

Richard stood at the altar in his family's ancient chapel, waiting for his bride. His wedding day – a day he'd often thought would never arrive. He'd had hopes and dreams, years ago, but his life had not been of the kind that encouraged settled habits of domesticity, or even an expectation of surviving till the end of the week. Lately, of course, the matter had become a pressing concern. But if he had ever imagined that mysterious person, his future wife, before the last few months – and he was not admitting, even to himself, that he had – he was perfectly sure he'd not expected her to be someone who loathed him and made little attempt to disguise it.

No, he mused, that wasn't right; she didn't loathe him, because despite everything, she barely knew him. It might be true, of course, that nobody did, and that he'd made sure of that himself, and should not complain. Perhaps when she knew him better, she'd truly hate him; that was a risk he had to take. But currently, she despised him, that was more accurate, and not without cause. It was stingingly ironic, because there were many other women who seemed to think he was rather wonderful, if dangerous, and yet he was marrying this angry, scornful one instead. And he couldn't honestly say he'd have it any other way. She no doubt felt differently. But that, too, was his own fault.

She was vexingly late, probably on purpose, and the congregation stirred restlessly, but he was reasonably confident she wouldn't fail.

There was a subdued bustle at the back of the small chapel now, and he turned, unable to help himself, and watched her progress up the aisle. She was magnificent: an undeniable fact. She'd not arrayed herself in pale colours, as young brides so often did, but that was reasonable, because she was a mature woman of nine and twenty, a mother and a widow. There were other people in the church, her family members rather than his, but he had no attention to spare for any of them, and they might easily not have been there. Her children, he knew, were not present to see their mother marry again and the only father they'd ever known replaced by a stranger.

Viola, Duchess of Winterflood, was wearing a dark red velvet riding habit, rather than the fine day-gown which would be more usual. Probably it was intended as an insult to him, as though she'd just wandered back from a morning's hard riding and strolled casually across to the family chapel to get married, because it wasn't even the second or third most important thing in her busy day. But he didn't care, because she looked so splendid. He'd wager she knew *that* too.

She was tall and voluptuous, fashionably dark – her hair was glossy raven black, in fact, save for the white streak at her widow's peak. She'd not had that, when he'd first known her, but it became her. He had no idea when it had made its appearance – when her first husband had died, perhaps. Her locks were piled up on her queenly head, and topped by an audaciously masculine black beaver hat, such as he might wear himself. A black eye-veil brushed her pale cheeks, and partially concealed her bright, dark, stormy eyes. He wondered, distractingly, what she'd done with her whip. Perhaps he'd find out later.

Her habit was not high-waisted, in the current mode, but made like a man's suit of clothes, at least above the waist: it was tight to her lush body, over a patterned silk waistcoat and a crisp white shirt worn with a rakish black cravat. Her breasts… this wasn't the place or time to be thinking about her breasts. But Jesus, her breasts.

The full velvet skirt swished over the flagstones as she grew closer, on the arm of her brother-in-law, Laurence Da Costa, who seemed a pleasant enough fellow but was a negligible creature beside her, and did not merit so much as a glance from the bridegroom, or anyone else. She stopped at Richard's side and the man melted rapidly away, as if anxious to disassociate himself from the proceedings if he could, perhaps because he feared that the bride was about to start throwing things – hymn books, maybe – or laying about her with the altar candlesticks.

She was here. So she really did mean to go through with it. That was something – everything, in truth, though she most definitely wasn't smiling or looking dewy-eyed with eagerness. If she ever smiled these days, it wasn't at him. Richard had no idea what sort of expression he might have on his face. Naked lust, most likely, rather than any more complicated feelings he might have revealed. Which wasn't calculated to win her over – but then, it wasn't calculated at all. It was a natural, honest reaction to one of the loveliest and most desirable women he'd ever seen in all his varied experience across the world. His reluctant bride.

They spoke the words in turn. His first time saying them – not hers. Her voice was deep for a woman, musical, and entirely devoid of any sort of emotion. She had stripped off her black leather gloves before she put her cold hand in his, so that he could put his ring on her. The other one, he noticed, Edward's ring, was gone now.

When all was done, he stepped forward instinctively to kiss her, and she turned her cheek sharply so that his lips just brushed her skin. The brief contact made her shiver, and he felt it as an electric jolt through his own responsive body, but he had no idea if her reaction was caused by desire or repulsion. Or some dangerous mixture of both. She whispered in his ear, 'You may fuck me, Lord Ventris, but you will never kiss me. That was the agreement.'

He said coolly, 'My apologies, madam. I thought to make a public show of affection, but you're right, of course.'

'Don't forget it again.'

'I assure you, I won't.'

She turned away from him – it would have appeared to the assembled guests that they had shared a tender little private moment instead of a stinging reproach – and they faced the throng together as husband and wife, ready to receive congratulations, her hand steady on his arm. Though he knew it was an illusion, Richard felt as though her touch was burning through the wool of his sleeve and the fine fabric of his shirt, to the skin beneath. Whatever other challenges they faced, and there were many, a lack of fierce mutual desire was not one of them, as they both had good cause to know.

Now she was his. But it was going to be a long, long evening till he could claim her.

1

A FEW WEEKS EARLIER

Viola stood on the steps with her arms wrapped tight around herself and watched as the carriage with its ducal crest rumbled off down the long drive. Loose strands of hair, black and stark white, had worked themselves free and whipped about her face in the strong breeze, blurring her vision along with the tears she had been suppressing. She'd normally be accompanied by a group of excited spaniels of varying ages, but they'd been locked away in the stables till the coach was safely out of the way, or they'd have chased after it. If they'd realised what it signified, they'd have been howling inconsolably, threatening her precious self-control.

Even when the vehicle had vanished from view, she still stood there, gazing pointlessly after it, tracking its progress in her mind. It would – barring accidents – have reached the post road at the edge of the estate before she turned away. And the estate was very large.

When she moved at last, her old governess and closest friend, Emily Naismith, who had been waiting in supportive silence beside her, took her arm and drew her inside the house. 'Let's have some tea,' the older woman said with an effort at cheerfulness. 'You must be chilled, love – I know I am.'

'I'm sorry, Em,' Viola said dully. 'You should not have waited with me in so sharp a wind. You know I don't feel the cold.'

'Nonsense,' said Miss Naismith sturdily. 'Of course I waited.' And then, after a moment's silence: 'They'll be fine. You know they will.'

The footmen sprang to open the doors for the two women, closing them behind them as they passed inside. Viola allowed Emily to draw her through the marble atrium and into the library, where a cheerful fire had dispersed any early autumn chill. Perhaps it wasn't really needed yet, but it was a comforting sight, or should be. There was a large, slightly battered sofa beside the fire, and the two women subsided into it. The big house seemed very quiet suddenly, the crackling of the flames and the shifting of the logs in the grate the only sound. How could a building that was still full of busy people seem so empty, just because two small boys had left it? They were noisy, of course, and always seemed to be in several places at once, sliding down bannisters, jumping on furniture, but it was more than that.

When the Duchess said nothing, staring into the flames in a brown study, Emily persisted in her futile attempts at consolation. 'You cannot doubt that William will take the best possible care of them,' she said softly, flushing a little.

'Of course I do not doubt it. You know I don't.'

The occupants of the coach had been Mr William Muncaster, the local magistrate, his twelve-year-old son, Sam, and Sam's fast friends, Viola's boys. These were two small persons with grand titles: His Grace the Duke of Winterflood, usually known as Ned, and the Honourable Lord Robert Armstrong, Robin, the Duke's younger brother by a mere twenty minutes. The boys would all be studying together at one of England's most distinguished boarding schools, and Mr Muncaster had most kindly agreed to take the twins with him when he delivered his own son to that institution. Viola had some while ago been made to understand, the message given by Mr Muncaster with a gentle concern that had made her eyes smart, that ladies – mothers – did not generally take their sons to school, and it would not be particularly helpful to the lads in question if their doting mama, even if she was a widowed duchess, broke with custom and did so.

Mr Muncaster was a good neighbour and a good friend, as well as being Emily's betrothed, and the Duchess had not the least fear that he would allow her boys to come to any harm while he was with them. But that did not mean that she could regard their prolonged absence with complaisance, nor cease worrying about their safety. She had never been separated from them before in all their almost eleven years. And they were all she had, as a widow of three years' standing. Their father, Edward, had been nigh on thirty years her senior, and had died as the result of a sudden heart attack – some congenital weakness, the doctors had said, which in hindsight the Duke had perhaps long suspected but kept secret from everyone – when his sons had been rising eight years old and she had only been six and twenty.

She shook her head. 'I'm sorry, Em,' she said again. 'I must be very dull company. It will take me a little time to accustom myself to their absence, you know. The silence. And I must, for I need to decide what I shall do. I can't put it off any longer.'

'I know you feel that,' said Miss Naismith softly, entirely ignoring the conventional apology, which was no more than it deserved, between such close friends. 'But does it have to be today?'

The two women were of very different appearance and character. Emily was small and trim, her hair a smooth blonde and her eyes warm blue – the kindest, gentlest face, a much younger Viola had once told her, in the whole world. The Duchess herself was taller, obviously quicker-tempered and more decisive, statuesque in build, and of a dramatic dark colouring that spoke of her mother's Italian background. They had been close since a nervously determined seventeen-year-old Emily had arrived as governess to Mrs Constantine's large family of daughters, among them Viola, a great gangly child only five years her teacher's junior. And Viola knew that soon, she must lose her too.

As if sensing her gloomy thoughts, Miss Naismith said fretfully, 'We can easily postpone the wedding for a while. I hate to leave you alone like this, when you are so bereft – it is unconscionably selfish of me. I am sure William will not mind.'

Her friend and employer smiled wryly. 'I am sure he would mind excessively, and it would be unnatural if he did not. It would be unconscionably selfish of *me* to let you put it off. You shall be married Thursday week as planned, and I shall be there to wish you very happy and cry over you. And you know that I will not be alone here, or not for long – not if I decide to accept Lord Ventris's offer of marriage, outrageous as it is.'

Emily's gentle face was troubled. 'Viola, my dear… please tell me you aren't contemplating such a rash step merely because you don't want to be on your own in this great barn of a house. I could not bear to think that it would be all my fault if you married that odiously rude, disagreeable, untrustworthy man.'

She laughed with genuine amusement. 'My God, Em, do you think me so feeble? If I feared loneliness, I could find quite a dozen ladies who would rush to be my companion, though not one of them, I hope I need not say, could be what you have been to me and always will be. I could ask one of my sisters to stay with me this winter, for that matter: Bea, or Cecilia. No, that is not even the smallest of my reasons for considering the offer, I promise you.'

'Then why...? My dear, putting aside all the rest, you hardly know him. How can you seriously contemplate tying yourself to a stranger so irrevocably? If he has set foot in this house once in the last decade, it must have been when I was absent, and I have so rarely been absent. Or am I mistaken?'

The Duchess said quietly, 'No, you are not mistaken. He has not visited of late years, and I have had no contact at all with him since Edward died and he wrote to condole with me. Probably you even replied to his letter on my behalf – you remember how distracted I was at that time, the boys so shocked and distressed as they were. But I knew him years ago, a little. He and Edward were very attached to each other – they were cousins, as you know, but the age gap was such that they were more like uncle and nephew.'

'If Lord Ventris had in fact been your husband's nephew, it would be illegal for you to marry him.' Emily's tone suggested that she thought the law sadly negligent in this respect. 'And I would be glad of it, for the man is a notorious rake, to say nothing of the rest. And even so, I wonder he was bold enough to write you such an extraordinary letter.'

The missive had come just over a week ago, brought in to the Duchess as she breakfasted with Emily one bright morning. The boys had been with them earlier, consuming improbably large quantities of food and then rushing off together to collect Sam for some mysterious errand that would, in Viola's experience, lead to bruised knees, torn and dirty clothing, and the consumption of another huge meal in order to sustain them in further adventures.

She had not been entirely sure she recognised the hand, her acquaintance with Lord Ventris not having been such that they had ever had occasion to carry out a regular correspondence, but he had scrawled his title and the legend *Ventris Castle* across the paper by way of a frank, so she had known before she opened it that it was from him. Her stomach had lurched at the sight in instinctive recoil, and she had been annoyed with herself for that before she even knew its contents. But when she had unsealed it and read it, and then read it again because she'd feared her eyes were deceiving her and it could not possibly say what she thought it said, she had impulsively uttered highly unladylike words that had had Emily staring at her in shock. Luckily, there had been no footmen or other servants in the room to overhear her curses.

Jumping to her feet, the Duchess had relieved her feelings by striding energetically up and down the small chamber, skirts swishing furiously. Eventually, she turned and blurted out, 'The audacity! The damnable audacity of the man!' She seized up the paper and pressed it into Emily's hands, saying, 'Read it! Only read it. Do not speak a word of censure till you have done so, or you will never get to the end. "Warm recollections of our earlier acquaintance," he says! Oh, I am so angry!'

It was a bolt out of the blue, from someone she had not set eyes on for an age. When she had known him, he had been merely Mr Richard Armstrong, younger half-brother of Mr Tarquin Armstrong. Tarquin was, before the birth of her sons, her husband's nearest male relation and heir. Edward had loathed Tarquin and never seen him if he could help it, but Richard had been a frequent visitor to the Duke of Winterflood's home from his youth, so Viola had encountered him a few months after her marriage.

That had been long ago, when his prospects for advancement were non-existent and he had worked for a living, in trade, despite his noble connections. But a curious quirk of English custom had made him Lord Ventris earlier this summer. Emily had read the news of his elevation to the peerage in the paper one day, and had innocently exclaimed over it, asking if the gentleman in question was not the late Duke's cousin, as the surname was the same. Viola had confirmed that this was true, and told her lightly that Tarquin must be quite furious at the intelligence; he was a jealous-natured, bitter man who had through her own marriage and pregnancy been thwarted of the dukedom he had so long expected to inherit, and now his disreputable younger brother had had a barony and an estate fall into his undeserving lap. Yet Tarquin was still a plain mister with no title and no fortune to speak of, and no chance of either. Or – not if her sons lived.

Tarquin and Richard had shared a father but not a mother, and this was the crucial point she had had to explain to her puzzled friend. The Duchess knew, and the newspaper article confirmed, that Richard's mother had been the youngest daughter of an ancient Border family, whose title by writ could descend through the female line. His mother's oldest sister, lacking brothers, had therefore been Lady Ventris in her own right. When she had died without issue or a sibling living to succeed her, her nephew had stepped into her shoes. He had found himself owner of a castle on a cliff and a great deal of windswept, empty moorland, home chiefly, the London gossip said, to sheep and red deer and scarce but surly inhabitants. It was the sort of place that bred hardiness and independence of spirit in all ranks of society. What would a man of his dark reputation find to do there?

Viola had assumed that Lady Ventris, that great lady of the north, had left her fortune, gained through shrewd marriage alliances, to Richard too; where else would she think to leave it? But the letter she had received told her – along with much more outrageous content – that this was not quite correct.

Richard's irreverent personality came strongly from the page – it was like speaking with him again after so many years. Whether this was a pleasant sensation for her was quite another matter.

When Emily had finished reading, mild blue eyes growing rounder and rounder with every paragraph, she had asked if Lord Ventris was quite mad, so peculiar did the missive appear to her. Even the gentle governess could not wonder at her friend's anger on receiving it. But Emily had never met Richard, and Viola, who had, knew that whatever else he might be, he wasn't deranged.

My dear madam,

It is a long time since we saw each other, and I trust you and the boys are well. I am sure they will be grown tall and strong by now, true Armstrongs in their father's image. I know Edward would have been so proud of them, and of you as their mother.

You will, I am sure, be aware of my accession to the Ventris title in my Aunt Alice's place. I gather it was quite a sensation in the polite world. You might perhaps have presumed, if you thought about me on hearing the news, that I fell heir to the lady's substantial financial assets also, but alas, it is not so. Or at least, not yet.

Aunt's heir was always to be my older cousin, Simon, son of another aunt now sadly deceased. Simon was in holy orders, and a person of whom she greatly approved, and furthermore, had recently engaged himself to be married to a Yorkshire-woman of equally tedious and conspicuous virtue. Every time I met Aunt Ventris of late years, she was pleased to dwell at length on the distinction between Simon's manner of life and my own, to my enormous disadvantage. But poor, dull Simon was carried off by an inflam-

mation of the lungs this last winter, still sadly unwed, and she was left, to her horror, with me. She did not refrain from telling me that she wished that Providence had seen fit to strike down my unworthy person instead of him. No doubt she had a stern word with Providence on the subject too; she was a very grand lady and I am sure they were upon terms.

Feeling her end approaching, my aunt summoned her lawyer and drew up a codicil to her will. Wherever she is now (of which I am by no means certain), she must be chuckling at her own cleverness. She could not keep the estate's lands from me, nor the name and title, but since her fortune came to her by marriage, she was free to dispose of it as she wished. And what she wished was to say that I might have it all with her blessing, as long as by my thirty-fifth birthday, I should be married and the father of a child. One small mercy is that she was not so inconsiderate as to specify the sex of the infant.

You may or may not recollect that I shall achieve that great age in eighteen months' time. I have now in my unworthy hands – you will appreciate the irony – a very large estate comprising many of the most inhospitable sections of the north of England, and scarcely a penny to maintain it, nor the ancient castle set upon it. If I wish to prevent everything falling into utter ruin, I must induce some unfortunate female to marry me very soon. This lady must then embark upon the chancy enterprise of attempting to conceive a child and bring it safe into the world, in the full knowledge that if she does not do so in very short order, through no fault of her own, she will live out the rest of her life penniless, and burdened with me as a husband into the bargain, in a crumbling castle in the middle of a howling wilderness.

I know my reputation is not the most shining, but I find in myself an odd scruple that may make you smile: I cannot ask anyone to marry me without revealing these uncomfortable particulars to her. I have not yet run about London looking for sufficiently desperate women, and I hope I never am obliged to do so, but I have no confidence at all in finding one prepared to take me on those terms.

Naturally, then, my thoughts turned to you, Duchess. (Admit, if only to yourself, that you knew that this was where all my elaborate preliminaries were leading.) I do not wish to be indelicate, but you are notoriously – even proverbially – fecund. To the wonder of all the world, you gave my cousin Edward two fine sons within two years of your marriage to him, when his previous unions had both been childless. Is it too crude to hope that you might do the same for me – with me?

Viola, will you marry me?

You will say – I can almost hear you saying it, dark eyes flashing splendidly – that I offer you no incentive. Why should you be different from any other woman who has the sense to think me a terrible bargain? But you are, your grace, because we can discuss this matter openly and honestly. If between us we cannot fulfil the conditions of my aunt's ridiculous testament, you will not be obliged to stay with me. I am all too aware that eighteen months is not so very long. Winterflood is your home, and I have no power or wish to take it from you. Even if we do succeed in our endeavours, I will not think of forcing you to remain with me if you do not desire to. You may make any stipulations as to your future that you care to, and I swear I will honour them.

I am sure that your boys are now of an age to need a father – a stepfather, at least, since no one can truly take Edward's place. I presume that one of the reasons a woman so lovely and so desirable in every way has not remarried is because you fear bringing a stranger into your sons' home as some poor substitute for my cousin. That too would be a chancy business. But you have my solemn assurance that I will care for them as if they were my own, if you let me, whether we give them siblings or not. I would do so for poor Edward's sake, for yours, and for theirs too.

I do not suppose you will receive this letter with any great joy, but I beg you to consider it very seriously. My offer, clumsy as it is, may well prove a lifeline for us both. I know you always preferred the word with no bark upon it, so I have not attempted to honey any part of my damnably awkward situation – or, for that matter, yours. Give me at least some credit for not making protestations of love that you would treat with the contempt that they deserved.

With continuing esteem, and warm recollections of our earlier acquaintance,

I remain yours,

Richard Armstrong, Baron Ventris

Emily, mild eyes sparkling with unaccustomed anger, agreed instantly that the letter was a grave insult, and one that should be rejected in the coldest terms, if indeed it merited a reply at all. But Viola, once she had overcome her initial impulse to have a fire lit in the breakfast room purely in order to throw the paper into it and watch it burn to ashes, was not so sure.

Damn him to hell along with his mad aunt, he was quite right when he said that her growing boys would benefit from the presence of a father figure. How could they not? Especially when one of them had succeeded far too early to the dignities, titles and looming responsibilities of the dukedom, and the other had not. What a burden to place on a young boy, and what a cruel division to make between him and his twin brother.

Ventris also pierced right to the heart of her reasons for not considering the suit of any other man she had met in the years of her widowhood. She hadn't spent very much time with her sisters and her mother in London society since she put off her black, being fully occupied with her children and the estate. But she had attended local assemblies and private parties often enough with Emily, and had been left in no doubt at all that if she wished to remarry tomorrow, she could find many candidates for her hand. It wasn't necessarily a flattering thought. No doubt the prospect of living at Winterflood as its master, at least till Ned came of age, which was more than ten years off, added to any attractions her person might hold. And her own widow's portion was respectable enough by itself. Not to mention her damned *proverbial fecundity,* and the salacious rumours about her bedroom skills that had plagued her in her youth.

It wasn't true to say that any of the men who had swarmed about her had wooed her – she had not let them go so far, having instead made it very clear that she had not the least interest in courtship nor any kind of flirtation. If she were ever to marry again – and a little voice inside her said, *After all, I am still only nine and twenty!* – it could only be to a man whom she could trust to care for the boys with genuine affection. Trust utterly, for she too might die and leave them in his sole care. And Ventris – damn him again – was the only man now living in the world in whom she could place unequivocal faith in that manner. She didn't have to like him or trust him in any other respect to admit the truth of that.

The quickest way to put herself at the risk of death, she thought with mordant humour as she sat gazing into the fire now and Miss Naismith watched her anxiously, was to engage, as Ventris had put it, in the chancy business of attempting to give birth again. It was no small thing he asked of her, and despite his flippancy, he knew it.

He was also right in saying that she appreciated honesty and disdained idle flattery, so, however shocked Emily was, however shocked she too had been at first, she could not judge him for his bluntness. She knew she *had* been a byword among the members of the haut ton for producing twin boys when her husband, quite five and forty when he wed her, had been married twice before and neither of his previous wives had, as far as anyone knew, ever even been in a delicate condition. His first ill-suited duchess had deserted him to run off with another man after five years of marriage and he had been obliged to divorce her, with great expense and scandal; his second, with whom he had shared a much happier and longer union, had died childless in an epidemic of some infectious disease that swept through London in 1800.

A year after that lady's death, fresh out of mourning and still grief-stricken, he had married Viola, who had been only seventeen and just out. Considerably less than two years later, she'd given birth to the twins. So she and Edward had indeed been the subject of a great deal of most prurient gossip; she knew this because her oldest sister had kindly told her so, in excessive detail. Sabrina, who in private loved a salty tale, had been most entertained at the wilder speculation over what, precisely, the nubile Viola must have done to stimulate Winterflood's previously sluggish masculine ardour to the point where she conceived; the Duchess herself had not been nearly so amused to know herself discussed in such a humiliating manner. Would the Duke have hated it too? Surely any man would, and especially him, but it didn't matter one jot now.

Viola refused to dwell on such unpleasant matters. She and Edward had been happy enough in a fashion, at least once the boys were born. Not passionately in love, on either part, but contented in their mutual love for their little sons, who were, as he had often told her, the greatest gift any man had ever been given. She moved uneasily in her seat; this letter had brought back long-buried memories that she was generally extremely adept at suppressing.

Ventris had wisely made no direct reference to the intimacy that must inevitably take place between them if she accepted him. Emily thought his letter indelicate, and it was, but it could have been a great deal more so, in Viola's opinion. There was an undertone to it, of course... Emily too had noticed that, she thought, but it was such a nebulous thing that she hadn't found words to refer to it. And that was not a conversation the Duchess herself had any intention of initiating. If she were to be honest, that part of it wasn't the problem, or not directly. Richard was an attractive man, had always been an attractive man even in his early twenties, and she'd been alone for a long time. Her bed was cold; she could not doubt that his presence would warm it.

And she would like another child. A daughter, perhaps, a baby in her arms again after so long. She didn't really care, boy or girl. The idea made tears rise to her eyes, the deep-seated yearning suddenly so strong, it took her by surprise. That was a stark fact.

What was the problem, then? Setting aside her shock and fury, taking into account the pressing reasons for acceptance that he had not failed to list, and those he had not listed but only referred obliquely to – the boys' safety not least among them – what *was* the problem? He didn't love her and made no bones about it; she really didn't expect him to, and, as he'd said in his letter, wouldn't have believed him if he'd said he did. Empty professions of love and devotion really would have been insulting.

Her concerns, then, should be her lost independence, won at such cost and too precious to give up lightly, and his appalling reputation. He was known as a rake who had engaged in scandalous relations with many ladies of the ton, as her friend had said, but that was not the whole of it. Many men were libertines; that would not make him in the least notable. But there were darker rumours that swirled about him; rumours that painted him as not merely dishonourable, but actually criminal. This was not a matter, as one might imagine, of cheating at cards or some such commonplace transgression of society's codes; the gossips, even around Winterflood, spoke of actual theft, theft of money and incriminating private documents. Of blackmail, based upon those thefts. And that was not by any means all. She had once heard it whispered – but surely, surely it could not be true – that he had killed a man in Yorkshire and somehow got away with it; that he was a cold-blooded murderer.

2

Viola saw her dearest friend married, shed tears that mingled joy and loss, and then left for London early the next day, carrying along with her, like so much extra baggage on the roof of the coach, a complicated mixture of feelings. She wasn't committing to anything by merely going to Town, she told herself. It would do her good to get away from the empty mansion full of memories and ghosts.

She had never travelled unaccompanied like this before, without husband, children, sister or friend, she realised as she gazed out of the carriage window at the unspectacular passing countryside, her maid Hannah Owen nodding sleepily at her side. She'd not made many journeys at all since Edward's death, apart from visiting her sisters occasionally with Emily and the children.

Not that she was alone now, or sparsely attended – far from it. She had several liveried outriders – her steward had insisted that they were necessary, both as a tribute to her status as duchess and a safety measure for a woman travelling without a gentleman to accompany her – and they, along with the crested ducal coach in all its shining state, were enough to make anyone stare. As they slowed to pass through one of the small but bustling Hertfordshire towns on the run into London, she heard through the open window one passerby asking another if it was a procession, and if so, what was it in aid of? *My enormous consequence*, she thought drily. *I am, like Ventris's late aunt, very grand. And if I want to drive sixty miles on a whim, I can do so without consulting another soul, because I am independent, and need explain myself to no man. And not even to my own mother, for that matter, who is more intimidating than most men. Do I really want to give that freedom up, and to a man I cannot trust, at that?*

The outriders performed their function, even if that was only deterrence, and they crossed Barnet and Finchley Commons unchecked by bold highwaymen or any other manner of delay. Late in the afternoon, the carriage rolled between the open gates of the big, old house on the edge of Hyde Park. The staff had been prepared for her arrival, naturally, and appeared to be very pleased to see her. She greeted them all, and ate her dinner in solitary state, sitting idle at table sipping wine for a while afterwards and then going up to yet another silent, silk-hung chamber with a large, empty bed in it. It wasn't cold, because it had been carefully heated for her by a well-trained maid with a warming pan, but that wasn't the sort of warmth she needed. She had thought she'd disciplined herself to overlook these persistent, nagging reminders of loneliness, but Ventris's offer had made her freshly conscious of such things. It was having an alternative, however complicated, she supposed. So many things to balance against each other, and no choice to be made that did not involve some kind of risk and potential loss.

When she put her hands on her body in an attempt to relieve her tension so that she could gain some much-needed rest, it was Richard Armstrong's face she saw behind her closed eyelids. His face as it had been when she had last seen it – ironical grey eyes, crisply curling black hair, beautifully sculpted mouth. His elegant hands on her instead of her own, his lips, pressing hot kisses onto hers, whispering endearments. She very much doubted if he was lying alone in his chamber dreaming of her; if his reputation was at all merited, he wouldn't be in his bed for hours, and when he finally got there, it wouldn't be empty or cold. She still found release despite that uncomfortable knowledge, but sleep was very slow to come, and when it came, her dreams were uneasy.

The next day she set off, with no outriders this time, to see her sister. One of them. Viola was one of six, the second-oldest child. Their father's small estate had been entailed, and so their mother's life had been ruled by a single, entirely rational obsession: that her many daughters should marry well and save the family from penury. Society might scoff at her for it, call her a shameless social climber, but she cared nothing for the opinion of others. Others, she was fond of saying, waspishly and in several languages for extra emphasis, were not facing destitution and homelessness because of their failure to produce a masculine child. God knows she had tried; her six daughters with their elaborate Italianate names were ample evidence of that.

Viola's marriage had been her shining success, dukes being rare and, normally, hard to catch. The fact that Winterflood was a couple of years older than her own husband had been shrugged off by Mrs Constantine as a mere detail. He was a good man, she had said, and would give her daughter a good life. Viola herself had been sensible of the duty she owed to her family; she had accepted Edward without hesitation when he called on her to ask for her hand, having first sought her father's (which was to say her mother's) permission and unsurprisingly been given it with promptness.

The Duke had been diffident, shy almost, and despite her own fears and a lingering sense of regret, as if for a possible future vanished forever, she had felt sympathy for him. He'd lost the wife he'd adored, making no attempt to conceal his continuing pain. He was no great bargain, he had said humbly, and she would be doing him enormous honour if she agreed to take him on. He was still handsome, a little careworn, anxious, and not at all puffed up about his status and wealth. She had said yes immediately. She did not waste time now picking over whether she had regrets or not. Of course she did – she was an adult, not a green girl.

Viola's oldest sister Sabrina had also married young and married well, given the regrettable scarcity of dukes, marquesses and even earls; her husband, Laurence Da Costa, had no title nor grand connections, but was wealthy, and also amiable and easy-going. He had loved her on sight, and Sabrina had grown to love him in return. As a pledge of her affection, she had obligingly presented him with a son nine months after their marriage, not long before Edward had offered for Viola's hand.

Mr Da Costa's substantial fortune had originated in trade, a generation or two back, but Mrs Constantine and her daughter were too sensible to care for that. The Da Costa pair now shared a contented, busy domestic life in a fine new London home, and a houseful of children. If Sabrina could be persuaded to sit down and listen for five minutes, she was the wise and steady one, much less impulsive than any of her younger sisters. And Viola desperately needed to talk to her.

Admitted to the untidy, comfortable sitting room, the Duchess checked swiftly that no children were in it, neither hiding behind the curtains nor under either of the sofas, and turned the key in the lock. 'Goodness,' said Sabrina placidly, 'you must be desperate, and I collect not just to talk of Emily's wedding. Locking the door doesn't ever work when I do it – if we are here alone for long enough, they will start coming down the chimney if they can't find another way in – so you had better tell me quickly what the matter is. Are the boys unhappy at school? Has Winterflood burned down and left you in the street in your shift?'

'No,' replied the Duchess, refusing to be diverted from her purpose. 'Obviously, it has not, or I would not be here, and yes, they have written; they are well, and settling in. Sam Muncaster confirms this in his own letters home. I've come to see you because I have had an offer of marriage.'

Sabrina blinked. 'You must have had others since Edward's death, and never came rushing pell-mell sixty miles to tell me of them.'

'I haven't, in fact; if anyone showed a disposition to be interested in me, I always became so chilly in my manner towards them that eventually, they gave up and moved on to easier targets.'

'I can well imagine it. But *targets*? You do know that it's perfectly possible a man might be interested you for yourself?'

'That would be a novel experience.' Viola uttered these words as flatly as she could manage. It wasn't quite true – there had been a man once, or so she had thought... But that could not signify now, and she had no intention of telling her sister about that, or even thinking about it too loudly in her presence, after keeping the dangerous secret for so long.

Mrs Da Costa absorbed her words. 'Oh – I suppose it would be, at that. I'm sorry, my dear Vee. I can see how that would sting. But you were content enough with Edward, weren't you, at least once the boys were born, after that first difficult time? You always seemed to be. I don't mean because he was a duke and all that nonsense, but because he was kind and gentle, and so grateful.'

There were faint scuffling noises outside the door already, but both women ignored them. No small Da Costas appeared to be breaking anything irreplaceable or injuring themselves or others just yet.

'He was all that. I don't mean to sound bitter, just honest. And this man doesn't want me for myself either, but for the same reason Edward wanted me – to have a child, and quickly.'

'He tells you so? That's... unusually frank.'

Viola pulled the letter from her reticule and handed it over. It was looking a little creased and tired by now – she must have read it dozens of times, looking for hidden meanings and not finding any, or rather finding different ones each time. Sabrina now scanned the missive rapidly as her sister looked at her with affection, noting the bloom of health in her soft cheeks. They saw little of each other these days, but the bond remained strong. They'd fought a lot as children, being so close in age, and they did not have the sort of easy, undemanding companionship she shared with Emily Naismith, but Sabrina could always be depended on to tell her the truth, even if it wasn't palatable. Perhaps especially if it wasn't, oldest sister that she was. That was what she needed now.

Sabrina's eyes too grew rounder as she read on, but her reaction was very different from Miss Naismith's. She was laughing by the time she came to the end. 'You are a dreadful person, Vee,' she said at last. 'You must have shown this to Emily, and yet you did not make sure that I was there to see her face. Was she terribly, terribly shocked?'

Viola grinned reluctantly. 'She asked me if Lord Ventris was mad. Not only does she think I cannot possibly accept his offer, she is strongly of the opinion that such a letter does not deserve a reply of any kind, least of all a civil one. I do love her so – she was like an angry kitten prepared to take on a very large dog.'

'I can easily picture it. And have you replied? I presume you have not said no outright, or you would not be here.'

'I wrote only to say that I would be in London soon and would give him his answer then. He said he would by good fortune be here too – that was all he said – and that he looked forward to seeing me.'

'I don't think I have ever met him,' Sabrina said pensively. 'He wasn't at your wedding, was he? I know, of course, that he and Edward were cousins. But I can tell even from this letter that they were nothing alike in character.'

'No. He is… you can see what he is. Cynical, clever, amusing. Careless, but not as careless as he would have you think. And of course he has the reputation of being a rake.'

'And more than that.'

Viola was both relieved and disturbed that her sister had heard the rumours too. It seemed everybody had. 'A criminal – a thief, perhaps, and worse. I don't even want to put it into words, the most outrageous part of it.'

Sabrina's good-natured face was troubled. 'There's no way of knowing if it's true, of course. It's so wild and unlikely, it easily might not be. You know how people love to gossip, and make something out of nothing.'

'Exactly. But even if he told me to my face that he was not what people say he is, how could I believe him? Surely such a person must be practised at deception. I can imagine him saying to me, smiling, that if I do not trust him, there would be no form of persuasion he could use to convince me that he was innocent.'

'So you *don't* trust him – you have it in your mind to believe the gossip, or at least some of it? In which case, it seems to me that you should not take him. We're not young girls who must marry for the sake of our family – not any more. You have complete freedom to choose now, and an independent life that you have valued, I think. I obviously would have chosen Laurence anyway, and still would, but that's not the point. We're not talking about me.'

'It's more complicated than that, Bree. It's not about what I want, or only partly. Of course there are disadvantages – there must be to any marriage outside of a fairy tale. I'm sure even Laurence has his flaws. But I do trust Ventris to have a care for the boys, and I ask myself if any of the rest of it matters much. I don't know if that's crazy or sensible.'

Sabrina didn't seem to want to discuss Laurence's flaws just now. 'You think he's telling the truth there, at least? That he could care for them as if they were his own?'

'Yes. Yes, I do. And there is no one else in the world I could say that about.'

'There's something you're not telling me. I want to help you, but there's no point in you asking for my advice or even my opinion if you haven't told me everything. You know that.'

Viola was silent for a moment, then she said slowly, 'I've always been scared of his brother. Mr Armstrong. You know he was Edward's heir, and Edward had been without a son for so long that Tarquin must surely have assumed that the dukedom was all but his, if he could only be patient. And then the boys were born.'

'No doubt his nose was put badly out of joint and he was furious. But to be frightened he might... I don't even know how to finish that sentence.'

'I know that he was uttering threats of violence towards Edward and me long after he should have reconciled himself to our marriage; I was told as much years ago, by someone who heard him in his cups. And Edward knew too, because he warned me against him. Almost the last words he said to me were, "Have a care he does not come near the twins. Promise me you will. He would do anything, I believe he would do anything..." Not the kind of words I am likely to forget, Bree. I have stayed away from London, for the most part, because he is usually here during the Season. And the boys have been safe at Winterflood, with people always looking out for them even though they did not know it, but now they are at school and out in the world. Vulnerable.'

'But is there anything more? Because you seem to be implying that this man, a family member, might be capable of murder – of killing two innocent young boys just because they stand in his way.' Sabrina, normally so unperturbable, was looking at her sister with very grave concern. Something solid – perhaps a youthful limb, or solid Da Costa head – thumped suddenly against the locked door, making them both jump, but they ignored it, continuing to gaze intently at each other.

'I know it sounds ridiculous. Hysterical. But I cannot afford to underestimate him, in case it is true.'

'I wonder you thought to send them away to school, if you are so worried for their safety. Could you not have kept them at home and engaged a tutor now that Emily has left you?'

This was a sore point. 'God knows I wanted to. But you know that Lord Marchett, Edward's oldest friend, is their trustee and guardian, and he would not be persuaded. They are of an age, he insisted. The more I tried to say that they should stay at home and be tutored, as many boys of rank still are, the more he thought I was a pathetic, clinging mother who could not bear to have them out of my sight. There was a great deal of talk of apron strings, and building manly character. He smiled at me and patted my hand in the most odious way. I have always known he disliked me, and thought Edward wrong to marry me. I had to concede the point, or else I would have lost my temper, and along with it, any influence at all I might have over him in anything. He was good enough to tell me,' Viola said through gritted teeth, 'that if I remarried and my husband should share my opinion on their education, he might concede. But he seriously doubted that any sensible man could possibly think anything so weak and foolish.'

'It's a wonder you didn't plant him a facer, as my boys would say. Silly old fool.'

'I wanted to, so badly, and what's worse is I probably could do it. He's not a robust man. I pictured myself knocking him down and standing over him in triumph. But I kept my temper. It's too important.'

'If he's so stuffy, he surely will not think someone like Lord Ventris a suitable husband, love. He must have heard the gossip too, unless he lives in a cave.'

'Of course he will disapprove enormously. I recall very well that he never liked Ventris either, even before all the rumours spread – and he actually wrote to me, years ago, and told me of them, can you imagine? But under the terms of Edward's will, it's not in his power to control whom I marry, thank God. And whatever Marchett thinks of him, Lord Ventris has one vital qualification for being taken seriously by another man – even if he truly is a rake and much worse – that I will never have.' The Duchess made a gesture that was unmistakeable, and both sisters laughed, though their mirth had an edge to it.

'Well, he certainly must have one of those, and the rumour is he knows what to do with it. That wouldn't play any part in your thinking, would it? I've never seen him, as I said – is he very handsome? Although I suppose it doesn't matter. If you are merely to be bedding him frequently until you conceive, you don't necessarily have to look at him.'

This comment brought a picture to Viola's mind that was so vivid, she felt herself colour hotly, and her sister said, 'Your face speaks for itself. He must indeed be virile and charming, whatever his other flaws! I won't be so indiscreet as to enquire further. Have you really come here to ask me if you should take him? Because it seems to me that you have decided already, no matter whether he's a criminal or not. Which is extraordinary, really, as you don't need me to tell you. And of course Mama will say you've run mad – I hope you're prepared for that.'

Viola winced at the truth of her sister's statement. 'Perhaps I have... No, there are solid reasons in favour of it. It's perfectly true that Ventris could no more guarantee to keep Ned and Robin safe at school than I can, but if I marry him, I would be able to withdraw them and have them taught at home, or at least in a smaller school near Winterflood, or near Ventris Castle, I don't care which. And also, I think perhaps Tarquin might be a little frightened of his younger brother. Of his unpredictability, of his low connections – even of violent retaliation from him if anything were to happen... If any fraction of my suspicions is correct, it might give him pause if Ventris and I were married. There's that to consider too.'

There had been a steadily growing racket outside in the hall for several minutes, which was reaching a house-shaking level that was hard to ignore. 'It's possible they're murdering each other,' said their fond mother with no particular appearance of concern. 'Still, there are quite a few of them, so I can probably spare one. Tell me quickly, has that helped at all?'

'I think so. I believe I must do it, despite my qualms, and I knew it already, but it is clearer now.'

'Will you ask him to come and see you?'

'I suppose so. What else can I do? It's not as though I'm likely to bump into him by chance in the street.' Though she would not dream of telling her sister, or anyone, Viola felt her heart start beating faster at the prospect.

'How thrilling. Well, let us go shopping together before you leave London, in that case. There at least I can be truly helpful.'

'You think I need new gowns? I purchased several not long since. I shouldn't think they are outmoded yet, and I don't really care if they are. I certainly don't mean to wreathe myself in orange blossom and white muslin like a virgin bride, and make myself ridiculous.'

Sabrina shook her dark locks and grinned at her wickedly. 'Virgin bride, indeed! Gowns are not what I had in mind, nor yet pelisses or spencers or bonnets. I think you urgently need alluring new nightgowns for your honeymoon, Lady Ventris!'

3

Viola drew in a deep, steadying breath as the liveried servant took her evening cloak in the hall of the townhouse. Twelve years ago, when she'd made her come-out, it would have been impossible for her to enter alone for such an evening party. She'd have been far too nervous and self-conscious, and worried that everyone would be looking at her, whispering about her, but that didn't matter, because it just wasn't done in any case. Young ladies did not go anywhere in London unaccompanied, no matter how they might behave elsewhere. They were strictly chaperoned at all times; not just supervised, but seen to be supervised, in a sort of public performance. Their virtue was too fragile and too important a thing to be left to chance.

She was no longer a young lady, and in theory should be freer, but it wasn't quite usual for widows to go about in society alone, either – someone of her standing should, according to custom and convention, have a companion living with her, going everywhere with her, and Emily had fulfilled that function until recently. Now she had no one. If she were to marry, of course, she would no longer have need of a female companion to give her respectability; a husband, any sort of husband, was supposed to do that.

Tonight, she could have called on one of her sisters, married or unmarried, or – God forbid – her mother to accompany her to this party. But she didn't want to. She didn't want to be questioned by anybody about what on earth she was doing. Even Sabrina, who knew what she was about, would have quizzed her unbearably, and then watched every second of her meeting with Ventris with a critical eye, and commented satirically on it afterwards. That wouldn't help her; it would only make her so self-conscious that she couldn't order her thoughts or behave naturally. She wanted to *see* him properly before she committed herself irrevocably to marrying him. And she wanted, for her own protection, to see him in public.

At first, this had seemed an insurmountable problem – she could hardly stroll into one of the low inns or other disreputable haunts she assumed he frequented and order herself a quart of gin – but she had applied her intelligence to the matter and found a solution. She'd written to Lord Ventris and told him she would be at Lady Granville's soirée that evening, if he cared to meet her there. Despite his shocking reputation, she knew he still moved in society occasionally. If there was a pattern or a purpose to his appearances, she had no idea what that might be, and didn't want to know. She'd now and then seen notice of his attendance at some ball or other in the scandal sheets – perhaps his dangerous presence added a touch of spice to a lady's entertainments. Perhaps some of them were his lovers or his blackmail victims; it seemed more than likely. Not her hostess, she hoped – that would be undeniably awkward, and out of character for what she knew of the woman. But she did not doubt his ability to obtain an invitation almost anywhere, if he wanted to.

She'd met Lady Granville, who'd then been Lady Harriet Cavendish, unmarried daughter of the late Duke of Devonshire, a few years ago, on one of her brief trips to London without Edward. They weren't exactly friends – Viola had few close friends besides Emily and her own sisters – but they'd become friendly, and corresponded in a desultory sort of way, though they rarely saw each other now. It had been easy enough to find out who was in Town at this odd season and who planned to hold parties, and easier still to write boldly to Harriet and ask if she could attend tonight's event, since she was unexpectedly in London. Of course she could, the swift and gracious reply came. This was no surprise; she wasn't Miss Viola Constantine any more, a nobody; she was a duchess. Lady Granville, though she was the daughter of a duke and his famously unhappy and unfaithful wife Georgiana, was married to the mere younger son of a marquess. Such things counted.

Harriet's husband, Granville, had been her Aunt Bessborough's lover for close on twenty years; that aunt had arranged their union. Even in the haut ton, this excessively intimate arrangement was a little unusual. But everyone knew of it and nobody seemed to care. Harriet herself was a woman of spotless reputation who plainly loved her husband, and wasn't the subject of any gossip, which must have made her unique in her scandalous family. But presumably she wouldn't blink at a whiff of shadiness, such as Ventris must carry with him. She was raising her husband's illegitimate children – her aunt's children, who were therefore also her cousins; it made one's head ache – as her own.

Viola wore her finest new gown. It seemed important that Ventris would see her at her best, if he came. It was red velvet, quite plain, low cut across the breasts and shoulders – this was the current fashion, and she knew it suited her – and with it, she wore the famous Winterflood jewel: a Tudor necklace that had been passed down through the Armstrong family. It was not hers in any meaningful sense, as she certainly couldn't have sold it even if she'd wanted to, but it looked well with crimson, since it consisted of a central ruby in an ornate setting embellished with pearls, sapphires and delicate coloured enamel, hanging down into her deep cleavage on an ornate gold chain. It gave her courage, and she could be confident that Ventris would recognise it. If he came. Surely, he'd come.

She entered alone, braving a few blatant stares, and was announced, her hostess coming forward to greet her, her urbane husband – who was sometimes described as the handsomest man in London – at her side. Viola had no eyes for him, though she had enough self-control not to scan the room for the man she was truly anxious to see.

The couple seemed pleased to welcome her, and were commenting on what a rare pleasure it was to see her in Town. Asking after her boys. She reciprocated – she knew that Lady Granville had had a baby last year: a daughter. They did seem happy and united, as far as one could tell, so perhaps it was truly possible for a man to change; perhaps Ventris might change, if he chose to. Lord Granville too had been a notorious philanderer in his day, which hadn't been so long ago. A famous lady had, it was rumoured, attempted to put a period to her existence when he had ended their irregular liaison, so desolated had she been at her loss. But then again, he was a politician of some repute, and an experienced and trusted ambassador, despite his scandalous private life – not anything more dishonourable or alarming than that. He'd just had to stop chasing women (Viola hoped for Harriet's sake that he'd stopped), not alter his whole manner of existence.

Her hosts moved on to greet other guests, and Viola fixed a smile on her face and entered into light conversation with various acquaintances who happened to be standing nearby. Lord This, Lady That, Mr Somebody-Or-Other. If she'd ever been practised at this sort of thing, she wasn't now, and she found it excruciating, though she trusted that wasn't obvious to anybody. To think she'd yearned for this sort of existence once, when she'd been marooned in the country alone with Edward for months at a time – now she merely endured it, with a goal in mind.

She knew that she must be an object of some interest here; she could feel eyes on her, assessing, judging, and hear a more than casual interest behind the polite questions she was being asked. It was understandable, she supposed, though she didn't have to like it. She was a high-ranking noblewoman, but she rarely appeared in society, and almost never participated in the London Season as others did, though she had at least been presented at Court, finally, eight or nine years ago. This had been done on her own insistence, because it looked so odd and somehow demeaning that she had not been previously. Her husband had been a notorious recluse, which perhaps explained the secluded life she'd lived with him – but he was dead now, and had been for some years. Did her surprising attendance at this party hold some deeper significance? they'd be wondering. Might she intend to come out of her shell for good, and remarry, even? Could she be considered a catch? Surely not, when there were so many dewy young heiresses and ladies of noble birth to choose from in the haut ton.

She did seem to be attracting a fair amount of masculine attention in particular. Ladies whispered; gentlemen looked her up and down quite openly. Maybe the low-cut gown had been a mistake. But almost all of the other women were wearing gowns as low, or lower. Lady Caroline Lamb's nipples were a presence in themselves. Why couldn't everyone go and drool over them instead? But perhaps they held no novelty, having been on show too often before. Lady Caroline and her nipples weren't received everywhere these days, after the scandalous affair with Lord Byron that had reached its public climax in the summer, but Lady Granville was her cousin, of course, and had grown up with her.

'You appear pensive, Duchess,' a cool voice said at her side, making her start. 'It's a long time since I've had the pleasure of seeing you, and you are magnificent as ever, but perhaps a little... abstracted? I conjecture that you are remembering with regret how dull London is out of season, and wondering why you have made the effort to be here. As indeed is everyone else.'

Viola turned with a fair assumption of delight to greet her interlocutor, ignoring the ambiguity of his last observation. He wasn't the man she'd come to see, but he was a personality, an arbiter of society still, and could not be snubbed. Not that she wished to snub him. She might find herself the target of one of his famous witticisms, but at least he could be relied upon not to peer down the front of her bodice; his manners were too good, where ladies were concerned, to commit such a solecism.

'Mr Brummell!' she said. 'How can you say that London is dull when you are present?' She hoped she didn't sound flirtatious; that was not her intention. To be out in company was a sad trial to her, and she wasn't confident she always hit the right notes when speaking, but she'd only herself to blame for being here tonight.

'It's true,' he sighed, apparently taking her comment as no more than a simple fact, 'but there is only so much that one can do alone to make a tedious evening memorable. I will require your aid, I think.' He was immaculate as ever, the cut of his coat and the perfection of his linen making most of the other men present appear shabby or over-dressed. He'd be five and thirty now, and despite the sober splendour of his dress, he looked it; his eyes were shrewd as ever, but perhaps a little tired. It would not be fanciful to say that his countenance held a slightly dissipated appearance. She'd heard rumours of huge gambling debts and vast sums owed to tradesmen, of a fortune wasted and public quarrels with his princely patron. 'Everyone is wondering why you honour us with your company so unexpectedly, madam, but they will not be rude enough to ask outright. Nor will I.'

He hardly needed to. 'Might I not just have wished for a change of scene?' She was striving for tranquillity, and a well-bred ease of manner to match his.

'Of course you might – the country is so dreary, all those vulgar, noisy farm animals making the place untidy, one shudders to think of it, and you have had years to grow thoroughly weary of a rustic existence – but the question is, why now?'

'I felt a little restless suddenly,' she said frankly. It was the truth, though not the whole truth.

Trust him to take her up on that. 'If your understandable discontent with life should carry you so far as the contemplation of matrimony once again, might I suggest myself as a possible husband? You wouldn't be a duchess any more, regrettably, but think what you would be.'

Such a suggestion would be outrageous, if he meant a word of it. This was her month for shocking proposals, it seemed. 'I would be the woman who captured George Brummell at last – what a triumph! It is a deliciously tempting offer, sir. But I don't think I can afford you, much as I might wish I could. I am no great heiress, you know. I have a jointure sufficient for my own needs, but that is all.' He was not serious – she need not be either. Timid little mice did not do well in his company. This cat had claws.

'It's such a pity,' he responded, smiling slightly, entirely unabashed. 'You make a good point, madam, but think what an outstandingly handsome couple we would make, which counts for a great deal. Penniless – or at least we would be, once I'd swiftly run through your modest fortune – but so very stylish and admired. And would it not almost be worth it to picture Lord Marchett's face when he heard the news? He would instantly be possessed with dark imaginings of how I would surely try to play at ducks and drakes with your sons' patrimony, compromise his position as guardian, and make his life a misery in his twilight years. You're far too sensible to marry me, but the old man won't realise that. If you were lucky, an apoplexy might carry him off at the mere thought, and then I should have done you a great service to outweigh all the rest.'

'That's perfectly true,' she said, laughing aloud at the thought. 'I wonder I did not think of it years ago. It would be worth a larger sum than I can scrape up to be rid of him forever.'

'Perhaps we should merely announce our engagement, and see how that serves,' he said lightly. She barely heard him, suddenly distracted. And then after a tense moment, he added, 'Or perhaps we should not, after all… I understand better now, Duchess. My apologies.' He was so quick; he'd seen her face alter midway through his teasing speech, when Lord Ventris was announced.

She'd betrayed herself, to Brummell at least – but just in that moment, she didn't care.

Richard Armstrong had been one or two and twenty when she'd last seen him, and though he'd reached his full, impressive height by then, he had filled out in the intervening years. His shoulders were broader and his frame was more robust. Whatever he'd been doing, it seemed to involve a fair amount of exercise. Riding, maybe, fleeing from pursuit – his thighs were unavoidably muscular in his tight black silk knee-breeches. He hadn't transformed into a tulip of the ton, or anything like one, nor even a dandy in Mr Brummell's mode; his clothes were of good enough quality, tailored to his strong frame, but not at all extreme or luxurious either in colour, fabric or fit. He wore no jewellery, not even a fob.

Viola discovered in herself an odd reluctance to look into his face, and overcame it. She met his watchful grey eyes, trying to push away the thought that he must be assessing her too, refusing to wonder what he might make of her. She was older, of course she was. No longer the girl he'd known.

And him? He was an adult of three and thirty now, not caught between boy and man as he had been before. His face had never been soft – it was too strongly boned for that – but it had taken on a certain added harshness in the intervening years. He looked uncompromising, remote, and oddly formidable. She wasn't sure if that was a good or bad thing for her purposes. There was a sprinkle of silver in his dark hair now, as there was in hers, and new lines about his eyes and mouth. He'd always looked a little like Edward, in features rather than in expression, and he resembled him more now that he was older. She wished he didn't.

Time seemed to be suspended for a moment, both of them frozen, but inevitably, it restarted with a jolt. He crossed the room with an athlete's fluid grace and bent over her hand, brushing it with his lips. She'd thought he might, and was prepared for the fleeting contact, which seemed to burn through her evening gloves to her sensitive skin beneath them. 'You are lovelier than ever, your grace,' he said, his voice seeming deeper than it had been years ago. She couldn't tell if he was mocking her.

'I am more than a decade older, so I doubt that can be true. You said in your letter that you knew I preferred the word with no bark upon it. There's no need to play off insinuating airs on me.'

'I'm not,' he said easily. 'I wouldn't say it if it weren't true. You were beautiful, and you are. I won't say "still" – that's an insult in itself. I daresay you will be so when you are eighty.' If she had been inclined to blush and simper at this compliment, which she decidedly was not, she would have been vexed beyond all measure by his next words. 'Your mother is everywhere spoken of as a remarkably attractive woman, so I expect you have inherited your looks from her.'

If George Brummell had spoken words of farewell, she hadn't heard them, but he'd gone from her side without her noticing, though she could not doubt he was watching her still from the crowd, eager for gossip, missing nothing. It must be a delicious sight – the widowed Duchess and the man of scandalous repute. They were observed by many, she did not doubt it, but nobody was standing close and so they could not be overheard. Which was just as well.

'My mother is a widow too, and even more notoriously fertile than I am, especially if you have no fixed objection to daughters,' Viola said with a glittering smile. 'But at fifty, perhaps a little too advanced in years for your purpose, Lord Ventris.'

'I had considered that,' he said, firm mouth quirking with inappropriate amusement. 'It's a pity, but there we are. I'll have to make do with you. I assure you, it will be no hardship.' His voice caressed her, just as if he'd trailed his long fingers very slowly over the exposed skin of her neck and upper breasts, and she could only be grateful that her gown was thick velvet, not thin, clinging silk like Lady Caroline's. She felt quite naked enough in his presence. Her skin was tingling as though he'd really touched her.

'In point of fact, I have not said a word to make you so confident that I will marry you.' This between gritted teeth.

'But you are here – despite the fact that you so rarely come to London since you were widowed. That must count for something.'

God, had he always been so irritating? 'I am free to come and go as I please. To socialise with whom I please. I am under no obligation to explain my movements to anybody.'

'And heaven forbid that I or anyone else should try to interfere with that,' he said piously. 'Why did you come, though, Viola, and summon me to your side? You know we can't talk here... or do anything else that we might wish to do.'

His voice was silky, deep, always teasing. Damn him. If only it were possible to control one's blushes. 'I wanted to see you,' she answered flatly and honestly. Useless to lie to him. 'Nothing more than that. In a public place.'

'Well, there we differ; you should know. I'd much rather see you in private. All of you.'

He was smiling, and she wanted to hit him. 'Don't,' she said involuntarily.

His smile grew broader, and his tone was that of tolerant understanding, which was unbearable. 'Will you write to me again? I can't help tormenting you a little, but I shouldn't. I'm sorry. Our situation is confoundedly awkward, and I have made it more so. Write to me, and I will come and call on you at any time or in any place you choose to appoint. We do need to talk in private, you must admit. You can always send me away... after.'

She didn't like the significant little pause and the sly way he said *after* – after what? But she nodded wordlessly, and he bowed over her hand and moved away from her. She did not watch him go, or seek to see with whom he spoke next. It was to be hoped that their little tête-à-tête had appeared to be nothing more than a conversation between cousins by marriage who had not met for a while, brief and now over, nothing to see. Brummell knew better, of course. He might gossip about it to half of London, or he might keep silent. He was famously quixotic, and she barely knew him; it was impossible to tell.

And here the Beau was, back at her side again, like a very stylish gadfly. He said evenly, 'Your face is calm – well done, Duchess, keep smiling just as you are – but a pulse is beating wildly in your throat. You're wondering if you should appeal to me to keep silent about whatever it was I just witnessed, or if speaking of the matter openly will show how much you care, and encourage a worthless fellow such as myself to gossip all the harder. And now you are wondering if I say all that merely to tempt you into further indiscretion. Do I have it right?'

Exactly right, but she need not tell him so. She had the headache suddenly, and wished she'd never come. 'I have not heard that you were ever unkind to a woman without cause,' she managed. 'I do not know how many other men in this room that could be said of, if truth be known. Isn't that shocking?'

'Including our host, of course, and your recent companion, as you so elegantly imply? His reputation is such that cruelty in a drawing room is the very least of it, to be sure. But you have done me no harm, you mean, and there is no reason I should do you any.'

She must not make this a tragedy when it was only an inconvenience at worst. If she married Ventris, it would not matter afterwards if there should be whispers about them. The marriage would soon confirm that that particular gossip at least was all too true. 'You owe me nothing. If you could just wait a day or so before you make public any speculations...'

'But scandal, unlike revenge, is only good if it's served hot,' he mourned. 'Yesterday's tittle-tattle is like yesterday's fish. No, I'll tell you what I shall do, because I admire you as a brave and beautiful woman, and also because I am frankly terrified of your mother. She and I are alike in many ways; we have invented ourselves out of nothing. You and I shall spend the rest of the evening flirting elegantly with each other, gazing into each other's eyes as if mutually bewitched, and then I shall put it about that I have offered for your hand, and you have refused me. A tragedy – for me. It's even true, if one should care about such quaintly moral matters. And the bustle that will be stirred up by *that* will instantly swamp any mention of the awkward little encounter you had just now. You shall have your day or so to do whatever it is you're doing with the infamous Lord Ventris, and then I and the rest of the world will be enlightened by some startling news, I would wager. But then perhaps I'm wrong, after all, because when I wager, I so often lose. What do you think, madam?'

She laughed in sheer relief. 'I am very willing. And grateful, though I make no admissions. But I'm not sure I remember how to flirt.'

'Which is not something one could say about your recent companion, who is now making Lady Caroline blush with his most marked attentions – surely a notable achievement in itself, given her history. I shall not conjecture as to why he chooses to make such a public display of himself, with one even more notorious than he; no doubt he has his reasons.'

Viola did not reply; she wasn't sure if Ventris was punishing her somehow by going straight to Lady Caroline's side from hers, or if he was being oddly considerate and making sure that when people spoke of this evening, they'd speak of him intriguing with London's most flagrant adulteress, rather than Viola herself.

Brummell quirked a mobile eyebrow at her lack of response. 'Oh, you are admirably discreet. What a wife you would have made me. There's no denying that any woman who was unfortunate enough to marry me would have so much opportunity for the exercise of discretion – as no doubt will the future

Lady Ventris, for that matter. I expect if the Bow Street Runners came calling, you wouldn't turn so much as a hair. Well, if you do not know how to flirt, Duchess, I shall teach you. It'll be something to tell your grandchildren.'

His confidence in his own enduring fame was extraordinary, but she wasn't sure he was wrong. He was a phenomenon, as well as being uncomfortably sharp and noticing. And she *was* grateful – he had given her a precious breathing space from gossip, to come to terms with Ventris – or to reject him utterly.

4

Viola's difficulties were not over, even if seeing His Lordship briefly yesterday could be said to have resolved anything. By now, half the world would be talking about her and Mr Brummell, and the other half about Ventris and Lady Caroline. She must exercise a little caution, then, in what she did next. The Duchess might not care much for her own reputation, but she had her younger unmarried sisters to think of.

Men, of course, could go where they liked and when they liked. The world was not equal in this respect, as in so many others. She could not doubt that Ventris often entertained female company at his rooms – it would be the height of folly to imagine him lonely – but ladies of quality would not go there, unless they came disguised. And Viola would not stoop to such a pantomime, though Lady Caroline's reputation – to pick a random example – suggested that she for one easily might.

It was obvious that the decisive interview with her suitor, if that was what he was, could not be carried out in a public place where they might be overheard and watched. Last night had made that sufficiently clear. That being so, she had no alternative but to ask him to call on her at Armstrong House as he had implied that she should, and hope that if anyone heard of it or saw him entering, they would not think it too odd. If she really did marry him soon, as she'd realised last night, it wouldn't matter in the least. Their relationship would be public knowledge and public property. It wasn't a pleasant thought.

Frowning, she sat down at her desk and dashed off a quick note, telling him that she would be free later that afternoon if he cared to call. She sent one of the footmen off with it, simultaneously hoping and fearing that he would be at home to receive it. Making him – and herself – wait until the next day because it seemed somehow more proper not to show unseemly haste felt like cowardice. It wasn't that she was eager to see him again, she told herself, but she knew she wouldn't sleep tonight or do anything but pace the room all day today if she'd arranged to see him tomorrow.

She wore a high-necked, amber-coloured day-gown, not one of her new ones, but she disdained to change for him. He'd seen her looking well last night, in velvet and jewels, but now he must accustom himself to her in her everyday dress – as indeed he'd have to if they married. There should be no pretence between them. He didn't want her for her fashion sense or any beauty she might possess, whatever he might say to her to charm her, but for her fertility alone. He'd said so plainly enough.

She'd surprised herself, showing a burst of anger over that when she'd been talking to Sabrina. If it had ever occurred to her to resent the reason she'd been chosen by Edward as his bride, she'd long since buried those feelings, and all but forgotten she'd ever harboured them. There had been a dark time in her life after she'd married that she chose not to dwell on if she could help it. Perhaps she'd been simmering with resentment all along, all these years, and never allowed herself to realise it till now. Perhaps her initial reaction had been right, and Ventris's offer was a grave insult – another one – as well as being a lifeline. It was ridiculous that she couldn't tell for certain what to think, but kept changing her mind. Marry him, don't marry him, and round and round. She told herself that it was only natural to be nervous; this was a life-changing decision she was contemplating.

Her private sitting room was comfortable, full of books, furniture and pictures that she had chosen for herself with great pleasure a couple of years after her marriage – the first time she'd ever had that luxury after her crowded, shabby-genteel childhood, and then Winterflood, which as a nervous young bride, she'd been unable to change in any respect. It looked out over the park, and was a tranquil space, decorated in harmonious shades of green, gold and plum but with no regard to whatever might be the latest mode in furnishings. She paced it now, its peacefulness having vanished along with her own.

He was punctual to the minute. The footman announced him – she had given instructions that he should be admitted without delay – and closed the door behind him. It was suddenly shocking to see him here in the flesh, alone, in her sanctuary. They stood looking at each other in silence, and the moment stretched, neither of them seeming inclined to break it. Once words were spoken, they could not be recalled. Last night had been the merest skirmish, and in front of others, where they could not speak their minds; now they would come to it properly.

He kissed her hand again; at home, she wore no gloves, of course, and the brief contact burned all the more on her bare skin. But she would not let desire prompt her into hasty speech that she might regret later. She would save her breath and make him speak first, for the sake of her own pride.

He said wryly, wasting no time at all on idle chatter, 'I understand that I have been outflanked, Duchess, and that you have had another fine offer for your hand. A much finer one than mine, indeed. Should I congratulate you on your conquest? He is not quite the catch that he would have been a few years ago, now that one hears that his fortune is entirely frittered away and the Regent no longer stands his friend, but still – a notable feather in your cap, madam, and if you must exchange your title for a humbler sobriquet, Mrs Brummell will sound very well.'

He almost sounded as though he believed it and was sorry, or was possessed by some other strong emotion, perhaps even common jealousy, but that could surely not be the case.

'Don't be ridiculous,' she said shortly. 'Mr Brummell merely decided to indulge himself in a little light flirtation, in his capricious way. He knew that I would cause a stir, since I have so rarely been seen in Town, and he thought he would add to it, for his own amusement, by creating this fantasy of a case between us. I assure you I have not the least intention of marrying him. I have not quite run mad.'

'But he offered for you?' He didn't sound as if he cared that much, but if he didn't, why had he asked?

She shrugged. 'In jest.'

'Whereas *I* was not jesting. And I am anxious to know if you have summoned me here today to accept me, all the more because I cannot expect the next man who offers for you, now you have emerged from your seclusion, to be making a joke of it as Brummell did. I cannot imagine why else you would have asked me to call on you, unless it was merely for the purpose of abusing me for my audacity in offering for you. In which case, madam, I beg you, say your piece and be done, and I shall go out into the street directly and find some flower-seller or milkmaid who has a fancy to be a baroness.'

'There must be one or two who might. I am right in thinking, then, that no ladies of your acquaintance would jump at the chance? Lady Caroline is married, of course, sadly, and therefore out of your reach, but still it seems most odd.'

She hadn't asked him to sit down. He had released her hand, so that she had not been obliged to pull it from his grasp, but he was still standing very close.

'You must be perfectly aware that I have as little genuine interest in Byron's poor discarded lover as you say you do in George Brummell. You know that my brief flirtation with her was all for show, and for your sake, to set idle tongues wagging on the wrong topic. But yes, it is curious, is it not, that I should be so limited in my choice of bride? Though I know I explained the peculiar circumstances to you with great frankness when I wrote to you.'

'My friend who was with me when your letter arrived thinks there are only two possibilities – that you meant to insult me gravely, or that you are mad.'

'She didn't think it could be both? I must be losing my touch.'

She had to stop herself from smiling, and knew he was aware of it. He said in a more serious tone, 'You must also know I didn't mean to insult you, Viola.'

This was too much. 'No, of course you didn't. Perhaps I am over-sensitive. I should be accustomed by now to being regarded as some sort of prized farm animal.' Unwelcome emotion made her voice waver, and she swung away from him, struggling to regain her composure, cursing herself inwardly.

'I am sorry,' he said from behind her, sounding as though he meant it, though how could she ever be sure, with this man? 'I had reason to know that, and it was never my intention to hurt you. That would be unconscionable in the circumstances. Sometimes, my humour is too dark for civilised company. I should have realised that my bitter jest, which I admit was not in the best of taste, would strike you in that manner and no other.'

'How else could it strike me?' She was furious suddenly; she turned to face him once more, wanting very badly to hit him, or at least to find some crack in his infuriating composure. 'Good God, my "notorious fecundity"? Is my life nothing but a joke to you?'

'It's not a joke. Far from it.' He sighed. 'Viola, you know my situation, and I have an inkling about yours. Unlike Brummell, I am entirely serious. I thought we might help each other – build something lasting out of the ruins of the past. Make life easier for both of us, not just me. Keep the boys safe.'

She could not afford to dwell on the rest of it, however much it stung; this was the heart of the matter, or should be. 'Have you any reason to think that they are not?'

'You speak of my brother, I presume?' At least she could depend on him to take her meaning, not beat about the bush and utter any sort of platitudes. That had never been his way.

She took a few restless steps away from him. 'Edward warned me against him when he was dying, as you did too, long ago. I haven't seen Mr Armstrong for many years – now that he is no longer the heir to Winterflood, he has no excuse to pay a visit. My only guests are my own family. I don't know if it's reasonable to fear him; I only know that Edward did, and it was not like him. I thought you might have a better idea of his state of mind, as his closest relative. I know you used to talk to him, at least occasionally.'

He grimaced and shook his head. 'I'm not on visiting terms with him either these days. I have heard that he is drinking heavily and talking wildly – keeping low company, and if *I* call it low, believe me, my dear, it really is of the lowest. I can't imagine my sudden elevation to the peerage has improved his temper one jot. Is he dangerous to your boys? I don't know. I'd tell you if I did. I do know that dogs cringe from him, and horses, and he can't keep servants. Being his younger half-brother was not an enjoyable experience until I grew big enough to fight back. It is fortunate for them and you that he is not your sons' guardian, I know that much. Marchett might be an old windbag, but at least he's not a villain.' He said these unreassuring words levelly, then added, 'Had you heard that Tarquin was recently married? I pity the poor woman.'

'So do I. Might it make things worse, with him, if I accepted your offer?' She said this quietly, half to herself.

'Well, he has done nothing so far, and he's had years; it's all just supposition. But you are asking me if I believe him to be a potential child killer.'

'I suppose I am. It sounds ridiculously Gothic when said aloud.'

He shrugged and said lightly, 'Perhaps tales of wicked uncles and villainous plots to trick people out of their fortunes thrill us partly because we know it does happen, or at least, has happened in the murky past. It's not impossible. Viola, I do not know. I have promised to look after the boys to the very best of my ability. You can be confident I will. I can set guards about them that no one will ever see – not even them. I can talk to my brother, if you wish. Threaten him. But if you are crediting me with supernatural powers of protection...'

'Of course I am not,' she said shortly. 'I'm not a complete fool. But they are at school now, against my wishes. I can see that you remember Lord Marchett well enough. He would not heed my desire to keep them at home, and patronised me in a manner I found close to unendurable. But he also conceded that if I were married and my husband supported me in this plan – this foolish female plan, he all but said – he must reconsider it.'

Ventris smiled rather wolfishly, and his eyes swept over her, his gaze that familiar slow caress across her body. 'He must assume, of course, that any man who was lucky enough to wed you would have no desire at all to have two great boys about the house when you should be focusing all your attentions on *him*. Therefore there is little chance of you receiving such support from any new husband, he must imagine.'

'That was the implication; I could not miss it, though I'm sure he didn't mean it to be even slightly flattering, since he dislikes me so. But it's not true of you, is it?'

'No. No, my dear, it isn't. So it is a little unfair of you to accuse me of regarding you in an agricultural light, like some prize cow, when your main reason for considering my offer – perhaps your only one – is to keep Ned and Robin safe from my brother. It seems we have both of us been reduced to a rather primitive level of existence. We might as well live in a cave and go about dressed in skins – not that Ventris is much better than a cave at present. But I am sure I shall not care, if you are with me. I think you'd look rather well in furs and nothing else, like some savage goddess I should worship on my knees.'

His voice was silky and dangerous, and her body flushed with heat, right to the core of her. *Some savage goddess*, indeed, and *on his knees*. There was a picture to torment her of a lonely night. She had a sudden thought that if she accepted him and told him so now, he might consider that there was no time like the present, and reach out and touch her... more than that. If she told him she wanted a child for herself, she'd almost be inviting his immediate and intimate attentions. Why wait? The words trembled on her tongue, but she did not utter them, though her whole body was suddenly hot with overwhelming and unwelcome desire.

'We have been tolerably plain in our discussion,' he said when she still did not answer him and the silence grew uncomfortably tense between them, with so many things still unspoken on each side. 'Painfully so, at moments, and yet for a wonder we have not quite fallen to abusing each other. Can it be true that we have a bargain?'

'I think so,' she said reluctantly, then realised that for her own pride, she should not allow herself to be swept away so easily. 'But I will need certain assurances from you, as to your state of health.'

He did blink then, surprised at last. 'Oh,' he said slowly. 'My terrible reputation for indiscriminate amours. Well, this is frank indeed, madam. You realise, of course, that I can give you the assurances you require, but they will only be words, in the very nature of things.'

'I know that. Nevertheless, I ask for them.' She saw the distaste on his face and said hotly, 'You are unfair, sir, to be so squeamish about it. I cannot afford to be so nice. I would risk my life attempting to have a child for you – every woman of childbearing age does, every time she lies down with a man. Men may treat it as a thing of no consequence, but a woman if she is wise does not. I am prepared to take that risk, but I would prefer not to put my life at hazard in any other manner, nor that of any innocent child I may have. I don't think there's anything unreasonable about that, so I will not apologise, even if my unladylike frankness does offend you.'

'You misunderstand the reason for my reaction,' he said, his face expressionless and unreadable now. 'I am never offended by honesty. It was self-disgust, perhaps, that such an assumption might be made about my mode of life. And yet I cannot say that it is entirely unfair in you, given what you must believe you know of me. I do not underestimate the risks you take, my dear, nor the size of the debt I shall owe you even for trying, so let us be plain: I do not have the pox, and I have never had it. I have been far more careful than you or anybody else would care to give me credit for. And recently, I have not... I promise you, that at least you need not fear. And Viola, if we marry, I will be faithful. I swear I will, and it is not just empty words, though I know you have little reason to believe me.'

'Very well.' She was proud of the steadiness of her voice. 'I will take you, then, Ventris.'

'Shall we perhaps celebrate our betrothal, or seal our agreement, if you prefer to look at it like that?' That silky, seductive tone in his voice again. He had moved yet closer to her. Why had she said *take,* of all words she could have chosen?

She looked up at him – she only had to raise her head a little.

'You are very brave,' he said, and reached out one well-shaped hand, his fingers lightly caressing her cheek and tracing the full shape of her lips. 'But I knew that already.' His touch sent shivers through her, and she had to fight not to close her eyes against the perilous sweetness of it.

It had been so long since she had had any real physical contact save for the boys' precious and increasingly rare embraces. At almost eleven, they were already beginning to consider themselves too grown-up for childish cuddles, which cracked her heart. And she did not even want to think how long it had been since anyone had touched her like this, though she could, if she wished, have tallied it up to the year, the month and the day, even the hour. He was going to kiss her, she knew.

All at once, she could not bear it. 'No,' she said, and turned her face away from his hand. 'You said you would respect any stipulation that I cared to make, and I have made none. Well, here is one. We will be married as soon as it can be arranged, I will live wherever you please as long as the boys are with me, but you shall not kiss me.'

His hand fell to his side. 'I did say that, didn't I? How rash of me. But madam, if you find me so repulsive, how are we to go on?'

'You know it's not that. It would bring back memories I do not care to have revived, that is all.'

'Let us be clear, then – apart from that, you place no other restrictions on my... conjugal behaviour?'

Damn him. 'No.' She looked him full in the face again, and she knew that if there was longing in her eyes despite everything, he would be able to see it.

'So I may not kiss your delectable lips, but with your consent, I may throw you down on that sofa there and *take you* now? For example?'

Trust him to put it into words, when she had only thought it. Her voice was almost level, but not quite. 'If you wish.'

'If I wish... Viola, you know I have always wanted you. Whatever else has changed, that has not.' They were chest to chest now, their bodies almost touching, then touching at last, and their breathing was coming faster. Whatever this was, they both felt it.

The tips of her suddenly aching breasts brushed his coat, and she could feel him pressing hard and insistent against the softness of her belly. Heat was pooling there, and lower. 'Well, then, my lord. My fecundity, as you so kindly pointed out, is so prodigious that I could be with child before we were even wed. Today. Now, before you quit this room. Think of the trouble it would save.'

He let out a crack of laughter. 'I'm not convinced that I want to save that kind of trouble. If we marry and we time it correctly, for which I depend on you, I will have at the very least a few weeks in your bed before we could be confident of the desired outcome. Whatever else I may doubt in our immediate future, I do not doubt that there would be a great deal of mutual pleasure in that. More – and I cannot believe I am saying this when the immediate prospect is so damn tempting – than fucking you hard and fast on a sofa and then leaving you.'

'Leaving me, at least, is something you have practice at.' This was something she had been determined not to say, but it had slipped out.

He reached out again and captured a tear from her lashes, and then, unforgivably, raised it to his lips and tasted it with the tip of his tongue. She had tried so hard not to cry, and he must draw attention to it.

'I know,' he murmured. 'My dear, I do. But it will be the last time I do so, our circumstances being so changed. Soon, you are to be my wife. Mine. And still we have not found a way to seal our bargain. You say we cannot kiss, but a cool handshake will hardly do, I fear.'

Desire was so bound up with anger and regret in her, and with the weight of so many long years of loneliness, loneliness that stretched far back before Edward's death, that she could not answer him. She wished he had put her over the sofa as he'd said, where she could not see his face nor he hers. She wished he'd pulled up her skirts and freed himself and taken her. Fucked her, hard and fast. It would have stopped her, at least for as long as it lasted, from *thinking*. From remembering.

Their eyes locked.

He put his hands upon her waist, where her stays ended. She knew he could feel that; through the material of the gown and petticoats that covered her, his thumb traced the line where the stiffened fabric of her corset met her soft, warm flesh, with only one layer beneath it: her fine lawn shift, covering her belly. Her thighs. Her core.

His touch was irresistible, despite everything. 'You want to seal our bargain, Richard? Do it, then. Make me forget for a little while. Use your clever fingers and give me a downpayment on all that pleasure you so rashly promised me.'

They were moving before she'd finished speaking. He backed her against the wall, his strong body pressing her to it, and dragged up her skirts with one efficient movement. She parted her thighs eagerly and his hand slipped between them, covering her, cupping her sex. His hand was warm; her body was hotter. She pressed herself against him, urging him on, and his fingers slipped between her lips. He did not taunt her by telling her how wet she was, how swollen her bud, how ready for him despite all her reservations. But when he felt it all, he swore and sank to his knees, his hands hard on her thighs. And as she leaned back against the wall of her private sanctuary and closed her eyes, he began devouring her. He was not slow or subtle; he ate her with a barely controlled fierceness that had her hoping, while she was still capable of coherent thought, that when he had done with this, he would not be able to prevent himself from unbuttoning himself and taking her, here against this wall, on the sofa or on the floor, she didn't care which, and spending inside her, even though he'd said he wouldn't. That would feel like some sort of victory, to break the iron control it seemed he had over himself, and she did not.

She came with shocking suddenness, biting the pad of her thumb to suppress her moans, but he did not stop, mercilessly prolonging her pleasure, and only when she began to fear that her legs would no longer support her did she put her hand on his forehead and push him away, not trusting herself to speak. She felt light-headed, sated, and ashamed of herself. She couldn't know what he was feeling. Triumphant, perhaps – she did not look for confirmation of it in his face. He'd got what he'd wanted, her submission, and he knew she was vulnerable to him still. But then, he'd known that already – or he'd never have written to her.

And then he rose to his feet, kissed her hand and left without a word.

5

It was easy enough to arrange a marriage, it seemed, when both parties were fully of age and the gentleman, even if he could not afford to restore a large, neglected estate in the north of England, could afford an expensive special licence. Viola was not privy to Lord Ventris's negotiations with the Archbishop of Canterbury (or, more realistically, some representative of his), but if either of those clergymen entertained any qualms, they overcame them, and the licence was granted without difficulty. Ventris's dubious reputation was apparently not grounds enough for refusal, perhaps because he was a peer now too, a member of the House of Lords, and therefore a person of influence and consequence.

Viola knew she had Sabrina's support in her equivocal undertaking; she now had the more difficult task of speaking to her mother. She didn't need her approval, but in common courtesy, she must tell her, and she couldn't put it off any longer. This would result, she knew, in something uncomfortably close to an interrogation. If a career had been open to her and matchmaker was not considered a profession, her mama could have made a success at the head of Bonaparte's secret police.

Mrs Constantine, who had been a widow for some years now, lived in a small rented house in Bloomsbury with her three younger daughters, their family estate having gone to a cousin. She had a modest jointure, which would not by itself have been enough to support life in London nor the cost of the younger girls' come-outs; Sabrina, Viola and their next sister Allegra split the bulk of the family's expenses between them, and so they went on very well. Nobody could doubt that soon enough, another Miss Constantine would be respectably betrothed, despite their lack of fortune, humble birth and unfashionable residence.

The Duchess found her mother alone when she called in Great Russell Street a couple of days after her encounter with Ventris. She hadn't seen him since, but he'd been keeping her updated with his progress by note, and they had discussed their plans by this medium, which was perhaps easier than face to face, given what had happened last time they'd met. It seemed the marriage was really happening. Tomorrow morning, early, they would be visiting their lawyers together.

'Mother,' she said abruptly, 'I'm getting married.'

Mrs Constantine had never been one for the social niceties or for any form of pretence. Though she had by the sheer force of her personality found good husbands for two of her daughters and made a most spectacular match for Viola, she hadn't done it through toadying manners or bowing and scraping to her social superiors. Perhaps she'd simply frightened the gentlemen into offering, or mesmerised them till they were utterly in her power.

'Sabrina informed me that you had had a proposal,' Leontina said calmly. 'And of course, I have heard the gossip about Brummell, which I was not foolish enough to believe.' She had set down her needlework upon her daughter's entrance and sat looking at her with sharp, dark eyes. The room was a little shabby, as London lodgings often were, but no one was likely to notice that when she was present, and she did not give a fig about such things herself. 'I should have realised that you would be vulnerable now that Emily Naismith has left you and you are all alone to brood. Why are you doing this, Viola? Please do not tell me that you are in love with him, whoever he is.'

'I would not dream of telling you that, Mama,' she said, feeling herself flushing as though she were eighteen again. 'That is an obvious absurdity. It is Lord Ventris – Edward's cousin, who was Mr Richard Armstrong. He has recently inherited an estate and title, but by some quirk of his aunt's will, he cannot gain the money to support it unless he marries and has a child within eighteen months.'

'I see why he offers for you; it is eminently sensible of him, so clearly he has a brain in his head. But I do not see why you accept him. You are as secure in life as any woman can ever hope to be, and you have your freedom besides.'

'The boys need a father, and he is the only man I can trust to care for them as Edward did. Also, I... I'm tired of being alone now they're growing up. It's nothing to do with Emily making a life for herself, as she is quite entitled to do. I'm sure she wants a baby before it is too late, and I'd like another child myself.' Leontina was intimidating even to her own daughters; Viola never felt less like a grown woman with children and responsibilities of her own than when she was in her mother's astringent presence, struggling to explain herself.

Mrs Constantine considered her dispassionately. 'Such folly. I speak of you, not Emily, of course; she has done well. I suppose it is of no use telling you to take up a hobby to fill your time. Watercolour drawing, perhaps, or philanthropy. Horticulture. Bee-keeping. No? I understand this man has a very poor reputation indeed, even if one discounts half the gossip, but I see that you are prepared to overlook it. You've always been impulsive; it is a fault. Have you told the boys yet?'

'Not yet. I mean to go and see them tomorrow and tell them in person, after we have met with the lawyers and agreed on the drawing-up of the papers. And then I'll go home to Winterflood. I hope you'll come, Mama, and bring the girls. Sabrina and Laurence are coming. We're to marry there; his estate is too far for everyone to travel, and besides needs extensive renovations to make it more habitable. He wrote to tell me that his aunt, despite her wealth, was allowing the castle to fall down around her ears in recent years. She was too old and stubborn to manage it as she should.' Before the end of this rather breathless and unnecessarily long speech, Viola was disagreeably aware of her own voice echoing fatuously in her ears. She ceased abruptly.

'As long as he does all this work with his own money and not yours. But do you think Winterflood is a good idea? Might it not be simpler to be married in London?'

'Ventris lives in lodgings in London, Mama. Wherever we choose to marry, we will be obliged afterwards to go and live either at Winterflood or Armstrong House, at least for a while. And I would prefer to be in the country. I mean to find a tutor and take the boys out of school after Christmas, perhaps sooner, and it will be better for them to be at home rather than in the dirt and smoke of London. There will be memories of Edward at both houses, if that's what concerns you. There is no difference.' Why was she talking so much?

Mrs Constantine said nothing more on the subject, perhaps seeing with her usual ruthless practicality that it was pointless to argue any further. 'Do you think they will mind?'

Viola shook her head. 'I honestly don't know. They adored Edward, and they've never met Ventris. It will be strange for them, to have someone new standing in the relation of a father. But I think it will be good for them in the long run, once they have accustomed themselves. Don't you?'

Her mother shrugged, reluctant to commit herself. 'It will be strange for you, too, and more than that, if he tries to exert fatherly authority over them when you have been their sole parent these past few years.'

There was no denying the truth of this. 'I expect we shall fight over that, and other things. I'm sure we shall, in fact. He is a provoking sort of a person, not calm like Edward or Father or Laurence. And you know I have a hot temper much like yours, so I do not suppose it will be a tranquil existence. I am prepared for that. I'm not suffering under any illusions that it will always be easy.'

'You're talking about passion.'

God, her mother was sharp. 'I don't know how you can tell that, but yes, I am. It seems we have that connection. But it's not why I'm marrying him.' She would not even allow herself to think further on that, not in her mother's presence. The woman was extraordinarily quick, and terrifyingly frank, and quite capable of plucking her most private thoughts from the air.

'Then I must wish you happy. Perhaps there is already a little Ventris on the way.'

'Mother! There is not.'

'That's a pity. You realise of course that if you do not give him a child in time, you will be saddled with him and his tumbledown castle for life, all for the sake of getting the boys a father and warming your own bed. Would it not be much easier to take a lover?'

Mrs Constantine's motherly advice was not always of a conventional nature, so Viola was not as taken aback as she might have been. 'I could do that, of course, but then my famous fertility would be a cause of anxiety rather than an advantage, would it not?'

Her mother agreed that it would, unless of course her lover was a woman, and after that, there seemed little more to be said. Few people would have believed that her mama's advice upon hearing she was to marry again had been that she should instead find a woman to take to her bed and keep her satisfied and happy; only members of the Constantine family would not have been surprised in the least.

The Duchess, eager to change the subject, enquired about her sisters and their suitors – there would surely be suitors – and after that, took her leave. The fact that her mama had merely questioned her with her habitual incisiveness, and had not expressed her inevitable disapproval anywhere nearly as forcefully as she might have done, had not made the interview anything close to pleasant. But at least she had not been obliged to share her own vague suspicions of Tarquin Armstrong. Mrs Constantine had no time for vagueness.

After the meeting with Ventris and the lawyers, which went smoothly enough from her point of view, she set off in her carriage to the school. She'd written to the headmaster and explained that she had some important news for her boys that she must deliver in person; mindful of Mr Muncaster's warning, she had arranged for them to be brought to meet her at a respectable local inn rather than appearing on the premises. This was apparently quite a usual sort of thing to do – at any rate, if one was a duchess.

It was a slow and rather anxious journey across London's bustling centre and out the other side, but eventually, she arrived, and sent one of her attendants to the school, which was just around the corner from the substantial old half-timbered inn that had been recommended to her. A little while later, her sons were ushered into the spacious private parlour she had reserved for the afternoon.

It had hardly been more than two weeks since she had seen them, and already it seemed to her that they had grown. She rushed across the room to embrace them, and this time, they suffered it with good grace, and clung to her for a precious moment. It seemed they secretly wanted that contact too. They might even have missed her, a little.

Once she had reassured them that she had no bad news for them – that no person nor animal they cared for was ill – they fell hungrily on the substantial meal she had had sent up for them from the inn kitchens. An inexperienced person might have assumed that the school was starving them, but Viola knew better. She also knew it was useless to attempt to ask them anything or tell them anything and expect them to pay heed to it until they had satisfied their hunger. While they ate prodigious quantities of meat pie and potatoes, followed by great slabs of fruitcake, they told her, indistinctly, fragments of detail of their new life, their new companions, and, as an afterthought, their lessons and those strange creatures, their masters. It seemed they liked school well enough – Robin more than Ned, perhaps, since he had always been more easy-going.

She listened intently, watching them, looking out for changes and for things they did not say. Though they were twins, they weren't identical; far from it. They were both dark, as all the Armstrongs were and as she was herself, but Ned was smaller and slighter, his face less symmetrical, habitually serious until it was lit up by one of his swift, beguiling smiles. Robin was bigger, more solid, more of an athlete, less of a worrier. They complemented each other in their skills and qualities, and were a formidable force for mischief when combined. They asked politely after Miss Naismith – now Mrs Muncaster – and about how things went at Winterflood. It was plain that they missed their dogs and horses above almost everything else.

At last, their rate of consumption slowed, and she said resolutely, 'I am very happy to see you, my loves, but I would not have come and taken you away from your studies and your friends if I had not had something important to tell you.' She paused for a moment. There was only one way to say it – straight out. 'A gentleman has offered for me, and I have accepted. I have come to tell you that I am to be married.'

They looked quickly at each other, but said nothing.

'He is Lord Ventris,' she told them. 'You do not know the name, because he has only recently inherited the title, but he is your father's cousin, Richard Armstrong, whom perhaps you have heard spoken of. He was very close to your father when he was younger.'

'We've never met him,' Ned said. 'Or I don't remember if we have.' He was understandably wary.

'He saw you when you were very small, but you could not possibly recall it. He has not visited Winterflood recently; his business has taken him abroad a great deal.'

'If Papa liked him, I am sure we will too,' said Robin stoutly.

'Do *you* like him, Mama?' That was, inevitably, Ned.

'I do,' she said, not even sure if she was lying. Her feelings towards Richard Armstrong were far too complicated to explain to a child, especially since she wasn't positive that she fully understood them herself. 'And I know that your father would be happy, not least because he would trust Lord Ventris to have every care for you.'

'I suppose that is good,' Robin said. 'Though we don't need care all that much. We are not *babies*. He could take us shooting, perhaps. Or teach us how to drive a bang-up pair in a high-perch phaeton, if he's a whip. That would be good.'

'Fishing,' said Ned absently. 'Papa was going to teach me fishing.' His brow was furrowed. 'You aren't marrying him just for our sakes, are you, Mama? Because you know that other fellows have fathers and we do not?'

'No,' she told him, blinking away a fugitive tear. 'No, of course not. I could have remarried long before this if that was all I cared for. But it is not so easy to find a good man – not every gentleman would want to have another man's children around, perhaps, when newly married. I promise you that Ventris will never make you feel unwanted. You will not *be* unwanted, not for a second. He will love you for your father's sake, and for your own. That is important, I think.'

'Is he very old?' Edward would have been close on sixty if he had lived, as old as many boys' grandparents; it was a natural question.

'No, Robin, he is three and thirty. Only a few years older than me. Not old at all, and he has no other children, since he has never been married before.'

'That's good.'

'Yes, I suppose so, but I expect he will want a son of his own, then,' Ned contributed.

'Well, Lord Ventris's title and estate can pass through the female line – it came to him through his aunt. So he would like to have a child, yes, quite naturally, but it need not be a boy. A girl could inherit.'

Robin's face reflected his horror at this new idea. 'Not just a nasty, smelly baby, but a girl!' He made a noise suggestive of profound masculine disgust.

'Mama would like that,' Ned said unexpectedly. 'I expect she has been lonely, especially now we are away at school, and Miss Naismith has left to marry Mr Muncaster. Is that why?'

'Partly,' she said resolutely. 'And I admit, I would like a baby, now you are both grown so big.'

'A puppy would be just as good,' grumbled Robin. 'And much more fun. Dogs can *do* things, even when they're quite young. Babies just…' He waved a hand to encompass all the chaos of which babies were capable, and knocked over a cream jug.

When order was restored, it was plain that the boys – or Robin, at least – had tired of the subject. They went outside together and walked about a little, chatting of this and that, and then it was time to return them to school and set out on the long drive back to Armstrong House. Viola embraced them, when they were certain nobody was looking, and watched as they went inside, heads close together as always.

They had taken it as well as she could have hoped; Robin would be won over if no baby was immediately forthcoming and if Richard involved him in suitably masculine pursuits, and Ned... Ned knew she had been lonely, wanted her to be happy, and would be to a large extent placated if he saw she was. His own relationship with Ventris would have to be built more slowly and cautiously.

But would she be happy in her new marriage, even if her boys were? How could she possibly know?

6

THE WEDDING NIGHT

Viola sat in bed, propped on pillows with her hair loose about her bare shoulders, and pretended to read. It was most unlikely that a woman in a situation such as hers would really be able to concentrate on the pages of a book, however gripping, and indeed she couldn't; the words were a blur to her. But she was damned if he was going to come in, when he finally did, and find her meekly waiting for him. If she picked up a volume when she heard the connecting door between their chambers open, he'd know she'd done it just for show. He'd be able to tell that she'd just been moving – he had a hunter's instinct for that sort of thing; she knew in her blood. Of course he did – it came from how he had chosen to live his life. Whatever he'd been when he was a youth, now he was a big, beautiful, sleek animal, a predator, and she would not be his prey. Not ever.

So she held *Pride and Prejudice* in front of her, open at some random page, and tried to breathe calmly. If he thought to tease her by asking her about the story, and he might, she was prepared. She'd read it before, upon its publication; given its premise, she and her sisters might have been said to have lived it. She wondered idly – her thoughts were buzzing about like flies trapped against a windowpane – if the lady author, whoever she might be, had ever envisaged that her clever book would be read in such scandalous circumstances, by a naked woman who was both dreading and longing for the arrival of the man she had married only a few hours since, and in many ways hardly knew.

The door opened at last, and he lounged in, closing it behind him. He was wearing a black silk banyan, carelessly done up – as if anything he ever did was careless – to expose a tantalising V of bare, muscular chest, and the dark hair upon it. He was the embodiment of every fantasy that a lonely woman had ever had at night (assuming she was not inclined to take Mrs Constantine's advice, and take it exclusively, in the matter of bedfellows). She would not lick her lips, though she wanted to. She closed the book with a little snap that sounded excessively loud in the quiet room, and set it down, and looked at him in silence.

The banyan now concealed much of his athletic frame, those hard thighs, the lean hips and the broadness of his shoulders, but his day clothes did not, fitting his form with tailored precision. The current mode for tight pantaloons and breeches meant that all of a gentleman's masculine endowments could quite easily be seen and assessed, not just the muscles of his thighs and torso but much, much more than that. When a man was aroused, it was shockingly obvious. Never discussed by ladies, at least not in public, but plain to see. And he had been visibly aroused earlier today. Provokingly, she became aware that her nipples were peaking, her breasts tightening, and not because the room was cold. Even ladies gave signs of arousal that they could not always hide. Foolish to imagine that those dangerously observant grey eyes would not have noticed.

He said, 'I confess I did not expect to see you already naked, my lady.' His voice was very deep, his tone caressing.

She replied with composure, 'I did not care for the idea of you undressing me, and still less did I care to undress myself while you watched, as if at your command. So I saved us both a little time.' When she had finished speaking, she threw back the covers before she lost her courage. To give him credit, he did not blink at what was revealed.

'But we have nothing but time. We have all night. All week. Longer. Or do you imagine,' he said, unfastening his robe and letting it fall, then crossing the room to her side, 'that I intend merely to fall on you like a thunderbolt, take my selfish pleasure from you, and then leave you alone and unsatisfied? I would expect that a woman of your experience should know better. Even from our last encounter, you should know better.'

She shrugged, taking a little wicked pleasure in the way it made her breasts move, and the way his eyes followed that movement. He was very close now, naked as she was, and it took a conscious effort not to let her gaze linger on him: his strong shoulders, his chest, the tautly muscled torso with the line of dark hair leading down to his proudly erect member. 'You don't doubt your ability to satisfy me, sir?'

It wasn't a fair gibe, or even a logical one, and she knew it. She did indeed have evidence that he could give her pleasure, from their explosive meeting when they'd agreed to marry. And that was not all. Nature had been generous in the gifts she had given him, as she could see for herself, and rumour had it that he had made good use of those gifts over the last few years, so *she* didn't doubt it for a second – but there was no need to tell him that. He didn't need to be any more smugly confident than he already was.

'Was that a challenge?'

Viola had a temper, she would have been the first to admit, and sometimes, it led her to say things she later regretted. For reasons she didn't care to dwell on, this man of all men riled her into incautious speech whenever she met him, which was perhaps a shame, since she'd just married him. 'Ventris,' she said crisply, 'we have wed for the purpose of conceiving a child. I have reason to believe that you need no instruction in the methods usually employed to do so, and you will be aware that I am similarly enlightened. And here we are, both naked and, to all appearances...' and now she did allow her eyes to linger, to caress and to appreciate, 'Ready. I assure you, I need no fine words, no delicate persuasion, no slow wooing. Shall we...?'

Before she had finished speaking, he was on her. *Be careful what you wish for*, she thought, as he moved between her legs – which had not before been spread wide to accommodate him between them, but somehow now mysteriously were, though he hadn't yet laid so much as a hand on her – and covered her body with his. And stopped. His member was at her entrance, nudging, seeking, but he stopped. They were belly to belly, hot skin to hot skin, his rough chest hair tickling her breasts, his arms taking most of his weight so that he did not crush her, his face close to hers. His breath caressed her cheek as he said, 'I cannot decide whether you need to paint me as a brute and a villain, perhaps in your own mind as much as anywhere else, or whether you really are... impatient. Again. If it is the first, I refuse to give you that particular twisted satisfaction, and if it is the second, well, despite appearances, I am not myself so hasty. You must know that good things come to she who waits.'

And then, silkily, 'I promised not to kiss your lips, and you reminded me of it earlier today when I forgot for a moment. In the spirit of fairness, I will extend that to your lovely face, lest you think that I am likely to be carried away and make a sneaking attempt on your mouth. That would be underhand; I shall not do it, however tempted I might be. But I made no undertaking not to kiss any other part of you. Did I?'

'No,' she said steadily. 'I did not ask that of you.' She had undertaken the formal marriage negotiations herself, though her father's old lawyer, who still looked after her affairs, had been so scandalised that he had almost died of it. He'd been there to put her stipulations into lawyers' dry words for her, but she had not stayed absent like some blushing virgin whose future could be decided for her behind her back. Not this time. Three men had been present in the dusty panelled office with her, two lawyers and Ventris himself. She had said baldly, careless what any of them thought, 'I have told you already that I will not kiss you – Mr Carlyle, I want it to be very clear, I will not kiss him,' and had it written into the agreement. Insisted upon it, or she would not have signed. If she'd said, *I do not want your lips anywhere upon my body*, the old man would have fallen down dead of an apoplexy on the spot. And besides... didn't she want that? Why deny herself such pleasure when she knew just how good it could be?

She could tell somehow that this provoking man she'd married was smiling. She could not see his face, because he was kissing his way down her neck, tiny butterfly kisses, and occasionally a nip of the teeth, just to unsettle her. His warm breath on her throat, the slight caress of his lips, the sudden, unexpected sharp jolt of his teeth... It had been so long. She would not moan. She would not whimper, gasp or sigh.

He'd reached her breast, and now his tongue came out and teased her nipple, the very tip of it, and she bit her lip, hard, in order to keep silent. She would not bury her face in his hair and drink in the scent of it, clean and masculine, no matter how much she wanted to. And then he made some wordless sound and took her whole nipple in his mouth and began sucking on it, laving it with his hot tongue, while his hand came up and began playing with her other breast, its erect peak stiffening even further at his touch.

And her resolution snapped. She had never promised or even intended to lie there like a log while he explored her body; so now her fingers tangled in his silky hair, and she wrapped her legs around him tightly. This was a sign, it seemed, for him to stop holding himself back too; he let his whole weight fall on her, pressing her urgently into the soft bed, and she welcomed it with a fierce emotion that she refused to describe as joy even to herself.

When he moved away a little, it was only so that his right hand could trace its way down her body, across the soft swell of her belly. She had stretch marks there, silvery and faded now since they were eleven years old, but if he saw them and they bothered him, he did not show it. Whatever he thought about them, and his thoughts must be as complicated as hers were, he did not share it with her, and she was glad.

His erection was no longer pressing at her core; because he had shifted, it lay heavy on her thigh, and his exploring fingers replaced it. He'd stopped talking some while since, his mouth being fully occupied, and she was grateful once more that he did not raise his head and think to comment mockingly on how wet she was, and what it signified. In fact, she was grateful that he did not raise his head at all. There was nothing that he was doing that she wished him to stop. Her hands had moved to trace the corded muscles of his shoulders and upper arms; she was greedy to touch more of him, but couldn't reach. She wanted to bite him, to leave a mark. Later, she would.

He wasn't tentative this time either. Far from it. His thumb stroked her pearl of Venus for a while, and then his fingers slid confidently inside her. She clenched on him, and arched her back, digging her nails into the hard muscle of his upper arms, pushing her breasts up to fill his mouth and fingers in a wordless plea she'd have been shot before she uttered aloud.

Now he did lift his head up, revealing his face, wet and dazed and curiously defenceless, and what he saw in hers made him shift again, to enter her at last, but then in one smooth movement he was rolling them both over, so that she straddled him. He had the sense not to speak to her now and ruin it. They were both breathing hard, and he reached down to cup her buttocks and squeeze her tightly. He filled her, stretched her in a way that was both familiar and new, and she put her hands on his chest and began to move. After a little while, she closed her eyes and gave herself up to the pure sensation of it, riding him, shamelessly using him to give her pleasure as he thrust up to meet her. She tried, but did not entirely succeed, to forget who he was – her husband, now – and why they were together. It had been so long.

She did not cry aloud when she came, though she badly wanted to, but she threw back her head and rode it out on him, grinding against his hardness. When he saw her cupping her breast and pinching her nipple, he urged her forward with gentle pressure of his hands so that he could get his mouth on her again to give her what she needed, what it seemed he needed too, and with a great groan of release, he spent himself deep inside her, his face smothered in her abundant flesh.

After a while, she said, 'Roll me over again,' and when he did not respond immediately, she repeated it, tugging sharply on his hair. He obeyed then, still inside her, and only pulled away from her when she was on her back. He lay beside her, propped on one elbow, and watched as she slipped a pillow under her pelvis, raising her knees to her chest.

Nobody had ever called him a fool. 'My precious seed,' he said in light, ironic tones that held a wealth of tangled meaning.

'Precisely. I have been talking to wise women of my acquaintance, my sister chiefly, and this is what she recommends, undignified though it undoubtedly is.' She could have given a longer explanation, curious details of feminine wisdom that she thought might have interested him, but she was trying hard not to let her tone towards him soften, drift towards intimacy. Whatever they had just done, they had not made love.

'I do not care a great deal for dignity, and if you are worried your posture appears odd to me, banish that concern from your mind. It is damnably erotic. *You* are.'

'Ridiculous,' she said shortly. If she had cared at all what he thought of her, she wouldn't have let him see her like this. But it was too important to neglect for the sake of mere appearances.

'Not so. You are a spectacularly beautiful woman, and you have just taken your pleasure from me, and I from you. And it was no common, fleeting pleasure, but exquisite release. Whatever else we both know, that remains true. It is very easy to forget our bargain. I have forgot it. Your lovely breasts are still flushed pink where I kissed and licked them. We are naked here together. You smell of me, and I of you. If I sucked my fingers, I would taste you. And in a little while, we will do it all again. And again and again, as often as we wish. How could that not be erotic? Do not lie to me and say you don't feel it. You're not a liar, Viola.'

Not taking his eyes from her, he raised the fingers that had been deep inside her to his mouth and slowly, slowly began sucking on them. Despite herself, she felt a fresh thrill of arousal and of need surge through her. Good God, she had feared this. She needed to keep up her barriers, fragile as they were, because however much she might tell herself that this was just a transaction between them, a cold bargain, the unbridled passion they ignited in each other could not be denied. There was nothing cold about that. And passion was so dangerous. She'd almost let it ruin her once before.

7

Emily Muncaster had been a wedding guest along with her new husband, naturally, but Viola had had little opportunity to speak with her amongst the clamour of the Constantine family. They'd snatched a moment together on the morning of the ceremony, no more than that, and Viola had been glad to see her best friend looking well and happy, though her pretty face was presently clouded with anxiety. 'Are you quite sure you want to go through with this madness?' Emily had hissed urgently when none of Viola's sisters was close enough to hear.

'I am. I am committed. And there is no need to be so concerned for me.'

'I am more concerned even than I was before, when I read that appalling letter. Perhaps you are not aware that sometimes, you look at Lord Ventris as if you hate him, Viola!'

'Only sometimes?' she said lightly.

'And the rest of the time...' The former governess's cheeks were flaming. She was a married woman herself now; perhaps she understood better, even if she didn't want to say so. 'And as for him, I can't tell what he's thinking at all, apart from the fact that he never takes his eyes off you for a second.'

Viola embraced her friend. 'Don't worry,' she said inadequately in her ear. And then, 'I'll write to you, I promise, when we leave here. We must not lose touch, ever. I will want to hear all your news, whether important or trivial.'

Emily's new home was close enough that she'd not been obliged to stay overnight, but Winterflood House was still full of Constantines in the days after the wedding – Viola's mother, all five of her sisters, Sabrina's and Allegra's husbands, and those of their children who were not away at school. The older ones, including Ned and Robin, hadn't been fetched here; it wasn't the custom, and Viola had judged that it would be unsettling and awkward for her sons, and for herself. They had never known her attention to be divided, and for a short while at least, it must be.

Their younger cousins would be running riot in the grounds even now, terrifying every animal for miles and making a nuisance of themselves in the stables and anywhere else they happened to be. The adults would be celebrating her marriage and their family reunion in the traditionally noisy, argumentative Constantine manner. There would be fallings-out and reconciliations. Drama. Old scores would be settled and new ones brooded over. Sabrina was calm and so was Laurence; the rest of them were anything but, and enjoyed nothing more than a good argument.

It was not an atmosphere conducive to a honeymoon of any kind, and so Viola had left her mother to act as hostess to the mayhem and decamped with her new husband and a few servants to the Dower House in the grounds. She'd always thought it would be her home on the distant day that Ned married, and perhaps it still would be – the future was so uncertain. But it was quiet and private, which was what they needed.

Despite her fine words to her mother that memories of Edward would be everywhere and so it didn't matter in the least, it had seemed sensible to start their married life together in a place that held no recollections of the late Duke at all, for her or for Ventris, who was after all his cousin. She had to rack her brains to remember her first husband ever setting foot in the Dower House. Maybe once, when he had first taken her around the estate, more than twelve years ago? She'd been so intimidated by all the grandeur he showed her that she couldn't remember any of those first days very clearly, and didn't want to. But this house was small and perfect, a Queen Anne jewel set in a lovely formal garden, and it had always been kept well maintained, as all of Winterflood was. She had a great fondness for it – it was on a human scale, unlike the big house.

It was very strange to wake with a man in her bed. Edward had always come to her, stayed a while to do what he had to, and then left, murmuring that he was sure she would sleep better undisturbed. When she had been in a delicate condition and after the boys were born, he had not visited her at all, so her bed had been cold for many years longer than she had been a widow.

As a young girl just married, though, she'd lain alone in her rumpled sheets after his departure and wondered if it was merely awkwardness that drove him away, or if he so desperately missed the wife he'd loved that he simply could not bear to see her take Elizabeth's place. But then, she had not known, because she'd never dared to ask, if her opulent, silk-hung bedchamber in the main house had once been Elizabeth's, and before that had been Julia's. One woman divorced and vanished, presumably abroad; the other dead and greatly missed. Edward had married Elizabeth around the time of her own birth; either of those women would have been easily old enough to be her own mother. People on the estate occasionally talked about Duchess Elizabeth, with respect and affection, and God knows Edward had spoken of her constantly, but no one ever dared to mention disgraced Julia.

Julia – there were no portraits of her anywhere, and her name had been so thoroughly crossed out in the family Bible, presumably by Edward, that it could no longer be read. Viola didn't even know if she was alive or dead, thirty years after she'd run from Winterflood and Edward with her lover. It gave her a sense of women's lives as impermanent and fleeting, leaving little trace, of no significance at all if they didn't produce heirs, if they otherwise failed to behave as they should, and she didn't like it. Her own fate could so easily have been similar; Winterflood could have been Tarquin Armstrong's, and she'd have been forgotten, or remembered only as another woman who had proved sadly unsatisfactory when it mattered most.

But it did no good to think like that. She'd not wanted to be alone any longer, and she was not. Here was Ventris in her bed, and he was certainly real enough. He took up a deal of space – he sprawled, utterly relaxed, at her side. He was lying face down, his dark head buried in a pillow, and the sheet and coverlets had slipped down to expose his strong arms, the broad expanse of his back, and a tantalising glimpse of his taut buttocks. She might have helped a little. Pulled the fabric down an inch or two, and then more. Made a frame for the picture. When he wasn't awake and annoying her, when she wasn't confused and uncertain and anticipating hurt – or even when she was – he was undeniably a sight worth looking at.

He was also unnaturally aware of his surroundings, despite the fact that she had thought he was sleeping soundly. He said lazily now, his voice muffled but perfectly audible, 'I'm a little cold, madam, but if you're enjoying the view, I don't want to deprive you of it.'

She sighed loudly. 'I like you so much better when you're not talking. But it never lasts.'

He made another of those uncannily swift movements and rolled over onto his back. But he didn't pull up the sheets, and neither did she. This view now was different, but just as good. Better, even.

'There was a time when you appreciated me for my enthralling conversation. But we don't have to talk,' he said.

'Thank God for that.' She'd been lying on her side as she looked at him, and his grey eyes were warmly appreciative as they ran over the full curves of her body once more.

'I can't get enough of you,' he said lazily. 'Wife.'

'That's because you're determined always to be talking about it instead of doing.' Again, she was being unjust, attempting deliberately to provoke him.

'You see, talking is but a poor substitute for kissing, and I can't do that,' he said, 'but very well. Not another word.' He moved again, this time to roll her unresisting onto her other side and bring his body close to hers, behind her, skin to skin along the full length of their frames, his chest to her back. It seemed to her that despite his teasing words, he wasn't cold at all.

They'd woken like this, his arms about her and his aroused member lying snugly between her thighs. She was pleasantly sore still from last night, another sensation that had been familiar once and now was strange. It would have been seductively easy to let the early-morning scene develop in the obvious manner, but she'd wriggled away into her own space instead, not liking the idea that he might choose to slip into her when he was half-asleep and she couldn't be entirely confident he remembered who she was. Not given his reputation. He might have murmured a name; for that matter, so might she. She feared she'd have said his, and she had no desire at all to know what he might have whispered in drowsy satiation. Best not. But he'd seen her now, they'd spoken, so she had not the least objection. On the contrary.

Viola had come to realise, perhaps because this unexpected second marriage had shaken up her ordered, uneventful life of widowhood and made her reflect on what she wanted for herself, that she had previously spent an excessive amount of time making things easy for people. The boys, of course – that was motherhood, and inevitable. Nobody wanted a mother who was all over prickles, like a hedgehog – she should know, she had one exactly like that and it had often been an uncomfortable experience. But often, with her mother and Edward above all others, she had smoothed things over, she had smiled and agreed when perhaps she should not have done. She had forgiven things that were unforgiveable because she had never wanted life to be difficult and awkward, and almost always avoided confrontation. She'd resolved not to be like that with Ventris. She was older now, she'd tasted independence, and she would be bloody-minded if she felt like it. She anticipated feeling like it quite often. There was an intoxicating pleasure in not censoring what she thought and said for a change.

But not everything had to be difficult. It wasn't a goal in itself, or shouldn't be. Richard was kissing her neck, lifting her long hair and burying his face in it, and all the while his fingers stroked her breasts again, doing the things he'd learned she liked. She was taut and heavy in his cupped hands, and his erection was making itself felt to good effect. She snuggled back against him and let him lie between her lips, against her entrance. His right hand moved down across her belly, caressing its soft swell, tangling in her curls. She remembered Sabrina's saucy comment – she didn't have to look at him – and chuckled.

'Since I'm not supposed to be talking, I won't ask,' he murmured in her ear, and nipped at her sensitive lobe, then drew it into his mouth and sucked on it. And then he was inside her, where she needed him to be, and there was no space for rational thought or for any sort of reply. She lost herself in pure sensation – their bodies moving in harmony, his hands and mouth on her, his ragged breathing, his knowledge – whether from instinct or experience – of how to please her. He held her hips tight when he spent himself inside her, and she pushed back against him and arched her back and maybe, this time, she cried aloud. But not his name, never that.

Afterwards, he handed her a pillow without speaking, and she repeated the ungainly exercise that supposedly would give her a better chance of conceiving. She wasn't quite sure if she was doing it for herself or for him, and perhaps it didn't matter. It would not help either of them if they – she would not say or even think *she*, for that was wrong – failed. They'd still be tied together, as her mother had warned her.

He was quiet now, for once, and his face was shuttered. He pulled the covers over her, which was not easy in her current position, and eventually, he said, his voice more serious than she had heard it in the last hectic weeks, 'I'm probably going to regret raising this, but I think it is time we talked about the past. Our past. We have grown very adept at avoiding it, I as well as you, but we cannot continue forever like this, ignoring everything that lies between us as though none of it had happened. The happiness, brief as it was, and the enduring pain of it. Everything.'

8

WINTER 1802

His cousin's new wife was a remarkably attractive woman, Richard thought as he sat with Edward in the library, sharing what would once have been, but now no longer was, companionable silence, the fire crackling between them and masking their new lack of easy conversation. And then, hearing the echo of his own unspoken words in his head – he'd perhaps had too much of Winterflood's fine old brandy, which was fatally smooth – he smiled wryly at his own pomposity. She was a lovely girl. Imagine how beautiful she'd be if she were happy.

Richard had been out of the country last summer, in America, when the Duke had married for the third time. He'd had a diffident letter from his cousin informing him of the fact, which only reached him months later because he was moving from place to place so much. It held a perceptible and rather affecting undertone of anxiety that he might disapprove of the match. He hadn't; it was obvious why Winterflood was doing it, poor old fellow, and no doubt, he'd thought, with a youthful cynicism that he was a little ashamed of now, it was a fair enough bargain. Her body, whoever she was, and her youth, in exchange for the title of Duchess of Winterflood and all the wealth, status and security that brought with it. Security for life, which was much more than most people of any rank had, and something he struggled to imagine ever having for himself. It was the sort of unequal union that happened every day, and nobody questioned any part of it. On the contrary, he supposed that almost everyone believed the young woman in question, who would be considered a mere nobody without title or connections, was lucky to have snared herself such a rich prize, the richest. A duke!

Back in London, his dangerous mission done with, he'd written to tell Edward of his return – though not of his recent activities, of course – and to reiterate his congratulations in case his previous letter of reply had gone astray, as seemed quite likely, given where he'd been over the past few months. Winterflood had written back with alacrity, flatteringly glad to hear from him, and invited him to come and stay immediately, for as long as he liked. Richard had just endured a long and perilous winter sea voyage on top of months of hard overland travelling and bursts of acute physical danger, and was delighted to accept. A few relaxing weeks in the country, riding, shooting and talking idly with his cousin and good friend, always the most undemanding of company, were exactly what he needed. And now here he was, enjoying his cousin's lavish hospitality and the much-needed opportunity to relax for a while.

Except he wasn't enjoying it, and for this, the presence of the new Duchess was responsible. It wasn't in any sense because she was a terrible hostess. Considering that she could have had no experience of overseeing a house of this size, things ran as smoothly as they ever had when her predecessor Elizabeth was alive. Perhaps it was the servants who knew exactly what they were about, and she had little to do with it; but even so, they seemed to defer to her and treat her with respect, as far as he could tell. And it wasn't her personality – she wasn't rude or standoffish, nor was she over-friendly, she was neither too loud nor too quiet for his taste, and her touching anxiety that he should be perfectly comfortable was not in any way overpowering. But he *wasn't* comfortable. He realised that now as he sat brooding by the fire and Edward nodded sleepily over a book opposite him, like a man of sixty.

It had been all very well to imagine, insofar as he had bothered to imagine it, his cousin marrying some faceless young woman who might just possibly give him the heir he so desperately needed at last. Richard had had no quarrel with that; he wanted the old fellow to be happy again, as he had not been since Elizabeth's death, and he was entirely in agreement with him that his own older brother was the last man in England who should ever get his grubby hands on the power and influence a dukedom brought. Winterflood had always been a tranquil place, but it wouldn't remain so for long if it fell into the grasp of a bully and spendthrift such as Tarquin Armstrong.

He'd recently encountered his brother by chance in a London tavern, and instead of greeting him with foul and unprovoked insults as he usually did, Tarquin had been almost friendly, for the first time that he could recall. Richard had soon realised that this novel behaviour did not reflect any welcome change in Tarquin's character or feelings towards him. No, it had come about only because his sibling was so incensed still at the thought of Edward's unexpected third marriage that he could not refrain from ranting about it to anybody within earshot, and all the better if the person forced to listen to his ravings actually knew the Duke. This vitriol seemed extraordinary, since Mr Armstrong had had many months to get used to the idea. But his fury, and his fear of being cut out when he'd thought himself secure, seemed to have grown stronger rather than waned. Clearly, he'd been brooding unhealthily on the subject; one might almost call it an obsession. He'd also been foxed, as usual, and after a while, Richard had tired of his drunken ramblings and – surely – idle threats towards Edward and his bride, and slipped away, with all kinds of slurs that encompassed the young Duchess's character and Winterflood's virility, or presumed lack of it, ringing unpleasantly in his ears.

And though five or six and forty wasn't any great age, even from the perspective of one and twenty, Edward was looking worn and anxious these days, and much older than his years, as Tarquin had implied. He claimed to be well, but he didn't look it. So the matter of an heir was sufficiently urgent, Richard could see that.

But the new Duchess wasn't a faceless young woman any longer – a mere cipher. She was an individual: Viola Constantine. She didn't smile very often, but when she did, it was like the sun breaking suddenly through a cloud and lighting up the scene. She was just eighteen, had been seventeen when she'd married Edward last year. Looked at objectively, that was surely wrong, the age gap verging on the grotesque, he thought now. His insufficiently considered views about the whole matter – about many matters – had undergone a radical shift since he had met her.

He'd heard fragments of gossip about the ill-assorted match in London, where people were still tittering cruelly and crudely over Winterflood's fresh burst of desperation to get himself a son after so many fruitless years. Remarks

Viola had let fall in conversation had confirmed what he'd heard about her background: her family was not a wealthy one, she had five sisters and no brothers, her father was in poor health, and his modest estate was entailed. Her older sister had been married for a couple of years to a wealthy man of no particular standing, and had given him a boy already, with another child on the way by now. If Edward felt he must throw the dice one last time and wasn't overly concerned with the social status of his bride, no better candidate could be imagined for his purposes. Of fertile stock, poor, and therefore likely to be grateful and compliant. *Compliant* – Jesus. He winced now when he thought of his earlier careless, heartless reaction.

Richard would not have found his conscience so suddenly tender if she'd turned out to be an obvious fortune-hunter, happy to sell herself for the highest rank any debutante could aspire to. If the bargain such a person entered into turned out not to be the one she had expected, if the reality of a husband old enough to be her father did not in the end please her, one could only shrug and be a little sorry for the way the world was ordered. But she was not in the least like that. She did not appear to take any great pleasure in hearing herself called Duchess, nor was she revelling in spending Edward's money on herself, or on anything, as far as he could see. Her gowns were simple, and she seemed happiest when riding out across the estate or playing with the dogs; if she was pining for London, it was her close family she missed – she'd admitted as much in an unguarded moment. Her new responsibilities seemed to cause her nothing more than anxiety, and what caused her the most distress, though she tried to conceal it, was Edward himself, and the uncaring way he treated her.

No doubt it was healthy and natural that his last duchess should not be entirely forgotten. They'd been married for fifteen years or so and loved each other deeply, so that her sudden death had been a terrible blow, and one from which Edward had obviously not yet recovered. But Richard thought that the vast portrait of the young Elizabeth by Thomas Gainsborough might tactfully have been removed from the dining room to some more obscure location, so that her replacement did not have the dead woman, more than life-size, looming pensive and misty-eyed over her shoulder every time she sat down to eat her dinner. Edward's gaze sometimes wandered to the enormous canvas during conversation; Richard had noticed it more than once since he had arrived, and he did not think that Viola, who appeared to be sufficiently quick in perception, could have failed to observe it either. The Duke also spoke of the lost Elizabeth quite frequently in front of his new wife, and Richard had never come so close as to becoming irritated by his cousin as when 'Elizabeth used to say...' had been mentioned more often than seemed necessary or considerate. The man had a history and his new wife knew it, but there was such a thing as tact.

He neglected his bride, too, and this was a surprise, given why he'd married her. Richard had no means of knowing how often Edward visited her at night – God knows he had no desire at all to be made party to such uncomfortably intimate knowledge – but in the daytime, he seemed preoccupied with the cares of his estate, much more than he'd ever been on previous occasions when he'd visited. It was clear that the Duchess was struggling to fill the long hours of her day, with very little help from her husband, and Richard had not been at Winterflood long when he began to suspect that he had been invited at least partly to entertain her. He was happy to do it, if that was his responsibility as the only guest, but it seemed odd.

They went out on horseback together every day, with Edward's entire approval and encouragement. Viola had been taught to ride in her youth, she told him, but she'd always lived in Town and did not have the easy familiarity with horses that a countrywoman would have developed in childhood. She was only now discovering that she loved them and had a natural feel for them; Richard wondered a little that his cousin had not thought to spend time with her in this, his own favourite pursuit. It could have been something they shared, something that helped build a much-needed bond between them, but instead Richard found himself showing Viola around the furthest reaches of the vast estate that was now her home.

One icy morning, they were heading back towards the house after their ride and paused to look down on it from a rise that offered the best view of the great pile. They had not gone fast or hard; the horses were not chilled, and though they shifted a little, they seemed content enough to stand for a while at their riders' command, nuzzling each other affectionately and blowing out great clouds of steaming breath. A couple of Edward's spaniels had accompanied them, but they were off snuffling about in the dead leaves under the trees.

The mansion was impressive, even intimidating – the vast frontage and the reflecting pond that ran towards it, the huge Renaissance fountain frozen in the centre, mantled in long icicles, and the stables and other outbuildings stretching back like a village in themselves. Smoke rose straight up from many chimneys into the still air, the only movement in the wintry scene.

His companion made a sudden sound that seemed like distress, and he turned to look at her in concern. She was dressed in a habit of rich, deep-blue velvet, with a jaunty little cap set on her lustrous, dark curls, trimmed with a matching feather. Her cheeks were rosy from the cold and the exercise, and she made an enchanting picture, he could not help but think. He also thought that there were tears in her eyes, and though he felt awkward to see such unconcealed emotion, he could not do anything but ask, 'What's the matter, your grace? I hope you are not unwell.'

She smiled at him, but it was a poor effort. 'I am quite well, thank you, sir. It's just that it takes me by surprise sometimes, the size of it.' She waved her gloved hand at one of the finest and largest baroque mansions in England. 'The responsibility.'

He did not know what to say to that, and she seemed to interpret his silence as disapproval. 'I know I am very lucky; I am always sensible of my good fortune. Edward could have married anyone.' It sounded very much as though she was trying to persuade herself rather than him. With a slightly different emphasis, she might easily have said, *Edward could have married anyone. Why did he have to choose me?*

And then she turned her large, dark eyes on him, and said devastatingly, 'Do you think your cousin is happy? With me, I mean.'

'I am sure he must be,' was all he could manage, and even that was an untruth.

'That's no answer, Mr Armstrong, when obviously, he isn't. Forgive my frankness, but you seem very close to Edward, and I have no one else to ask. He has friends his own age, I know, like Lord Marchett, but I do not know if he would talk openly with them. I am sure many of them must disapprove of his marriage to me, the disparity in rank as well as age, which might check his confidences. You are family, though, and he always speaks of you with such affection, I thought he might have confided in you.'

Richard was glad that he was able to say with perfect truth that his cousin had not said one word in private to him that might not have been uttered to the Duchess's face. He hadn't spoken of affection either – in fact, he hadn't spoken of her at all, not a word – but there was no need to say that. He could be tactful even if his cousin apparently could not.

'What do you fear?' he asked her bluntly. He'd rather not be having this conversation, but he was committed now.

She did not answer him directly. 'I know he loved his late wife, and I cannot wonder that he still misses her.'

'He certainly makes that plain enough. I can understand why it is hard for you.'

'It should not be,' she said resolutely, shaking her head, and his heart ached for her. 'He was the soul of frankness when he offered for my hand. He told me of his enduring grief, and made no pretence of love. I pitied him, and appreciated his gentleness and directness, and, of course, the great honour that he did me.'

Good God, the poor girl, he thought. *What a sad proposal it must have been. Especially if she had cherished hopes of romance, and what girl of seventeen does not?*

'Of course I accepted him. I know my duty to my family – my mother did not have to urge me in the slightest. I was quite content. But perhaps I did not fully realise…' She broke off. 'Oh, forget I spoke, please, Mr Armstrong. It was very wrong in me. I should not spill all my pathetic little secrets to you just because you are another young person in the house and seem sympathetic. It is just that I am not used to being so alone – I have always had my sisters about me, and we have such a busy, lively household at home, it is no wonder that my new life seems quiet to me sometimes. It is merely a matter of accustoming myself to it. This is my home now, and I am very lucky,' she repeated, and the phrase sounded even less convincing even than it had before. 'I shall be well served indeed if you go to my husband and tell him that I have been complaining without cause, like some spoiled brat.' She did not ask him not to; she seemed resigned to the fact that he easily might. He wasn't even sure she cared much. *She really is deeply unhappy*, he thought with sudden heat. *Quite blue-devilled. Damn Edward for an inconsiderate old fool.*

'I promise I would not do that,' he said, aware that his voice was a little unsteady, so great was his pity for her, and his regret. 'Of course I will respect your confidence. I can see that you are far from content, and though it is none of my affair, I can also see that you have cause. But my cousin is the best of good fellows, and I am sure that, as you said, it is just a matter of learning to live with each other, which will take time. It cannot be easy for him, after so long…' It was entirely inadequate comfort, he knew even as he said it. What did he know of married life, orphan vagabond that he was, and these serious and irrevocable matters that this girl not yet twenty was struggling with so earnestly? But he had to say something to console her.

'I am prepared to learn, to adapt,' she answered with suppressed passion, 'but I wonder, is he?'

He was not obliged to find some reply to that, for with a sudden burst of movement, she was urging her horse on, and the dappled grey gelding, eager for his warm stable, responded with alacrity and carried her off down the slope at increasing speed, the dogs darting out to follow them, ears flying. Richard sat for a moment, watching her blue habit stream behind her across the beast's flanks, and then his own mount's restlessness became apparent and he hastened after her.

9

It was hard for Mr Armstrong to face his hosts across the dinner table, and grew harder as the days passed. The Duchess was plainly aware, since Edward's vague manner towards her did not change in the slightest, that Richard had kept his promise of silence to her, though she said nothing of it to him. For his own part, Richard became increasingly conscious of the effort she was making to please her husband, or at least to conform to his unspoken expectations, and how bloody oblivious he was to all of it.

To give the man credit, he did not stand at all upon his dignity as a duke and never had, so that could not be why he was so blind. It wasn't that he thought she should be grateful for her startling elevation and content with her lot; he just didn't seem to be aware of his wife as a person with her own thoughts, feelings and interests, just like the dead wife he missed so much. It was an unnatural and lonely life for any woman, cooped up here in this big, empty barn of a house with a man who didn't seem to notice her from one day to the next, and all the more so for a girl of eighteen whose childhood had been so very different, full of life and laughter and people who cared about her. Richard began to wonder uneasily how long it could go on without a disaster.

There was thick, chilling fog one afternoon, and – Edward having vanished into some private fastness as usual without explanation or excuse –

Richard and his hostess were pacing the long picture gallery, surveying, for want of anything else to do, the portraits of previous Armstrongs, beginning in the Tudor era. It was mid-afternoon and the long green damask curtains were still open, but it was already growing dark; they'd brought candles with them. Spring seemed a long way off on days like this.

'The family emerged from well-deserved obscurity about this time,' he told her, eager to offer her what poor entertainment he could, 'having somehow become part of Henry Tudor's disreputable train in his exile abroad. Look at my illustrious ancestor, Thomas Armstrong. Did you ever see a more untrustworthy face in your life – can you not imagine him bilking a French innkeeper out of his due, or stealing coins from a church poor-box? Thomas came to England with the Tudor when he invaded, and was later rewarded for his years of loyalty with these lands. No doubt he could have told a tale or two about the seventh Henry's wandering years on the Continent if he wished.'

The Duchess smiled and seemed diverted, but was, not unnaturally, most interested in the women's portraits. There was nothing to be gleaned from the closed countenance of Thomas's wife, the Lady Alys, who still kept her secrets, eyes modestly downcast and mouth pursed tight, head bundled up in a curiously unflattering headdress like a great square box. 'She was a lady-in-waiting to Dame Margaret Beaufort, the King's mother, which can't have been enormously entertaining. Lots of sermons and very few parties, I should think, don't you, ma'am? But the next couple of generations made up for it, as you can see.'

Viola stared, arrested by the magnificence of the first Duke of Winterflood, Edmund. He stood four-square and massive, much like his friend and contemporary the eighth Henry, and sported an enormous bushy black beard, and a hat that resembled nothing so much as a squashed velvet cushion. The parts of his garments that were not slashed to show rich silken linings were heavily encrusted with jewels of many colours. His codpiece, which neither Richard nor his companion referred to, was easily the size of a loaf of bread, and was studded with yet more jewels. His wife was dressed with equal opulence, bore just as many jewels, and must have experienced a great deal of difficulty in sitting down, her gown was so stiff with gold embroidery. Above them was emblazoned the Winterflood motto – then and now: *Quod habeo teneo*. What I have, I hold. It wasn't a particularly comforting sentiment, and Richard wondered for the first time how hard it might be to live up to, for his cousin.

The current Duchess mused, 'It's hard to see them as ordinary people underneath all their finery; they are so concerned to show us their wealth and power, they scarcely look human. And yet aristocrats today laugh at those they are pleased to call cits, and call them vulgar. What could be more vulgar and ostentatious than this?'

He grinned in complete agreement. 'We all came from nowhere once, and the Armstrongs comparatively recently; it's just a matter of timing.'

'I suppose those who came over with the Conqueror still look down on parvenu such as the Armstrong family, then. That's comforting somehow to a complete nobody like me. But I've seen that ruby necklace before – the Duchess, the late Duchess, is wearing it in the Gainsborough portrait, I think. Strange that objects should endure, when the people who wore them so proudly are long dead.'

You are the Duchess, he thought, *but it is no wonder that you don't really seem to realise it. It must be so fatiguing, feeling like an interloper all the time.* 'I can only think that it is yours now. Have you not seen it, and the other family jewels?'

She shrugged, seeming not terribly interested. 'A few of them, but not that particular piece. I don't really have occasion to wear such priceless treasures.'

Of course she did not, if they never went anywhere or entertained parties of guests. 'Does Edward mean to take you to appear at Court as a married woman?' he asked carefully. He didn't know if she'd been presented on her come-out; he didn't want to assume she hadn't, though he knew that it was an extremely costly exercise and doing it for six daughters could bankrupt a family. 'If so, you could wear it then if you wished, or some of the other historic pieces. Court presentation is an occasion for the grandest of jewels, especially for a duchess.' The higher a family's status, the more customary it was for them to show themselves to the King and Queen after a marriage or some other notable event. Surely Edward would go to Town for that, and stay for a while and let his wife have some amusement for a change. Throw her a ball, perhaps, to honour her. Do *something* for her to vary the monotony of her life and make her feel valued.

'I don't know. He hasn't mentioned it,' she said in a low tone, as if she could not help herself, 'He doesn't really... talk to me more than is necessary. Or than he feels necessary.'

'I am sorry you are so lonely and unhappy. I wish I could help you in some way.' He didn't feel disloyal to his cousin, saying this openly to her; he was out of all patience with Edward by now, and would have to speak to him or hate himself for his cowardice, for all the good he expected it would do.

'But you have helped me a great deal,' she said with false brightness. 'You talk to me, and I am very grateful for it. Before you came, I don't think I'd spoken to anyone my own age, or nearly so, for weeks. Or anyone at all, really, apart from the servants, who are always so busy and discreet. The local ladies call on me sometimes, of course, and I on them – I know it is my duty to maintain contact, and Edward has made it clear that he wishes it. But they are all of them older than me, and very few of them have daughters my age. I don't know what to say to them. They all talk about the late Duchess, too, in such a pointed way. They loved her, and tell me so at length. Recite her virtues. Tell me what I've done wrong, and how she would have done it better. You'd think I'd murdered her, the way they look at me. As if I ever *wanted*...'

She broke off then, and said in a stifled voice, 'Ignore me, sir, I beg you. I am a trifle out of sorts today – a woman's complaint. I hope you will disregard my foolish words, and not mind if I leave you now; I don't think I am fit company this afternoon. Forgive me – you have been very kind as always.' She curtseyed to him, her face pale, and all but fled along the darkening gallery, vanishing into the shadows at the end.

Again, he watched her leave him, frowning. Richard was not entirely without experience of women, and he could not mistake the feminine complaint to which she had referred. *Another month gone*, he thought, *and one can only hope that Edward does not upbraid her for it. But probably he does not, because he does not speak to her more than is necessary. What a hideous picture of their intimate life that conjures up. Which does not mean that she is not acutely conscious of her 'failure'. The ladies of the county will no doubt remind her of it soon enough, even if nobody else does; trust them for that.*

Viola avoided him for the rest of the day and took her dinner in her room, pleading the headache, and Richard took the opportunity her absence offered to speak to Edward. When the dishes had been removed and the servants left the two cousins alone over their port, he declined another glass – he didn't like the sticky stuff anyway – and said rather stiltedly, 'I am sorry to see that the Duchess is unwell.'

'The Duchess?' Edward appeared rather startled, and glanced reflexively at Elizabeth's portrait. *Give me strength*, thought Richard. *He's forgotten his new wife even exists*. 'Oh – Viola. Yes, poor child. A trifling ailment – I am sure she will be better directly.' His expression didn't suggest he found it trifling at all; more like a tragedy, and a familiar one at that. But that really wasn't a subject Richard wanted to discuss with him.

'It must be quite lonely for her here, especially as she is from a large family and is used to having a great number of people around her,' he ventured. 'It might be pleasant if you made up a party to give her some entertainment, if you mean to remain here till the Season starts. You told me you had a very quiet Christmas.'

'Well,' said Edward, not seeming particularly concerned, 'the Constantines are all fixed in London, and I am obliged to be here on the estate, so there is nothing to be done about it. I assure you, I have no thoughts of entertaining anyone but you, my dear boy, or perhaps my old friend Henry Marchett. Such a lot of noise and trouble, the house full of strangers, which is not at all to my taste. And as for the Season, I am glad to be free of that nonsense, and so, I am sure, must my wife be, if she is sensible. The air of London is so unhealthy, too. How unfortunate she was, growing up mostly there; I wonder anyone can bear it for more than a month. This is her life now, and she must accustom herself to it.' And his gaze drifted inexorably to the portrait again. 'I am sure she will do so soon enough. Elizabeth was happy here, and never had any difficulty entertaining herself and keeping busy. She often said it was the most idyllic spot in the world.'

'It is, of course. But you...' Richard broke off, and Edward was so abstracted, looking down into his glass broodingly, that he did not press his young companion to finish his sentence, or even appear to notice the omission. There was no point saying that his cousin had loved Elizabeth, and she him, and that had made all the difference. If he couldn't see the truth of it for himself, and he was an intelligent man, it seemed unlikely he could be brought to acknowledge it by a cousin five and twenty years his junior. It was not Richard's business to suggest that Edward's first wife Julia hadn't been happy either, and look what she had decided to do about it. He had no reason to think that Viola was contemplating such extreme action, or that there was anybody for her to run off with even if she wanted to. She was entirely alone, and her husband knew and didn't give a damn, wrapped in what Mr Armstrong could only see as his self-indulgent grief and determination not to change his life one jot to accommodate the young woman he had married. *She* must be the one who made the accommodation. It distressed him and made him angry, and more out of charity with a man he'd always respected and admired than he'd ever been in his life before.

It was a recipe for disaster, of course. All of it.

10

There was a little constraint between the Duchess and her lone guest when they encountered each other the next day, after their rather too frank conversation when they'd last met, but they both dealt with the matter in the traditional English fashion: by resolutely ignoring it. She had not felt like riding, so they strolled together about the frosty gardens, admiring the filigree patterns on the cobwebs and the seedheads of last year's plants. Their breath was visible in clouds, and their footsteps crunched on the gravel paths, which were frozen into solid but treacherous clumps in places and quite awkward to walk on; he was afraid that she would slip and fall, and so offered her his arm. It was an innocent gesture – or that was how it began. He hadn't realised how much the lightest touch from her would affect him.

'It will be lovely here in the summer,' he said fatuously, aware that he was spouting rubbish, aware most of all of the forbidden thrill of feeling her gloved hand on his sleeve, and her body tantalisingly close to his. 'So different.'

'It was beautiful last year,' she agreed sedately, apparently quite willing to talk nonsense too. 'And the autumn colours, of course, were magnificent.'

It was the sort of thing a woman three times her age might say, and a defeated one at that: one who'd given up all hope and spoke only in commonplaces. There was no eighteen-year-old alive who gave a fig for autumn colours, in his estimation. She'd been here for seven or eight months, he realised, with no company. No wonder she pined so much for her family. It was a wonder she hadn't gone crazy, and if she hadn't, she soon would.

'Do you ever attend the local assemblies?' he asked, confident of knowing the answer already. 'I am sure there must be such events, in St Neots or Bedford or even Cambridge.'

'I daresay there are, but Edward does not care for them and will not consent to go,' she responded in a carefully expressionless voice. 'And when our neighbours have parties with dancing, he declines the invitations, as even such private events are not in the least agreeable to him, not even if his old friends and their wives hold them. Not that I'm eager to see any more of *them* myself, just so they can show me even more plainly how they disapprove of my very existence.'

'Nonetheless, he should be made to care for society and a little pleasure, and cease thinking only of himself! I shall tell him that he is grown prodigiously dull, and is in danger of making you dull too, and that we must attend some public celebration without loss of time. You have been here so long without any diversion that I expect you have almost forgotten how to dance.'

'I should think I might have,' she said wistfully, 'and perhaps he will agree, if it is you that proposes it.' This matter-of-fact comment stabbed at his heart. 'I should enjoy that, I think, if it could be managed, and if you would stand up with me.' She let go of his arm, to his regret, and stepped onto the frozen grass. It was a safer surface, and once on it, she essayed a few tentative steps, smiling to herself, giving Richard a precious glimpse of the woman – the girl – she could be in happier circumstances. He bowed with a flourish, and offered her his hand, and they moved through the figure of a country dance together, managing without any of the other members of their imagined set as best they could, hearing the lively music in their heads, keeping time without the least difficulty. It was very quiet out in the frosty garden, and they were entirely alone, as though they were the only two people left in the world.

They were both laughing at their own absurdity by the end. Her face was flushed, her eyes sparkling like stars, and she was so enchanting and so different – both from her usual self and from any other woman he had ever known – that Richard, hardly knowing what he did, possessed by an overpowering impulse, bent his head and brushed her lips with his.

It was a brief contact, but it sent a jolt of electricity through him that astonished him. She looked up at him, startled, and he was about to leap away from her and burst into abject apologies – tell her he had no idea what he had been thinking of and promise on his honour it would never happen again – when she put her gloved hand up to his cheek and left it there for a moment. He closed his eyes against the sudden sweetness of her touch, and when he did not pull away or speak, she kissed him back.

Perhaps what had happened before could have been glossed over as a mere nothing, an accidental contact that did not signify and could easily be forgotten if they both agreed to do so. But not this. Their lips locked and soon, they were devouring each other hungrily, bumping noses, clinging to each other and staggering a little on the icy ground at the impact of sudden and unexpected mutual passion, fierce and overwhelming in its intensity. His arms went out by instinct to pull her close, and hers were locked about his neck in equal need.

He did not know how long it was before she turned her face away, but he knew, because she'd done it twice before now, that her impulse when she went too far into intimacy with him was always to flee.

'Don't run away from me this time, please, Viola,' he said raggedly, as she stirred restlessly in his arms. 'We can't possibly pretend this did not happen.'

'It should not have done,' she said flatly, and he let her go, but he did not move away from her, and her desire to escape him seemed to have deserted her for the moment, for she too did not put any greater distance between them.

'My dear, I know it was wrong, and the blame is all mine. But I hate to see you so sad, and when I saw you happy for the first time – happy as you deserve to be – my desire to touch you overmastered me. I should say that I am sorry, but the truth is that I am not.'

'Nor I,' she said very low. 'How can I regret something so rare and precious? Mr Armstrong, Richard, I have thought in recent months that I was going mad. I know that most of the people in the world are worse off than I am. I know what the little maid who lights my fire each morning and the girls who scrub the vegetables till their fingers are numb and work till they are fit to drop each evening would think of me, for not being grateful for everything that I have been given. So many things – it's not even as though I was born wealthy and don't appreciate them. Maybe I am selfish and spoiled, and marriage to a duke has turned my head. I want for nothing in terms of possessions, my future is secure whatever happens, and how many women in the world can say as much? But the thought of living like this for years – forever – fills me with terror. I feel as though I'm turning into one of the statues, all covered in icicles. All the dead people in the pictures are more real than me. At least when we kissed, I knew I was alive for a moment.'

'I tried to talk to him…' Richard said helplessly. 'He doesn't mean to take you to London; he doesn't intend to invite anyone to stay here apart from his own friends. He thinks because Elizabeth was happy here, you must be too. I could see that it was no use telling him that Elizabeth was happy with him only because they loved each other, and shared a life they chose together.'

'I have chosen this, and I must live with it. But sometimes, I'm not sure that I can.'

'I cannot wonder at it. You didn't know what you were choosing. You were only seventeen! And I am positive your family put you under a great deal of pressure to accept him. It is no wonder that you could not resist – few people could.'

She shook her head and said resolutely, 'I could say that that was so, to excuse myself, but it would not be true. There was no need. It would have been my mother, not my poor father, but there was no need for anyone to say as much as a word to me. I was too conscious of what it would mean to the whole family if I accepted him, and the consequences if I refused. My papa has never been strong, and when he dies, my mother and my unmarried sisters will be close to penniless. Bianca, the youngest, is only six! We could not expect my sister Sabrina's husband to support us all, excessively good-natured though he is. I never expected to be able to choose a husband for myself.' She shivered in the frigid air. 'I thought I had no illusions. I could see that Edward was a good man, not a cruel one, not a libertine, not… personally unpleasant in any way. He could have been so many things that scared me, and I still would have been obliged to accept him. The law gives him the right to beat me, you know, and he would never do that, never even dream of it. As I have said to you before, I am only too aware that I am… lucky.' But her voice broke on the last word.

He reached out to hold her again, his hands on her arms. 'It's so unfair,' he said inadequately.

'It isn't, really. And I think it would be bearable, perhaps, if I had a child to love. But I don't think there's going to be a child, Richard.'

'You've not been married a year. Just a few months. It's still so soon – too soon.' He did not like to hear himself saying these words, as if he was urging her back to Edward's bed, which was the last thing he wanted to do, God knows. But if he didn't want that, what did he want? Nothing he could ever have.

'But Edward has been married twice before, and he has always wanted an heir. Needed one, to keep the title in the family and away from your brother, whom he so dislikes. He can hardly have failed to... he does not fail to now. I don't think he's had the uncommon bad luck to marry three infertile women in succession. I think it's him. Surely, he must suspect as much himself.'

'It's unendurable!' he said passionately and confusedly, for just as she was eighteen, he was only one and twenty, and then he kissed her again, and they clung together.

11

Viola had read once – having had a great deal of time for reading in the last few months since her marriage to Edward – of a French king who had believed he was made of glass. She understood that this was a pitiful delusion, a symptom of some illness of the mind, but the idea had lodged in her brain all the same. It was not that she was afraid that she would shatter into a thousand pieces, which had been the king's great terror, for in her bleakest moods, that would almost have been a relief: oblivion. No, she feared that she was becoming invisible. It was increasingly easy to believe this, when days passed with only the briefest of conversation with another human being. Sometimes, even on the rare occasions when she was in company, she was afraid to speak, and did not, in case it became horribly plain that, while she could hear her own voice, echoing in her head, others could not. What would she do then? If she screamed, and she felt like screaming, nobody would hear her.

Edward's visits to her bed did not mend matters. Sometimes, at night, she found herself formulating the thought that she must be real because he put his hands on her, because he had marital relations with her, was doing so now as she lay there under him, and this was no help at all. It hardly made her a human being, just some sort of passive vessel. She wasn't even sure she wanted him to stop. It wasn't *bad*. It wasn't anything. It passed the time, and she had so much time. She knew that her state of mind could not be healthy.

He didn't speak to her, barely said a word, but he did try to please her. She thought – something else she'd read, or heard whispered – that he probably believed that women could not conceive unless they experienced orgasm. To her, just using female common sense and looking at the world around her and the casual couplings, not to mention violent assaults, that so often seemed to bear unwelcome fruit, this seemed unlikely. But then *she* was not the desperate one. If her husband had read that in order to fall pregnant, a woman must paint herself orange and run naked around the grounds at midnight, she had no doubt that she'd be freezing her toes off on a nightly basis. But he hadn't heard that – nothing so outlandish, though she suspected that some of the peculiar dishes she, and she alone, was served at dinner were not just there to keep her fed, but had another purpose. She was beginning to hate the sight of eggs, however ingeniously they were cooked.

So, he tried to please her when he was in her bedchamber. Diligently. Doggedly. Sometimes, he achieved his goal through sheer persistence; sometimes, she pretended, to speed matters along. Sometimes, recently, she'd helped him gain his objective by imagining that the man touching her was Mr Richard Armstrong instead. That worked. So she'd already been unfaithful to Edward, in her own mind. But that was all. Did kissing constitute infidelity? Were there rules on such matters? She could hardly ask anyone.

Because now, since Mr Armstrong had arrived, since he had been so kind to her and they had kissed, Viola was walking on air. She was giddy with happiness. She knew that it was wrong, she was refusing to think about what might happen next, but she could not deny all she was feeling inside. All she could do was struggle to conceal it, most of all from Edward. Not that her husband appeared to notice her moods – he hadn't seemed to be aware of her profound unhappiness, so it seemed unlikely that he'd notice the recent joyful change in her, which was all due to Richard's presence.

Once they'd kissed, there didn't seem to be any reason not to do it again. She would never have imagined that so much time could be spent, nor so much pleasure taken, from kissing. Nothing in her previous experience with Edward had prepared her for this; he rarely kissed her, and when he did, it could not be described as magical.

Sometimes, she and Richard rode out to some distant part of the estate and found a secluded spot where they could embrace in private, but more often, they walked sedately through the gardens, side by side, not touching, to one of the distant summerhouses or follies, of which there were many dotted here and there. Winterflood had an abundance of gardeners to maintain its splendour, but none of them were doing any work outdoors with the weather so cold. There was little chance of being interrupted, and they flattered themselves that they were being careful and discreet.

It was chilly in the places they found, of course, but they kept warm in each other's arms. Though they talked, they didn't speak about the future – they didn't take their intimacy any further – they just kissed for hours. Richard kissed her hands, worshipping them in minute detail, and pressed his lips against the blue veins at her wrists with an intensity that almost made her swoon. She did the same to him, dropping soft kisses into his palms, sometimes just holding his hand against her cheek with her eyes closed and his arm about her. They explored each other's faces with lips and fingers, and sometimes, as when he kissed her eyelids or her hair, his gentleness brought hot tears to her eyes, though in general, his presence made her purely happy, happier than she had ever been in her life. The contrast between Edward, who barely seemed to see her, and Richard, who saw her as no one else ever had before, was so overpowering that she dared not dwell too much upon it, or on what was to become of them both. Nothing, she assumed, on the odd occasions she allowed herself to think about it seriously. This could not last, and nothing could come of it, and eventually, he would go away, back to his mysterious life out in the world. She would be left here with Edward. At least she'd have some memories, some reason to believe that she existed. Or had existed, once.

She told Richard everything – all about her family, their characters, from her parents and Sabrina down to tiny Bianca. It was trivial stuff, she thought, and must appear all the more so to him, who'd journeyed so widely and seen so much, but he seemed fascinated by all of it, because it was so different from his own life. His only sibling was his older half-brother, and their relationship, he told her, had never been close. Far from it, since Tarquin was a bully and a person not to be trusted; she knew because he had told her so that his brother was not at all happy Edward had married again, and must be counted her enemy. Both his parents were long dead, and he had few other relatives apart from a terrifying old aunt, his mother's sister, and some older Yorkshire cousins he barely knew.

He didn't talk much about his day-to-day life now, but she knew he had some training as a lawyer and was employed by a City firm to oversee their foreign interests. His situation involved a great deal of travelling, and he was happy enough to talk about that, making her laugh with his descriptions of his comical misadventures in various far-flung locations. But as for his job itself, he said that it was very dull, consisting mostly of peering at goods in warehouses – which were always either freezing cold or hideously hot – and pretending he knew what the great piles of things were supposed to look like. And smell like, for that matter. Often, they did smell most unpleasant. He could read a ledger, he said – he had learned, and he had developed an instinct for when people were trying to cheat him, which they usually were. But all that was boring and he'd much rather talk about her.

She knew he desired her – her experience over the last eight months had taught her that much, at least, the mechanics of the human body – and she found that she desired him. She blushed when their eyes met, she felt dizzy when she knew she would see him soon, and every inch of her body tingled when he touched her, or even when he looked at her across a room. She felt heat pooling between her legs when she was with him, and even when she was not, and touched herself when she was alone late at night, imagining he was touching her, was with her in her bed, holding her. Wishing he could be. That was a new experience for her. Her intimate life with Edward was not by any means unpleasant – he was experienced enough to be able to make her body react to his touch, even if her mind and her heart were left entirely unaffected – but she'd never been aroused by the mere sight of him, nor did his attentions make her want to caress him in return, or cling to him, or kiss every inch of him. He didn't seem to want that either. Probably excessive passion was not required of a duchess. Not this duchess, at any rate. Perhaps the previous one...

Viola thought later that it was possible that this stalemate would have continued until Richard was obliged to leave to go back to work, and all of their lives – many people's lives – would have been very different, if Lord Marchett had not come to visit his old friend at Winterflood that cold February.

12

His Lordship was Edward's oldest friend, in every possible sense of the word. He was, in fact, only a year or two senior to the Duke, and therefore barely fifty, but, as Richard said, he was the sort of man who must have been born pompous, and bored his nursemaids witless in the cradle.

The noble pair had undertaken the Grand Tour together, round about the time of the American Revolution, and remained as thick as inkle-weavers ever since. The Earl had even written a book on the unique experience, a weighty tome, and had it privately published in lavish, gold-tooled binding. There were several presentation copies in the Winterflood library, many of them with the pages still uncut. In anticipation of the gentleman's arrival, Viola had attempted out of curiosity to read one of them, but had lost her will to live among the stately, relentlessly self-regarding paragraphs within a few moments of picking it up. It didn't signify much; she'd met the Earl briefly before, and knew that he had never in his life cared to know a woman's opinion about anything, or even admitted that she might have one. He'd be as likely to ask a table or a chair what it thought about the current political upheavals and the chances of peace. He was married, and had a great number of children and grandchildren, and they all had her heartiest sympathy, especially his long-suffering wife.

One evening, the two old friends had been left together over their port, while Viola withdrew to sit alone by the drawing-room fire, bored, but less so than she would have been in their company. Richard had also tactfully left the older men to enjoy each other's conversation and reminisce about their shared past and unimaginable youthful adventures. He had some urgent work to do, he said – papers to look over. He'd kissed the Duchess passionately but all too briefly in a dark corner and then really had gone off to his dull task. He'd said, and she reluctantly agreed, that they dared not risk being caught together in a compromising situation, all the more because unlike Edward, who noticed nothing, Lord Marchett seemed sharp, and had already worried them both by the pronounced coldness of his manner towards them, and his penetrating gaze that seemed to follow them about and judge them harshly.

She'd been reading a novel by Miss Burney earlier in the day, and most provokingly put it down somewhere; now, she wanted it to help while away the long evening, and could not find it anywhere. She'd already looked in the library – not on the crowded shelves, that would have taken days, but on all the tables. It wasn't in the hall or any of the rooms she used most often, and she was sure she hadn't taken it upstairs. Irritated with her own absent-mindedness, she thought she might as well search the one place in this part of the house where she hadn't looked – the little antechamber to the dining room – before she admitted defeat. Positive it was a waste of time but reluctant to give up, she slipped quietly in there from the salon that adjoined it.

This antechamber was a curious little space, hardly more than a closet – it had two doors, and no furniture apart from a cushioned window seat that spanned the meagre width of the room. It would have been wonderfully cosy to sit with Richard there one cold afternoon, except that the chances of being observed when one emerged, dishevelled and guilty from kissing, into one of the adjoining rooms, or from outside through the tall sash window, were too great.

And her book was there on the seat. Someone – perhaps one of the servants – must have picked it up elsewhere and left it there by accident; she certainly hadn't done it herself, however distracted she was by her current state of euphoria. She took it with a low sound of mingled exasperation and triumph, just about to leave and go back to the warmer drawing room, when she froze at the sound of voices. The door to the dining room wasn't fully closed, she saw now, and it was possible to overhear Edward and Lord Marchett in conversation as they sat together at the table. She was no eavesdropper, and besides, nothing could be more tedious, since she'd have more than enough of their platitudes later – except that the subject of their discussion had her rooted to the spot with horror, then creeping closer to the crack to make sure she missed nothing.

'I wonder that you have that tricksy young cub Armstrong to stay with you, Winterflood,' the Earl grumbled in his habitually ponderous tones. 'He's just the kind of creature silly chits find handsome and lose their empty heads over, and I wouldn't trust him as far as I could throw him, myself. Especially not if I had a flighty young wife, which, I am happy to say, I do not.'

'He is my cousin,' Edward said mildly, 'and I have always been fond of him, unlike his complete scoundrel of a brother. And he of me, I like to think.'

'That may be so, but he's a damn sight fonder of your new duchess, and looking to make a damn fool of you by cuckolding you under your own roof, if you ask me.'

Viola felt a wave of horror wash over her, a rush of dizziness, but she could not move. She would have liked to flee, but realised that she must remain and hear all that was said – it was vital to know how far the man's suspicions went, and whether her husband meant to pay any attention to them.

Edward said nothing, and Marchett ploughed on, clearly determined to shake him out of his strange apathy. 'I'm not sure you understand me, old fellow,' he rumbled with a touch of friendly contempt. 'I'm telling you that your young cousin means to put a pair of horns on you, if he hasn't already. And although the boy should be horsewhipped, and the ungrateful doxy turned out into the street in her shift, I'm bound to say that you deserve some share of the blame for not putting a stop to it long before this. You leave them alone for hours every day – of course they'll be up to mischief. It'd take a far slower lad than that Armstrong not to take advantage of the situation. He's probably got her skirts up around her waist in one of your best bedchambers as we sit here like a pair of blinking idiots.'

'Oh, I don't think it's come to that yet,' Edward said without any particular appearance of concern. 'But you're quite right; it will, and soon enough.'

The Earl's tone betrayed his utter astonishment as much as his words did. 'I don't understand you, man! You know, and yet you let it continue? Have you completely lost your mind?'

'Henry,' said Edward slowly, 'I will remind you later that you have forced this conversation on me, so do not show me a shocked face when I am honest with you in response. You are a man with three sons and as many grandsons, so, despite our long friendship, I cannot expect you to understand my predicament. I am desperate. I know you disapproved when I remarried last year – you thought it damned undignified, and I suppose it was. But it was the last throw of the dice for me. And I can see already that I have lost. My marriage to a young woman from a conspicuously fertile family – and let us be clear, that's the only reason I chose her, for if I'd felt I had a choice, I would far rather have remained single now my dear Elizabeth has been taken from me – has confirmed what I had already suspected. The fault is mine: I am unable to sire a child. I could have fifty wives and concubines, like the Grand Turk, and fuck three or four of them nightly in rotation, supposing I could manage anything so exhausting, and I would still die childless.'

Lord Marchett made a curious wordless noise that combined polite but insincere disagreement with pity, and then huffed, 'I feel for you, old man, I do. But I still don't see...'

'Yes, you do,' the Duke said dispassionately. 'You just don't want to. My heir is the boy's half-brother, and he truly is a reprobate. A shameless libertine, of course, but much more than that. He will bring the Winterflood name to disgrace and ruin within five years, once I am dead. I cannot countenance it. I will do anything to prevent that from happening. Do you hear me, Henry? *Anything*.' After a tense little pause, he went on, 'Years ago, I tried to persuade Elizabeth to pass off some beggar's brat I'd found as hers – as ours – but she would not do so. She was too good, too honest, for such a subterfuge. It caused the only serious disagreement in all our years together, and that was a great grief to me. In comparison with that pain, this is easy.'

'Good God in heaven,' Marchett muttered.

Viola could hear the shrug in her husband's voice. 'You make too much of it. I daresay fellows of all ranks are cuckolded every day of the week – damn it, you know they are. Some of them don't know, and of the ones that know, some care and some don't. I'm of the latter party. The boy is of my blood, and looks a little like me. Enough like me, at any rate. If he puts her in farrow, the child will be an Armstrong. If I have some ordinary luck for a change, a son. And that damn vicious whelp Tarquin will be cut out forever. *Quod habeo teneo*, you know, Henry. I have an obligation to my inheritance.'

In farrow. Viola collapsed into the seat, her trembling hands at her face.

'And if it's not a boy?' said Marchett, obviously shaken. 'Do you mean to keep on pimping the girl out till you get the result you want? I presume she knows nothing of this – do you mean to tell her? If she has six daughters like her dam, what will you do then? Keep smiling and hoping and quoting Latin?'

'She won't. Her sister has a son, with some City mushroom the mother married her to, and I hear tell that she is in pup again. I like my odds. It's my only hope, you must see that. And no, I don't mean to tell her. Why should I? In herself, she is of little consequence, though she's not a bad chit. She will be creeping around feeling terrible that she has betrayed me, but doing it all the same because she can't help herself, not knowing it's exactly what I want. I wonder you cannot see the bitter humour in it.'

'I damn well can't! Good God, man, you have shocked me!'

Viola heard the sound of glasses being filled and drained and set down, and roused herself enough to creep away. She doubted very much if she could face them if they came looking for her, and it would be safer not to, lest she betrayed her secret knowledge to Marchett's sharp eyes.

In farrow. In pup. Of little consequence. She was still shaking; she had the quickness of mind to take her book with her so as not to betray her presence to anyone, and almost ran up the stairs.

13

Richard was frowning over the pile of documents on his desk by candlelight when his chamber door opened and he turned to see who had interrupted him. There was an art to covering up sensitive material from the gaze of others without appearing to do so, and he had mastered it. That, and not looking guilty.

He'd expected a maid with a warming pan, but it was Viola, and she was distraught. Her lovely face was white, and she was trembling. The fact that she'd come to his bedchamber without any thought of concealment already told him something was very wrong, but her face and demeanour said that whatever it was, it must be quite disastrous.

'My love, what's the matter?' he asked, going to her side and shutting and locking the door behind her before he took her hand in his.

She was struggling hard to regain her composure. He drew her to sit in the chair by the fire and put his glass of brandy in her grasp. Without looking at it, she drained it, then fell to coughing. When at last she could speak, she said dazedly, 'I was just looking for my book... I'd never have known anything about it if I hadn't been looking for my book. It was *Evelina*.'

'Go on,' he said. He didn't think she could hear him, so great was her distress, but he hoped his tone would be encouraging and soothing.

'I found it in the small chamber between the dining room and the blue saloon. The one with the window seat – you know it?'

He nodded; he'd used to hide from his bullying brother in the easily overlooked little space when he was a small boy.

'I didn't leave it there, but I suppose one of the servants... It doesn't matter in the slightest. I had picked it up and was turning to go, but I heard Lord Marchett talking to Edward, and I had to stay and listen, because he was talking about us.'

Richard was conscious of a sinking feeling in the pit of his stomach. And then, apparently a little recovered, she turned on him unexpectedly in a peculiar sort of cold fury. 'Tell me you didn't know,' she said stonily. 'Swear to me that you were not a party to this... to this foulness.'

He had not the least idea what she was talking about, and told her so. His face must have convinced her of his honesty – he was a good liar, his life demanded it, but on this occasion, he happened to be telling the truth – because she said, 'I see you were as ignorant as I was. Thank God for that, at least. It's almost unbelievable... In the first place, Marchett warned Edward about us. Said that it was obvious to him that we were about to become lovers, if we weren't already.'

Richard cursed, but she went on regardless, 'He pressed the point, and at last Edward said that he knew. He knew! Oh, but he wasn't angry. He was perfectly calm. Because it's exactly what he wants. I think – he didn't exactly say so, but it's been dawning on me – I think he planned it. Our closeness. That's why he invited you here, and why he's left us alone so much. He was deliberately throwing us together.'

'For what purpose?' He was beginning to suspect that he knew, but it was best to have all the information that might be got from what she had overheard. This sort of thing was his life, after all, when it was other people's secrets at stake rather than his own.

'For the purpose of you...' Her voice cracked and she had to take a couple of deep breaths before she could speak again. 'For the purpose of you *getting me in farrow*.'

'He said that?'

'He used those very words. "At least the child would be an Armstrong," he said. And if he was lucky – he said that too – a son. He was quite calm about it. Lord Marchett was not. He was appalled.'

'I cannot wonder at it,' he said, pouring a little more brandy and tossing it down, then yet more, which he passed to her.

She held the glass between her hands and looked away from him, into the depths of the fire. 'I don't know why I should be so shocked. It's not as though I ever thought he loved me, or even cared for me a little. He never pretended to. He told Lord Marchett I was of little consequence, but I already knew he felt that; it shows every day in the way he treats me. And I need not be self-pitying about it, because I don't love him either, or even like him now. The strongest emotion I have ever felt towards him was pity, and that left me months ago. I always knew he just wanted me for my supposed fertility. But this... Lord Marchett said he was pimping me out to you, and that's quite right, isn't it? I thought for a horrible moment that you knew, that you were colluding...'

'No,' he said quickly. 'No. I swear on my mother's grave, I had no idea. You know I tried to talk to him about you, about the way he neglects you. What a fool I was. He must have been laughing at me all the while.'

'Laughing, mentally rubbing his hands because his plan was working and you were beginning to be interested in me, just as he had hoped. I could hate him now, Richard, now that the shock is wearing off. I think I do hate him.'

'I cannot wonder at it. I would never have believed such a thing of my cousin if anybody but you had told me. You have not been unfaithful to him, and I have not betrayed his friendship. Kissing is not infidelity, or, if it is, it is a small form of treason, because you have not given away anything he valued or wanted. He has no use for your kisses, or your precious affection, or anything that makes you the person that you are.'

'No. No, it seems to me that he has betrayed us, if anything,' she said, looking back at him with dark, tragic eyes. 'Your friendship, and my wedding vows. I meant them when I said them, for though I did not love him, I earnestly hoped that I could one day; I don't know what *he* was thinking. This, maybe, even then? Which is revolting. Despicable. I was only seventeen, and he stood in a church with me, and lied. He told Lord Marchett a moment ago that you and I were bound to make love sooner or later – though of course, he did not call it that. I don't know if that's true, if we would have. I'll never know now.'

'What will you do? What should *we* do?'

She said slowly, 'Much as I hate to lose you, I must think you should leave. I don't see how you can stay here, knowing how the cousin you once respected so much has tried to manipulate you and make use of you, for his own selfish purposes.'

He shifted uncomfortably, unable to deny her logic but reluctant to admit it. 'I don't want to abandon you to him. You told me you felt as though you were going mad. The situation is worse now, and surely unendurable for you.'

'Then take me with you.'

14

He looked at her for a moment and she could not tell what he was thinking. 'I can't,' he said heavily at last. 'I love you – Viola, I do, more than I can adequately express. I could ask for nothing more than to spend my life with you. But I have no money to support a wife, or...'

'Or a mistress.' She was surprised at how level her voice sounded in her own ears.

He looked shame-faced, and did not try to deny that that was what she would be. She knew it would be childish for either of them to pretend otherwise. 'We could say that we were married, and strangers at least would believe it, but I live in a squalid little room when I am not travelling. And I'm away for months at a time. You'd be no better off than you are here, no less alone. It would be so wonderful when we were together, but we so rarely would be. What would you do all day long?'

'What do I do now? Nothing with any point to it.' But she didn't say this with any energy. She knew he was right.

'But at least you're safe. You would be all alone in London, in a down-at-heel area, which is all I can afford. Your family might easily cast you off if you left Edward – they would have to, if I understand their situation, because your reputation as a runaway wife, an adulteress...'

'Would damage that of my sisters, and utterly ruin their chances of making decent marriages. Threaten the whole family's future, in fact, and fill my poor father's last years with terrible anxiety. Destroy everything my mother has worked for. Mean that if Laurence did not support them for the rest of their lives, they would all be close to destitute.' She laid out all the horrors of her situation in quite a matter-of-fact manner, and she was proud of her ability to do it when she felt her heart was breaking apart in her chest. She needed to be strong.

'It is so wrong,' he said passionately, 'that you should have so much pressure placed on you. Your life is pulled out of any natural shape by what your family want from you, and what Edward wants from you. There is no space for what *you* want, and the damnable fact is, there's nothing I can do for you. I cannot even ask you to wait, because I have no prospects. Even if I make my way in the world through my own efforts, which I hope to, it may take years till I have any security. There is none at present.'

'I know. The horrible truth is, however furious I am, however much I hate him now, I am tied to Edward forever. There can be no escape for me save through his death, or mine. Even if it were possible for me to free myself through divorce, my family situation, my concern for my sisters' futures, means I could never contemplate such a scandalous course of action. It would ruin them as well as me. That would still be a fact even if I could afford the enormous cost, which of course, I cannot. It was a foolish, selfish thing to say – forget it, if you can.'

He fell to his knees at her feet, taking her cold hands in his and kissing them fervently. 'It was not foolish. Don't say that, or even think it. I would wish for nothing better in the world than that we could be together always, and as happy and secure as we deserve. Both of us. But the forces that seek to keep us apart are so powerful – it's not even the people, it's not even your mother and your sisters and bloody Edward, or my employers; it's great impersonal forces of circumstance.'

'They can't keep us apart tonight, however powerful they are,' she told him with sudden heat. 'I absolutely refuse to go back to my room and wait meekly for Edward to come to me again, or not to come, if he has stayed up drinking too late with Marchett and feels himself to be incapable. He knows he is infertile, he says – well then, he might as well leave me alone. I am sorry if he needs the pretence – no, I am not. I don't know if I want to lie with you tonight, Richard, as a woman does with a man – I feel cold and sick and used. And I don't want to think, or for you to think, that if I give myself to you fully, it might be out of shock or even some perverse desire for revenge on Edward. We both deserve better than that. But I would like to sleep in your bed, in your arms. If you will have me.'

'Come, my love,' he said, rising and taking her in his arms. 'At least we can give each other comfort.'

With great tenderness, he helped her undress down to her shift, and in a little while, they were embracing. She lay close against him with her head on his chest, and he stroked her dark hair and held her, and after a while, she cried silently at the hopelessness of it all, and he wiped her wet cheeks, and kissed them. But he did no more than that, and she did not want him to.

Perhaps the Duke went to her chamber to seek her out and found her absent, or perhaps that night he did not – they had no means of knowing. At last, they fell asleep and lay curled together until early morning, when Richard woke her and she left him wordlessly. She went creeping along the silent corridors with her gown bundled in her arms, realising as he had that it really would be folly to allow the servants to know that she had not slept in her own bed. Her situation was quite complicated enough without that fresh danger.

15

Viola remained in her chamber the next morning, and Richard could not blame her for it. He sat down to breakfast with his cousin and Lord Marchett, and he hoped his face did not betray any of the turmoil he was feeling, and especially his burning anger with Winterflood. He could not detect any difference in Edward's manner towards him, and so was still unsure whether the Duke had attempted to visit his wife last night or not; if he had, and found her absent, he was concealing his feelings about the matter exceedingly well. Richard would not have suspected him capable of such subterfuge, such ruthlessness, but then, perhaps he'd never really known him. He should have realised that everyone had secrets – not just him.

The butler came in to tell his master that the estate steward Thompson would be grateful for a word as a matter of some urgency, and Edward excused himself, leaving his friend and his young cousin alone in uneasy silence. Richard drank coffee with a show of unconcern and waited for what he had a shrewd idea was coming. Marchett struck him as the interfering type. 'Mean to make a long visit here, do you, Armstrong?' the older man said with no marked degree of friendliness.

Here it comes, Richard thought resignedly.

'Edward has been good enough to tell me he is happy to host me for as long as I am able to stay,' he responded with a show of calmness. 'But the necessity of earning a living will take me away soon enough, I am sorry to say.

This has been a brief holiday for me.' *Not that it's any of your affair, you nosey old toast,* he wanted to add.

'You're employed in some capacity in the City, I understand.' The man's tone suggested he might as well have asked if Richard emptied privies for a living. And perhaps he did, in a sense – after all, someone had to.

Richard met the Earl's gaze steadily. The old man was something high up in the Foreign Office, he knew, and therefore could not be a complete fool. 'I am, sir. My cousin paid for my education and offered to make me an allowance when I was grown, but I did not think it right to take him up on it, not least because he has made no such offer to my brother, his heir, saying with justice that he would only squander it. And – unlike my brother – I am not one for sitting idle when I can be filling my time more usefully.'

'I can see that,' Marchett said drily. 'Very busy, active sort of a fellow, it's quite plain. I'm sure your business in London – and elsewhere – must be pressing. Best you go back to it, don't you think?'

'Do you mean to report the matter of this conversation to Edward?' Richard asked with a spark of anger.

'I do not.'

'So then I may speak openly. You want me gone, which is understandable, but my cousin, as you know very well, wants me here, for his own reasons that have nothing at all to do with the pleasure of my company, or any such normal feeling. If he heard that you had warned me off, he would be angry with you, furious, I daresay, and ask you, with some justice, what gave you licence to meddle so egregiously in his private business.'

'Good God, boy, I've heard unsavoury rumours about you in Town, but I didn't know the half of it. You are very cool and high-and-mighty, and so I must assume that you know what he's about, and you... you are colluding in it! Taking advantage of his addle-pated folly!'

'You have not the least right to say that, and you know it. I have done nothing of which I need be ashamed – I have broken no vows, and I assure you, though it is not in the least your affair, neither has the Duchess. I would be interested to see if you can tell me honestly that you think the same of Edward.'

Marchett's bluster seemed to collapse suddenly, like one of Lunardi's balloons coming down in a field. 'Very well, then,' he said gruffly. 'What I think is, he's run stark mad. I've never heard of such a thing. Don't tell me if the girl knows of it – I don't want to hear anything I may later feel obliged to tell him. I won't stay here and appear to condone this dangerous folly of his. What a confounded mess he's made for himself. But the last thing I mean to do is to make more trouble for the poor old fellow. I don't give a damn about you or the silly chit otherwise.'

'The poor old fellow, as you call him, is treating his wife appallingly. Jesus Christ, man, she was seventeen when he married her last year! But it's quite clear to me that you don't care a button for that.'

The Earl waved his hand as if such womanish sentiments were not of the least consequence. 'And it's quite clear to me that you do, for all your fine words and protestations of innocence. More than you should.'

Richard laughed mirthlessly. 'What do you suppose he'll do, if you tell him of it? Call me out? Threaten me with a horsewhip? Because – let me be sure I understand you, sir – it would be perfectly acceptable for me to play him false under his own roof if I don't give a damn for his unfortunate wife, but somehow, it would not if I do happen to care for her?'

'None of it's perfectly acceptable!' the much-tried Earl said. But after a moment, he recovered himself and said, 'It's shaken me, this, I don't mind admitting. But I don't see how in all honour you can stay either, knowing what you do.'

'Then I should leave her alone with him, you think? You wouldn't be at all worried that if I fail him, he'll start looking measuringly at the footmen?'

Marchett rubbed his hand over his reddened face, and groaned behind it. 'He wouldn't,' was the muffled response. 'He's a gentleman, and he wouldn't.'

'I wouldn't have thought he'd do this either, and yet here we are. I doubt either of us knows him in the least, or what he's capable of. It seems to me he is quite ruthless in the pursuit of his ends, and entirely careless of the feelings of others.'

'I was afraid of this, but the fool can't see it,' the older man said. 'You'd have to be a scoundrel to co-operate knowingly with his damned unsavoury scheme and if you're not a scoundrel, if you care for the girl as you seem to... If she runs off and leaves him for another man like the other one did, it'll break him. Twice – can you imagine what people would say that he must have done to drive them both to it? He couldn't endure that again, the shame of it, the whispering, never mind this business of his precious heir. I know that much.'

'I can see why you think I might just care about all that, as an Armstrong, but there's no reason the Duchess should. You know there's a name for what he's doing to her, and it's not a pretty one.'

'Don't you think I tried to tell him that?'

'And yet if any sort of legal proceedings were brought on her behalf, in the manner of Mrs Addison's notorious case against her husband last year, and you were asked on oath if your friend had told you of his infamous plan, I'll wager you'd lie through your teeth to protect him and say you knew nothing of it. Leave her swinging in the wind.'

'Damn it, man, the Addison case was different! That was a matter of incest – quite exceptional circumstances, and the husband considered not in his right mind! You can't possibly be telling me that this girl would think to seek a divorce from Edward on her own account, tell the world what he's been up to, with all the cost and scandal that would involve!'

Richard would not dream of sharing anything that Viola had said to him in private with this man, and so his reply was somewhat evasive. 'No doubt she is aware that last year, for the first time, a woman was granted a divorce because of her husband's gross betrayal of her, but I have no reason to think that she has any intention of trying such a thing for herself. And I don't suppose for a moment she'd get one even if she did seek it. I'm sure she should if there was any justice in the world, but that's a different matter, as we both know there isn't. I doubt you and I could ever come to agree on the rights and wrongs of this, and God forbid that the precious status quo of England should be threatened for the sake of a mere woman's wish for decent treatment from her husband.'

Lord Marchett did not have an answer to that, or not one he was prepared to say out loud, and Richard, disgusted, left him to his breakfast.

16

Much as he was tempted to confront his cousin that very morning and relieve his own bruised feelings by telling him exactly what he thought of his behaviour, Richard could see it would be of no use, and might do actual harm. He was not the one with most at stake. How to proceed from here must be Viola's decision, and she knew already that her case was hopeless. Damn his own situation that made her even more trapped – he'd driven that home to her last night himself. But it would have been cruel to give her false hope, and he couldn't do it. This was not a world in which they could be together.

Despite Mrs Addison's success last year as the first woman to divorce and shame her husband through Act of Parliament, and gain custody of her children into the bargain, the old booby Marchett had been right to say that the circumstances were very different. Addison's incestuous affair with his wife's sister had been vouched for by witnesses – there was nothing so definite here. Edward's crime had been one of intention and manipulation only. And furthermore, the determined Scottish lady had had substantial financial resources and a shocked, supportive family behind her – Viola knew only too well that she could boast of neither. Marchett and Winterflood would lie to save themselves; it would be their word against hers, and society was not currently arranged to favour women's interests over those of rich, powerful, titled men. It seemed doubtful if it ever would be. No – there'd be a huge scandal, as she'd said last night, and she'd be the one to suffer most even though she was entirely blameless. Who could doubt it? Her family would be pulled down with her too – it would be a comprehensive disaster.

She emerged later in the morning, finding him doing nothing in particular in the library as he waited for her, and his heart was wrung by her pale, unhappy face. 'Let's walk,' she said. She was already wrapped in a grey velvet pelisse and holding her bonnet carelessly by the ribbons. He fetched his overcoat and hat and accompanied her outside. It didn't seem to matter where they went, but by tacit consent, they climbed the winding path up the slope that would have them out of sight of the house as quickly as possible. It was a looming presence that pointed up the vast disparity in power and influence between the Duke and themselves.

'Have you seen Edward?' he asked her, and she shook her head. 'Marchett accosted me this morning over breakfast – tried to get me to leave, prosed on about honour, as if I were the one behaving dishonourably here. But I confronted him with the horror of what his old companion is trying to do you, not to mention me, and he had nothing to say to me in his defence. He told me he would not report our conversation back, and I believed him. He's appalled, but you won't be surprised to hear that he isn't actually going to take any action on your behalf.'

'What could he do, after all?' she said with an air of indifference, almost of apathy. 'What can anyone do? I was never foolish enough to imagine that Lord Marchett, Edward's oldest and closest friend, would support me, and I'm not sure it would help much even if he did. How is it possible to be surrounded by such splendour, to supposedly be mistress of it, to be widely envied, and yet to be so powerless? I have no money beside the allowance my husband makes me, which is a great deal by most people's standards but is entirely dependent on his continuing to pay it, and my family has nothing to spare. I am a duchess, but it is an empty title, product of my marriage – people would bow and scrape to me wherever I went, I'd get endless credit at the modiste's so I could buy another stupid gown I don't need, but that is all. In law, I am no more than Edward's possession. It makes me feel sick and furious to think of it.'

There was nothing to be said to all this, because it was true.

They made their way to one of the summerhouses, and took some comfort in holding each other, but today, their kisses were desperate and feverish, as if they both knew that a shadow hung over their relationship and a time limit had been placed on it. That had always been so, of course, but it had been possible to ignore the facts before – now, it was not.

When they returned to the house, they found a great and unexpected bustle in the hall, with servants running to and fro; it soon became clear that Lord Marchett was leaving, and the Duke was bidding him a punctilious farewell. The carriage was already drawn up by the door, the luggage was almost loaded, and the horses could not be kept waiting long in the chill air. The Earl shook hands with Richard with a tolerable show of friendliness, and bowed over Viola's hand with an artificial smile pasted on his face, thanking her for her hospitality as he told her that he had been summoned home by an urgent letter in the day's post. Every single person present knew that this was untrue, and they all pretended to believe it.

'I am sorry to see you go, old fellow,' Edward said, appearing to mean it. Whatever had passed between the two old friends in the last hour, it did not seem as though they had had a falling-out: nothing so severe as to be irrevocable, at any rate. 'But perhaps it is as well, since I too must be absent from home for a day or two, and so would not be here to entertain you as I should.' He turned to Viola and said with perfect composure, 'I hope you will forgive me, my dear, but Thompson came this morning with an urgent message about a serious outbreak of some infectious disease among the stock on the farms over towards Cambridge. I feel I must go and make sure all is being done to prevent it spreading and causing a great deal of damage, even panic among the tenants. If I leave soon, I shall be there in good time this evening, and I shall be busy with it all day tomorrow, and put up at an inn, or at Thompson's house, for two nights at least. My valet is packing a bag for me, and you should not expect me back before Friday. But Richard will keep you entertained, I am confident of it.'

Viola was plainly taken aback by this news, and murmured some incoherent response; Richard could only be grateful for Lord Marchett's intervention, for once. The Earl raised what Mr Armstrong could not help but see as a satirical eyebrow, and said with a touch of impatience that it was time he was away, and any awkwardness was lost in the flurry of farewells. By the time his carriage had rolled away, Edward had said it was time for him to leave also, or it would be pitch-dark when he reached his destination. He made his way round to the stables for a less ceremonious departure, brushing away with a sudden vagueness his wife's insincere offer to come and see him off. The pair were left alone, save for the servants, looking at each other in silent consternation.

They wandered into the library and sat by the fire, both chilled. 'Thompson did come in and ask to see him urgently when we were at the breakfast table,' Richard told her. 'So it could be true, but it seems an odd coincidence all the same.'

'It may all be true, but it's still a pretext to leave us alone together,' she said, her voice rich with contempt directed at her husband. 'I do not believe he would normally go haring across the countryside in February because a few sheep have a cough. He has people to tend to such matters for him, surely. I know he does. Perhaps in the end, he cannot stomach the idea of being in the house while we... Or perhaps, and more likely, Lord Marchett has told him that if he insists on make a cuckold of himself, at least he need not be present while it happens.'

'Is it going to happen, Viola? You weren't sure last night.'

She looked at him, straight in the face, and then incredibly, she smiled. 'Yes, it is,' she said. 'If you want me, I am yours, even if it can only be for a night or two, and then we must part forever.'

17

Having taken that decision made a difference, Viola found. No matter that she had been manipulated into it, almost pushed into her lover's arms, no matter that when she thought about Edward, she felt sick and angry; still, she was choosing this for herself. She would not think now about the fact that she might be also giving Winterflood what he wanted – that didn't seem to signify much at the moment. This was what *she* wanted, and what Richard wanted, and tonight, that would be all that was allowed to matter. Something for themselves.

It was a day of flirting, of pretending that she was as free to flirt decorously with the man of her choice as any other girl her age. The reflecting pool was frozen still, and Richard found skates in some cupboard that he remembered from his childhood. Once they had strapped these metal contraptions securely over their boots, he took her out on the ice, both of them bundled up against the penetrating cold. He was a superb skater, and she was indifferent at best, wobbling comically at first and clinging to him, but he held her and did not let her fall. Once she became a little more confident and steadier on her feet, they glided together in exhilarating motion – like dancing in a ballroom, but so much better, fast and breathless and always with an edge of danger.

When they began to feel the cold and the sun was setting in an orange ball behind the bare tree branches of the park, and the white mist rising, they went inside and took tea by the fire. It was all very sedate, but occasionally, her hand would brush his, or his hers, and always their glances locked and held, their eyes bright with promise and with their ever-present desire for each other.

After tea, she bathed, lying in the cooling water and soaping herself slowly and languorously, anticipating his touch, refusing to think any further than the night ahead. She wanted to array herself in her best for their first dinner tête-à-tête, but resisted the temptation because her maid would undoubtedly think it odd to see her dressed as if for some special occasion. She chose instead a blue silk gown that he had admired when she had worn it a few days earlier. It was embroidered with tiny brilliants around the neckline and the sleeves, and she wore no jewellery with it. Everything she had, apart from a simple locket from her mama, belonged really to Edward – had been worn by his other wives first, and would be worn by other unknown women after her. She would not go to Richard decked in another man's diamonds.

They were waited on by the footmen over dinner, and so could discuss nothing but commonplaces, but there was a pleasure in that too – every word, every look, had an underlying meaning, and though his hands could not caress her, his eyes did. For the sake of appearances, she left him to sit in solitary splendour over the port she knew he did not care for, and it was worth the brief time alone – it was very brief – to see the glad expression on his face when he came to join her. They played silly card games together for ridiculously high and entirely imaginary stakes, laughing over their hands and teasing each other over mistakes as they had never been able to do when Edward was present. It was a piercing reminder that there was happiness in the world, that even this place where she'd almost lost her mind need not be quiet and miserable unless it was made so, and she found herself consciously storing away the memories against the lonely years ahead. She tried not to wonder if he was doing the same; his life was so much fuller than hers, she must think it unlikely.

Eventually, the clock struck ten, which seemed to her to be a reasonable time for a respectable lady whose husband was absent to go to her chaste bed. She said goodnight to Richard and climbed the stairs, a small figure amid such grandeur, alone as always but for once not lonely, ignoring, as ordinarily she could not, the intimidating marble magnificence all around her – the statues brought from Rome, the vast battle scenes, the writhing gods and goddesses in the frescoes on the ceilings high above her, the displays of ancient weapons. Tonight, they were not real and she was.

Her maid came to help her undress, and she tried very hard to behave as though it was just a normal evening like any other. Jennings was a woman in her thirties, small in stature and quick in her movements, always quiet and respectful, highly skilled at her profession, and a complete mystery to Viola. She'd tried in her loneliness to prise anything more than commonplaces from her attendant, and thus she was aware that Mary had grown up on the estate and had several siblings and her parents still living, but she knew nothing more. She did not doubt that the woman had opinions of her own about everything, including her new mistress, but it was impossible to divine what they might be. The new Duchess suspected, with no basis for these suspicions, that Mary Jennings had been Elizabeth's abigail for years, and a particular favourite of hers, but if she was glad to find herself serving her successor, or if she found each day a trial and an affront, Viola had not the least idea. It was impossible to dislike her, since she displayed no personality traits apart from diligence, competence and courtesy, and equally impossible to like or trust her. She, after all, was not really the woman's employer, but a mere newcomer.

She'd never had a maid before, not even a shared one, and her new personal servant had been selected for her without any consultation, presumably by Edward or the equally enigmatic housekeeper, the intimidating Mrs Bradford. If either of these women ever had a choice to make over where their loyalty lay, it would be foolish in the extreme to assume that they would choose *her*. At best, their allegiance was to Winterflood as some kind of abstract idea, but more likely, it was to Edward, and to his regrettably dead second wife. So she must never relax her vigilance in their company.

Once the maid had left her, she tried to sit calmly as she waited for the house to fall quiet and for the servants to retreat to their own quarters for the night. It was clearly inadvisable for Richard to come to her, for reasons to do with the state of the linens when the housemaid came in in the morning that were too sordid to put into words, even in her own mind. She would go to him, as soon as she felt it safe to do so. And she was glad to do it, because it was so very different from lying in her bed and waiting to see if Edward would appear or not. She would be active, not passive, for the first time ever. The fact that it might also be the last was something she pushed resolutely from her mind.

Eventually, she thought that she would be safe from detection as she could be, and wrapped herself in her robe, taking up her candle and very carefully closing her chamber door behind her. There was no point locking it – a locked door would give her away as completely as an empty bed, or a bed occupied by what the world would call the wrong man. She crept along the passageway, her heart in her mouth, until she reached her destination. Taking a deep breath, she opened the door and went inside.

18

Richard was waiting for her, dressed in his robe, and he came to her as soon as she entered. 'The maid has been and warmed the bed with the pan,' he told her. 'We are safe.'

'If only that were true,' she said, and pulled down his head so that she could kiss him with fierce urgency. It was different, doing that here, both of them lightly clad, both of them knowing that they need not stop. She gave free rein to all the desire that she'd been feeling for him over the last week or two, her tongue in his mouth, her hands fumbling for the fastening of his robe. She found it and released it, pushing it from his shoulders so that it fell to the floor, and discovered that he was gloriously naked beneath it. 'I want to touch you,' she said against his mouth, her hands exploring his broad chest. 'I want to know you, and for you to know me. I want you to show me the things that people do when they aren't coming together with one purpose in mind, and that purpose very little to do with pleasure.'

'Viola,' he said, 'my love, my darling, it shall be exactly as you wish. We don't have to do anything at all that would fit with Edward's plans, if you don't want to. There are many, many things that we can share that will give us both all the pleasure in the world and yet not risk giving him what he wants from us.' He was unfastening her robe too as he spoke, and caressing her body through the thin fabric of her night-rail.

'I want to do everything,' she said, unfastening the buttons of the flimsy muslin garment, aware that every minute was important when the time they had was so brief. 'These two nights with you will be all I have, I fear. I want to know passion as I have not yet, and if it does bring me a child, whether it is his precious heir or not, that will be a comfort too, and a reminder of you when you are gone. I had reconciled myself to having his child – why in the world would I not want yours instead, as long as I am able to choose it freely for myself? But I don't want to think about him or talk about him any more, only about you. There is no one in the world but you and me tonight.'

'Come to bed, my love.'

They slipped naked between the sheets, and he pushed them back so that he could look at her, all of her; they had neither of them blown out the candles, and this was new for her, and exactly what she wanted.

'You are so beautiful, it breaks my heart,' he said, and then his lips claimed hers as his hands explored her.

Edward had never kissed her as he kissed her – she had not wanted to make comparisons, but it was impossible not to, because she had never felt worshipped before, and the pleasure she had known had been but a pale shadow of this. She touched Richard too, and explored his beloved body with her mouth and her hands, imprinting every inch of it upon her mind so that she would always remember. And when their passion had exhausted them, they slept naked in each other's arms, and that was new for her too.

19

Richard had developed a useful habit of coming wide awake very early in the morning, fully alert in an instant and ready for anything the day might bring at the sort of ungodly hour when most people were fast asleep, dreaming and defenceless. Often, the path he had chosen in life – or perhaps it had chosen him – meant that he was obliged to sneak away when nobody else was up and about to catch him. Sometimes, he needed to explore and map the place he happened to be staying in, unobserved; sometimes, there was a vital object or objects – papers, usually – that must be stolen and concealed, or copied and put back, as the case might be. Once or twice, there'd been violence to be done: a smothering cloth, a blade in the dark, and then an innocent return to bed.

This late February morning brought a different kind of anxiety; though he had not the least desire in the world to drive her away, Viola had to be awakened and sent back to her cold chamber, so that she could make a credible pretence of sleeping in it once more to ensure that the servants suspected nothing. Or, to be painfully accurate, if indeed they suspected something already, as well they might, given the Duke's recent peculiar behaviour, she must make certain that their suspicions couldn't be proved correct by any physical evidence, such as a missing duchess and an empty bed.

God knows he wished she could stay. If she were his wife, he wouldn't be on the other side of the county peering at sickly sheep in a freezing field. Let some other poor bastard do that. She was warm and glorious in his arms, and when he kissed her tenderly awake, she responded with such instant trust and passion that they made love again, fast and urgent and fiercely, heart-shakingly moving. And then she slipped reluctantly from his embrace, dressed herself in the dark and left him, after more lingering kisses, not forgetting to take her burnt-down candle with her so that it too would be in its proper place if anyone thought to check. He rolled over to where her warmth lingered and buried his face in the pillow that held the scent of her hair. Which, of course, had much better be gone by the time the maid came to make the bed.

They did not meet at breakfast. He ate alone, but when she did appear, they went riding together as they had so often done before, and later took luncheon. It was bitterly cold today, an icy wind cutting across the frozen landscape and sneaking into the house here and there to make one shiver. They spent the afternoon reading quietly in the library rather than going out onto the ice or for a walk. They didn't have a great deal to say to each other in this semi-public place, and anyone who happened to see them together would have sensed a certain constraint between them, such as might easily fall between a young married woman and a male relative she didn't know very well with whom she had unexpectedly and awkwardly been left unchaperoned in her home. That wasn't the true cause of their discomfort, of course – in reality, it was the shared knowledge that tonight would be the last that they could be sure of spending together. Tomorrow was Friday, and Edward had said he would be back. Perhaps they might have a final stolen night, if he failed to return, but they could not assume as much until late the next evening, and perhaps not even then. They neither of them wished to grow complacent, or to play out some farce where he caught them together because they had been careless. Would he simply turn and walk away, or would he be hypocrite enough to pretend he minded? Would they be disgusted by his falseness and tell him that they knew what he was about, provoke an argument – and what then? Viola, who was nothing less than trapped here, should not be put in such a precarious position.

'I think I should leave tomorrow,' he told her soberly after dinner. 'I hate to go, but I do not see what else is to be done. I'll write to Edward, tell him I have been called back to work unexpectedly, and apologise for my discourtesy in not waiting to say farewell to him, and in leaving you alone in his absence. I don't think I can face him; I think if he sees me, he will know straight away.'

'It's what he wanted, isn't it?' she responded with a trace of bitterness. 'He should be pleased if he thinks something has happened between us. Though he'll be sorry you have gone so soon, and not stayed and made sure... Oh, don't look at me like that, Richard. I know you are right. I agree, in fact. It would be unbearable, the three of us alone together in such a false situation, pretending nothing was wrong. If you did not give our secret away by looking conscious, I would. My nature is deplorably hasty, my mother is always telling me so; I'd lose my temper and cause a scene, and things would be said on all sides that could never be taken back. However much I want to upbraid him as he deserves, I know I cannot risk it.'

'This way,' he said, taking her hand, 'if... nothing happens, if there are no consequences of our lovemaking, then he will never know for sure. He may suspect, but he cannot know. Perhaps that will be easier for you? Though I know there is no real comfort for you in any of this, my love.'

'Easier? Perhaps. Even he, we must hope, cannot really be angry with me just because he thinks I have failed to play him false. As soon as I put it into words, it's plain how ridiculous it is. He certainly can't *say* anything on the subject to me, not even a hint, if he believes I may possibly still be ignorant of his plans, and innocent. Yes, it might be easier for me. Safer, certainly, to have his suspicions unconfirmed, until and unless...'

'We will have tonight.'

'And I must be content with that, I know. I should not be greedy and want more of you than I can have.'

'If there was any way—'

She cut him off. 'There is not. We both know it. I don't need to be soothed with childish fantasies, my dear. I can face up to the truth. I have no choice.'

They repeated the farce of saying goodnight like virtual strangers and going off to their separate chambers, and once again, she crept along the silent corridors to join him an agonising while later.

Their lovemaking tonight was desperate, almost frantic – they both knew without speaking of it that it was possible that they'd never see each other again after this, or only meet very rarely, in public, where no private communication would be possible. It was not quite true to say that the future was uncertain, because the possibilities were not infinite: Viola would either have a child or she would not, and from there, the road forked to two very different destinations, but neither of the lives that she might have as a consequence would ever include him.

It occurred to him now while they lay silent in his bed, their bodies touching but their thoughts private and unshared, that he really might in a few short months have a son or daughter in the world whom he would never get to know, never be a father to, possibly never even see as they grew. Edward would be his or her father, in law and in day-to-day life. He'd never considered the question of fatherhood before, except to take trouble to avoid it – he was still only one and twenty, after all – and the sense of anticipatory loss, almost of pain that swept over him took him entirely by surprise. It seemed so wrong, he might even have said obscene. How could Edward, who had so much already, steal his child from him, the child of the woman he loved that they'd made together? But he didn't mention any of it to Viola; what was the point? They were both the losers here, but he had a great deal to do in the world, a great deal of danger to face that might easily bring his life to a premature conclusion before he could even know if a child was to be born, while she would remain here with Edward whatever happened. It would be nothing more than selfish and cruel to make matters worse for her than they already were by babbling about his own potential hurt and loss.

20

Eventually, they had to talk about it, in these their last moments alone together. They had barely slept, and it was close on six, almost time for her to creep away, when he spoke at last, his breath brushing her hair. 'When should I leave? I know Edward might easily not come back till late today or even tomorrow, and God knows I want nothing more than another night in your arms, but it seems to me to be a great risk to take, to linger here with you, however precious every moment in your presence is to me. I swear I am not concerned for myself – he has no power over me unless he attempts to call on the memory of our past closeness, and our relationship as cousins and friends is already irrevocably broken by his actions, by his heartless treatment of you. I am quite prepared to tell him so. But you have no such freedom...'

'I know,' she said, her voice a little muffled in his chest. She could feel his heart beating under her cheek, and she pressed closer to him. It felt so safe and permanent and right, but it was all an illusion. 'I hate the picture that my mind presents – of him entering some room and finding us together, however innocently we might be sitting reading or talking. If I saw a sort of avid, hopeful expression on his face as he looked at us, I swear I would cross the room and slap him. How dare he manipulate us so, as if he were one of the Olympian gods on the ceiling downstairs, and we mere helpless mortal pawns? If it ever occurred to him that we might develop feelings for each other, I am sure he brushed the idea aside as quite irrelevant. And so, much as it hurts me to say it, I would rather you were gone before there is any chance of him coming back. Write your letter to him and leave it in his study, and I will arrange for one of the grooms to drive you into Bedford or Cambridge – wherever there will be a stage or mail coach soonest that you can take to London. That is what would normally be done when you departed, is it not? And the servants will know what is best, and when you should leave.'

'Probably Cambridge,' he murmured dully. 'That's how I came. But it does not matter. It feels as though it were months ago since I came here and first saw you, so beautiful and so unhappy, but it is only weeks. Oh, my love...'

'Don't,' she told him fiercely. 'Don't, or I will break down and cling to you and beg you to take me with you again, when I already know the dozens of reasons why you cannot. I don't want your last memory of me to be in helpless tears. Don't tell me you love me when it's all so hopeless. Make love to me again; make me forget everything.'

She left him a while later, and was back in her own bed, pretending to sleep though she was unable to, long before the maid came to light her chamber fire and bring her tea. When her abigail came to help her dress, she said casually, 'Jennings, Mr Armstrong said yesterday that his correspondence was preying on his thoughts and that he thought he should leave as soon as possible and return to London. Perhaps he may have changed his mind this morning. But in case he has not, can you ask Fletcher where it would be best for one of the coachmen to drive him so that he can conveniently catch the next stage or mail?'

Mary said sedately that she would, not appearing to think anything odd at all about the request. In a short while, Viola had her answer, and the thing was set in motion with an ease that made her want to scream, to find some way to stop it because it was all so wrong.

A couple of short hours later, she stood bundled in her warmest coat in the coach-house yard, watching her lover climb up into Edward's curricle beside the waiting driver, his meagre baggage stowed behind him, his face pale and set. He'd bowed over her gloved hand a moment earlier, and they had spoken commonplace words of thanks, farewell and Godspeed that came nowhere near to the truth of what they both felt. It was as well that they were observed by the people around them, she thought, and therefore obliged to maintain the strictest propriety in their speech, appearance and actions – if she'd been alone with him, she'd surely have disgraced herself by falling sobbing to the cobbles. Her heart was shattering into thousands of tiny, sharp pieces in her chest, and she felt cold and sick and desolate.

He raised his hand in final goodbye, the coachman set the two horses in motion and the vehicle swept out through the gateway in a creak of wood and a rattle of harness. She was left alone.

She turned and walked back into the house, and its chilly walls closed about her like the grandest of prisons.

21

Edward did not come back that day, and a great part of Viola cursed him for it – not that she wanted him there in the slightest, but because he had told her to expect him – and cursed herself and Richard for their excess of caution, and for the loss of time together that they'd never have again. But in the end, she became reconciled, and in a numb way was glad to have a little space to herself, so that she might set her thoughts in some sort of order and face Edward with more composure than she felt she could manage at present.

Her courses were due in a little less than a fortnight. She had always been regular, and the circumstances of her married life had made her take good note of them – when they arrived and how long they lasted; she made discreet marks in her diary signifying as much. She thought it very likely that Edward also kept careful record of her cycle, though they had never spoken of it, naturally. When she was suffering with her female complaint, she merely told him after dinner that she was unwell – nothing more – and he understood her perfectly and did not trouble her. It was what her mother had advised her to do; it must be some sort of commonly used code, she supposed. Certainly, he must be used to it by now, since he'd had so many years of it with one wife after another, month after weary month.

But one thing she knew: he was not welcome in her bed any longer. Perhaps she could not keep him away forever, if she bled in a few days' time and he knew himself disappointed again. But he was damn well not lying with her, on her, touching her, while her whole body still tingled from Richard's welcome caress, and her arms longed to hold him and never let him go. She would feign some other kind of trivial illness – say she had a cold. Something, anything. He might jump to certain conclusions about why her door was suddenly closed to him, but just now, she did not care. Let him worry; let him wonder.

But he did not come, she dined alone, and went alone to her chamber. Her healthy constitution had a little mercy on her profound unhappiness; she slept heavily and long, and once she had risen, she went for a long walk about the estate, well wrapped against the chill. She found rather to her surprise that she looked on it all with more fondness now, because she had shared the walks and rides with Richard; here they had danced together, here they sat on their horses and looked down at Winterflood and he had first shown her sympathy, here and here and here they had kissed and spoken words of love. It still pierced her heart that he was gone, but whatever happened now, no one could ever take these memories away.

When she made her slow way back to the house, Wilkinson told her that Edward had returned a short while since, and was in his study. She would not wait for him to seek her out; she went to him. She had decided in her time alone that she would be braver than she had previously been.

He was reading when she entered – Richard's letter, she supposed, or one of the others that had come for him in the days that he had been absent. 'How were the sheep?' she asked, not troubling overmuch to make it sound as though she cared.

He made to rise to his feet, but she waved off the instinctive courtesy. 'The sheep...? Oh, there is still some cause for concern, but Thompson and the good farmers have it in hand. All possible quarantine precautions are being taken; I may have to go back in a week or two... I am sorry to see that Cousin Richard has left us. There is nothing wrong, I hope?'

'He had a number of letters, and they seemed to worry him; at last, he said he felt he had no choice but to go back and deal with the matters that were piling up in his absence. He made his apologies to me for not waiting till you returned, and said he would write to you to make his excuses also. I presume he has done so.'

'Yes, yes, he has. Well, I am sorry this should have happened; it will be sadly dull for you here without him while the weather continues so cold.' She thought he was looking at her with unaccustomed attention and sharpness as he said this, seeking some reaction, and for a moment, she could think of no answer to make him that would not betray anything of what she felt; she only shrugged wordlessly and turned away. He still could not *know*; it was perfectly possible for her to miss her pleasant companion, for her to cherish a tendre for him, even to be deep in love with him, and him with her, without anything in the least improper having taken place between them.

'It will be a little quiet without him, that is true, until we grow used to his absence. But I have walked for too long,' she said with hard-won, cool composure, 'and I fear I have taken a chill. Excuse me, Edward, I am going to lie down for a little while in bed and get warm.'

He was instantly all solicitude, and urged her – so that she did not have to suggest it herself – to take her dinner in her bedchamber and be sure to keep warm.

The succeeding days passed in similar fashion, and when she was not in bed, she bundled herself up in shawls and had no difficulty at all in looking wan and miserable as she drifted about the house, coughing occasionally when it occurred to her to do so. She was very tired suddenly, with no need for feigning, and slept a great deal. He did not come to her, and when he suggested sending for the doctor, she told him that there was not the least need. She just needed to rest.

Nor did her courses arrive. By the time they were three days late, then four, she was tolerably certain that they were not going to make an appearance at all. She felt the same, and yet different – her breasts were a little sore, as usual, but she had not a twinge of the dragging pain in her belly, her back and thighs that ordinarily accompanied her unwelcome monthly visitor. She did now feel a compulsion to weep at odd moments in the long, cold days – but she could not wonder at it. Well might she weep, or rage.

Viola thought her husband must be on tenterhooks, but for several days, he dared not ask her in plain words how she did. In other circumstances, she might have felt pity for his anxiety and the dawning hope that she saw him struggling to suppress. But she had none to spare for him – after all, it seemed he was getting exactly what he wanted. His wicked plan had worked to perfection, and if there was a price, he was not the one paying it.

22

1813 – THE PRESENT

'Yes,' said Viola slowly. 'Yes, I suppose we must discuss it. Though I do not know how much there is to be said. The past cannot be altered.'

'Of course it cannot. It is years too late for that and we both know it. Viola, I should tell you now that I had wondered if I should approach you after Edward died, once your mourning was over. You'd been married to him for so many years that any sensation over the match and its outcome must have been long forgotten, and it wasn't very likely anyone would assume that the boys could possibly be mine. Not when he had accepted them and lived with them as their father for so long. But the disparity in our fortunes was still so great, I still had so little to offer you.'

That sounded very much like a convenient excuse to her, and it didn't matter anyway, except that she wished he wouldn't lie to her. Again. 'Far too much time had elapsed by then,' she told him crisply. She was agreeing with him, on this at least, but that didn't mean that they were in accord. She let down her knees and moved to sit more upright against the pillows; it was impossible to have a discussion of such a serious nature lying on her back like a stranded turtle. She could not afford to feel so vulnerable in his presence.

'If we ever knew each other or cared for each other – and at this distance, I cannot be sure we did; we were both so young – the passage of years had driven us too far apart for us simply to resume where we left off. You said in your letter that I would not believe or accept declarations of love if you made them now, and you were quite right. Especially because you were never honest with me, Richard, were you? Not even when you were swearing undying love to me.'

He made no immediate response, his face closed and bleak. If she had expected him to rush into some smooth denial, plainly, she was to be disappointed. Would she never learn?

Angry with herself as much as him now, she went on, 'You have made me think about the past when I have learned to be very adept at pushing it away, deep down where I need never confront it. To stir it all up again was your choice, not mine. And now that you have done that, you must live with the consequences. Even you, with all your audacity, can hardly expect that such a dangerous exercise will put me in charity with you, and come cuddling up to you begging for caresses. I think I'd like you to leave me alone for a while now, Ventris.'

'Are you saying...?'

'I don't know what I'm saying, other than just now, I want you gone.'

She saw a flash of something in his face that looked very much like anguish, and went on roughly, desperate to drive him out of her presence before she softened towards him when he did not deserve it, 'I need some time alone. There is no need to make any more of it than that. I am your wife, and nothing can change that fact. I am committed, however much I might sometimes wish I wasn't; I will have your child if I can. But just now, I do not wish to look at you.'

'That is your right,' he said desolately, and left her without another word.

Viola sank back against the pillows, suddenly exhausted, and let the memories come flooding back. All of them, as he had said, damn him – the brief moments of joy, and the searing pain. Perhaps wherever he was – and just now, she didn't much care – he might be doing the same. God knows he had as much to regret as she did, and maybe even more.

23

SPRING 1802

It was her maid who spoke to her first, and really, she had no option. 'Your grace,' Mary said tentatively one morning, when in the middle of dressing, Viola was overwhelmed by a violent spasm of nausea that had her grabbing for the bowl she'd just used to wash, 'do you think you might be... in a delicate condition?'

'I think it's just possible, don't you?' said the Duchess faintly, raising her head and then lowering it swiftly again.

It was folly, of course, to imagine that Edward, who so rarely spoke to her at any length unless it was entirely necessary by his lights, would not speak to her of this. *This* was an event of great moment in his life. She could not make out if Jennings had told him, though much later, she had reason to suspect that she might have done, or if he'd counted and noticed the signs himself; at any rate, he came to her in the sitting room one day and said tentatively, 'My dear... my dear girl, you have been unwell, these last few days, and I wonder if you might possibly...'

'I believe I am with child, yes, Edward,' she said quietly. 'Of course, I have no experience of it, other than what I have seen in my mama and my oldest sister, but Jennings tells me that the symptoms... Yes.'

There were tears in his eyes, she saw, and they stood in her own too, though not for the same reason. He reached out a hand as if he might touch her, then thought better of it. 'It is wonderful news, the best news in the world, but it is early, of course,' he said gruffly. 'We must take the best possible care of you. Dr McAllister shall attend on you immediately, just to reassure us that all is proceeding as it should. Does Jennings, do you...?'

'Some time in November, she thinks,' Viola said. Seeing an opportunity, she added craftily, 'My mother might be able to advise me better, having such great experience in these matters. If she came to stay and brought the girls, it would be a great comfort to me. There is none of my sisters preparing to come out at the moment, Allegra is still too young this year even by Mama's standards, so they will not be constrained by the demands of the Season that will soon begin.'

Edward had always been notably unenthusiastic about the prospect of having his mama-in-law, who was some six or seven years his junior, to stay at Winterflood with her large and noisy brood. He and Viola had married in London and left immediately and alone for their honeymoon at Winterflood, and that had plainly suited him very well. But matters were different now, it seemed – now Mrs Constantine could be of practical help. He hastened to agree to his wife's suggestion, letters were written and replies sent, and in an astonishingly short time, a vast, old-fashioned hired vehicle, paid for by the Duke and full to the brim of Constantines, plus Miss Naismith, the young governess, was to be seen pulling up in front of the grand entrance to the mansion.

The weather had grown warmer over the last few days, and it seemed that spring might be on its way at last. The ice on the reflecting pool where they had skated a few weeks ago had melted, and all the icicles that had decorated the statues and the grottoes were gone. Swelling buds could be seen on the stark fingers of the trees, and tiny shoots were beginning to push up through the soil. Noticing them, Viola felt a little embarrassed, almost as though she embodied a cliché, but pushed away the thought as fanciful. The change of seasons was welcome, and her family were welcome too, and her dear friend Emily. They could not replace Richard, they could not transform Edward into the husband she wanted and could never have, but the bustle and drama they created would make her life seem a little less empty.

Leontina had left her meek husband at home on his small estate just to the south of London; he would do very well by himself, she said ruthlessly, and it was probably true that he would welcome the unaccustomed peace and quiet. But she had brought her four younger daughters with her: Allegra, who was almost sixteen, Beatrice, who was twelve, Cecilia, nine, and little Bianca. They tumbled out of the coach in a torrent of femininity that made the Duke blanch visibly, and seized upon Viola to hug her fiercely and exclaim over her. But they parted to let their mother and Miss Naismith pass between them.

Leontina looked her second daughter up and down and said, 'You are pale, which is bad. I am positive your foolish husband has been keeping you wrapped in swansdown and not letting you walk more than a few paces at a time. And what is the result? You have no energy and no appetite! Yes, yes, I am sure you feel sick – of course you do; one does. But you need fresh air and some exercise. Only then can you thrive, and the child with you.'

The Duke was heard to murmur mildly that it had been excessively cold for exercise, to which Mrs Constantine retorted unanswerably that it was not cold now. They went inside, and for the first time since Richard had left, the young Duchess was smiling.

Viola knew it was possible that the Duke had harboured a suspicion regarding her family: once the Constantines moved in, they might – like mice, or clothes moths – never leave. That was very likely one of the reasons he had been reluctant to invite them to stay previously. As the weeks passed and then the months, his fears might be considered justified. Mrs Constantine went back to London for a brief time, to be with Sabrina when she gave birth to her second child, but left her younger daughters and their governess behind at Winterflood in her absence and soon returned when it was plain that all was well with Mrs da Costa and her hearty infant son. Edward, of course, had been visibly delighted at the news that his sister-in-law had presented her husband with another boy. His own hopes were written sufficiently clearly on his face; Viola could scarcely bear to look at him.

Since the family's presence made Viola happy, and a happy Viola was one who seemed likeliest to bring a healthy baby – a son, an heir – to term, which she knew was really all he cared about, Edward swallowed any distress he might feel, and stayed out of their way, at least in the daytime. He wasn't spending any more time with his duchess than he'd done previously – but at least she wasn't alone day in, day out as she'd been before.

He had not visited his wife's bed since Richard's departure. One day, when they were alone, Leontina asked her daughter bluntly if he did, and was given an equally blunt answer: 'No. He married me to get a child, and he will do nothing at all that might put that child in jeopardy. God knows I don't want him to.' That was an ambiguous statement, and she didn't really care if her mother interpreted it correctly.

It was June by now, and Viola was beginning to show, though the current high-waisted fashions concealed a great deal. She'd had no word from Richard, and had expected none. He could not write to her and display honest feeling in case his words were seen by others, and what was the point of letters full of empty platitudes? She didn't even know if he had been told that she was in a delicate condition, and if he had written to his cousin at all – which seemed unlikely – she was not in a position to ask. Edward never mentioned him. He might be abroad; now that a peace treaty had been signed, the opportunities for international trade such as he was engaged in were surely much greater than before, and she knew he spoke French fluently. His absence was a secret pain that did not seem to lessen over time. But she could mourn it with nobody.

'He is... displeasing to you?' Mrs Constantine asked with rare delicacy. She meant Winterflood, of course. It was important to be alert, when speaking with her, not drift off into daydreams of Richard and answer all at hazard.

'There is nothing to dislike about Edward's embraces. But I do not miss them either. They neither please nor displease me, except in the most obvious physical, animal sense, which, Mama, we are really not going to talk about.'

Leontina shook her dark head. 'Pleasing or not, if your child is a daughter, you will need to welcome him back into your bed after a time. If you cannot keep him away for long enough to ensure your health, or fear you cannot, I will speak to him, never doubt it, and make sure he heeds me and has some patience.' This was an alarming prospect, but it was a sign of caring on her mother's part, and Viola could only welcome it, knowing it was lovingly meant. Other mothers might perhaps show their maternal affection in soft words and embraces; Leontina had a fiercer and more practical way about her.

'That is a bridge that I will cross when I come to it, and not before,' she said shortly. 'Worrying about that now will make no difference to the outcome. If one could have a healthy boy child by willing it, we'd not be having this conversation, would we?'

'And you would have a brother, or more than one. Indeed. What will be will be, I suppose,' said Mrs Constantine, apparently recognising that sometimes, even she could do nothing to alter the course of events. 'And you are young, if he is not. There is time.'

Naturally, Viola was not in a position to be able to explain to her mother why this statement, so eminently reasonable on the surface, was untrue. She'd never had secrets from her mama before – but then, she'd never had secrets from anyone. She was in uncharted territory here, and she could not share her love for Richard and the shocking truth about her child's parentage with anybody at Winterflood. If she told her mama that she had been unfaithful and conceived because of it, she'd be horrified, and probably angry at her recklessness; if she revealed the full circumstances, there was no knowing what would be unleashed upon Edward. Much as he might deserve chastisement, the consequences of an enraged and outraged Italian mother speaking her mind to him were too unpredictable to contemplate. So, silence was her only option, difficult as it was to have no one at all in whom she might confide. Emily – no. Emily was a dear friend, but she was very easily shocked and would not comprehend any part of this dreadful muddle, innocent as she was. Sabrina, perhaps, would be more understanding… but Sabrina was not here. This wasn't the sort of news you could put in a letter, and probably it was best not to tell her at all, but to keep her secret safe from everyone.

They couldn't stay forever. Even as mild-mannered a man as Mr Constantine required that his wife and family should eventually return to his side. Perhaps the unaccustomed peace and quiet had begun to make him nervous. In the end, it was agreed that Allegra would remain to keep Viola amused (and, as a bonus, learn more thoroughly how to go on in a grand house and in grand company, in preparation for her debut and a great match of her own) while the rest of the family and their governess returned home. It was several months yet before the happy event could be expected, and Leontina would be sure to come back in good time for it.

Viola had previously spent very little time alone with her next sister, who had just celebrated her sixteenth birthday here at Winterflood, and was a little ashamed to acknowledge that she barely knew her. She and Sabrina had always been a pair, whether they'd been fighting or sharing confidences, and their come-outs had been just a year apart. She realised now that she hadn't always treated Allegra, whom in her youthful arrogance she'd always viewed as a very poor substitute for Sabrina, as kindly as she might have done. Though Allie was little more than two years her junior, the gulf between a fine young lady of seventeen who was out in society – and thought herself very grown-up even before she had been courted by a duke – and her jealous fourteen- or fifteen-year-old sister had not been easily bridged, all the more because Viola hadn't cared enough in her self-absorption to bridge it. But now she didn't feel grown-up at all, but making life up as she went along, and looked at her ignorant, confident younger self with a sort of pitying horror. It was hard not to see Allegra as the next potential victim – although of what, Viola would have struggled to say. Not of their mother – Leontina was only responding to the situation in which she found herself. Of the way the world had always worked, perhaps.

They were walking slowly together in the shade of the trees that lined the carriage drive late one August morning, and Viola, though she was in two minds about it still, thought she must speak seriously. This moment was as good as any, and certainly private enough. 'You know, Allie,' she said with elaborate casualness, 'now that Sabrina and I are married and will be able to support you all if poor Papa were to die, which of course we all hope he will not for many years, there is no great urgency for you to rush into marriage when Mama brings you out, whether it is next year or the year after. You can afford to take a little time and look about you.'

None of Mrs Constantine's daughters were stupid. 'You almost talk as though you regret marrying Edward at the end of your first Season,' Allegra replied, going straight to the heart of the matter in a manner that would have made her mother proud.

Her only Season. 'I don't think anyone should get married at seventeen,' Viola countered evasively.

'Especially not to a man of five and forty?'

She sighed, fanning herself in the growing heat and trying to remember where the nearest seat was. 'I don't criticise Mama's choice for me. She would never let any of us marry someone whom she thought was unkind or unpleasant or unreliable, and she is a shrewd enough judge of people. But no, since you ask me, I don't think a gap of almost thirty years between husband and wife is a good idea. I am reminding you – not Mama, but you – that your situation is different from mine, and you need not marry the first man who offers for you, nor the second or third, even if Mama is confident he is a good man. I am sure she will work her magic and find you someone unexceptionable – but it might also be possible to wait, and look about you, and one day, when you are ready, choose for yourself.' *Maybe someone not unexceptionable but whom you love and who loves you, assuming you should be lucky enough to meet him before it is too late,* she thought but did not say.

'Do you regret it? You have... all this.' Allegra gestured vaguely at the trees and placid sheep and the low wooded hills beyond them, everything that they could see being part of the extensive Winterflood estate. 'But I have observed that you and Edward are not close.'

'I'm not surprised you have noticed that; anyone might. He is still in love with his dead wife and probably always will be; he married me simply in order to have a child. All men do, I suppose, unless they are in love, or of course if they are marrying a woman for her money and connections. As to regrets... it's complicated. I do not underestimate what I have when I know that many people have so little, but it's hard, Allie, to spend weeks and months alone with someone with whom you have very little in common and who barely converses with you. I am very grateful that you have stayed with me this summer, or I might as well be alone. I am sorry if I have not told you so before.'

Her usually lively sister looked up at her, dark brows drawn together in a frown. 'I've always been impatient to grow up – I expect it comes of having older sisters who thought I was a child, and younger sisters who *are* just little children. I've always longed to be out in the world as you are, and Sabrina, and have a house of my own and fine clothes and some *space,* but I'm beginning to see that it's not so simple. It's beautiful here, but you never go anywhere else, do you? And before we came, you hardly had any visitors apart from Edward's stuffy old friends and relations. I'd go screaming mad, I think.'

Viola shrugged. 'Edward does not want to travel, and so we do not travel. It's not as though he discusses it with me. Women have very little power, if they are married or if they are not – do not deceive yourself about that for a moment. If you are married to a man who loves you, as Laurence love Bree, he may choose to share everything with you; he may give you power. But you cannot take it for yourself if he does not. Most men are not like Laurence or like Papa. I once thought, as you did, that if I need not worry endlessly about money as Mama has always been obliged to, I would be happy. And perhaps I should be – perhaps it is some flaw in me – but I have not been. Maybe things will be different when my child is born. But don't get married at seventeen, Allie, please. I thought I knew everything then, and I knew nothing.'

Allegra said tentatively, 'Are you scared of having a baby? You're only two years older than me, and I can't imagine it for myself, not for ages.'

'And that is an excellent reason not to be married for a good while yet,' Viola said drily. 'Yes, of course I am. Of childbirth, naturally, as everyone must be, and of being a mother – the responsibility of it. I will have a great deal of help, as most women do not, and it's not as though I don't have experience of babies – I have plenty, as do we all; they hold no mystery for me. But my own... that's daunting, when I allow myself to think about it. And if I do not have a son...'

'You will love your daughter as Mama and Papa love all of us,' said her sister stoutly, and Viola, from the eminence of eighteen, was reminded of how young Allie truly was. She would love her daughter – of course she would, all the more fiercely because she was Richard's. But would Edward? Would he love or even treat kindly a girl who was a profound disappointment to him by her very existence – and was not even his own child?

24

DECEMBER 1802

Richard rode round to the stables and left his exhausted, muddy horse with the surprised grooms there. He only had a small bag that he'd carried strapped to the saddle; he was used to travelling light, and he had no intention of spending the night here. He'd find an inn later, not too close to Winterflood so they wouldn't recognise him as local innkeepers might. He'd been in France, often in perilous circumstances, for most of the past six months and he was dog-tired – so tired, in fact, that he had to consciously remind himself to speak English to the sleepy boy who took his mount and promised to look after it. The words of thanks felt awkward on his tongue after so long away. There was no danger here – or danger of a completely different kind from what he'd become accustomed to since the peace treaty had been signed.

He'd returned to his London lodging yesterday and found a letter from Edward waiting for him. Before this, they hadn't had any communication at all since he'd left here in February. This wasn't normal – they usually exchanged letters in a casual but frequent manner, despite the interruptions that inevitably came when he was abroad for long periods. He didn't imagine for a moment that the Duke had taken offence at his abrupt departure; it seemed more likely that Winterflood had been reluctant to open a correspondence that might lead to Richard upbraiding him in frank terms for his appalling behaviour. It was so much safer for him to say nothing and see what happened. And then when it became apparent that Viola was with child, probably the Duke had forgotten about his young cousin altogether, all his attention focused on the extraordinary fact that he just might be about to get his precious heir at last. Both Richard and Viola were merely means to an end and nothing else.

And Edward had got all he'd wanted and more. Not just one heir, but two. Two strong, healthy boys, born a couple of weeks ago. Winterflood had written to tell his cousin of it. His joy and incredulity rose from the page in an almost palpable fashion, and Richard couldn't be sure – not entirely sure – that in his delirium, the Duke even remembered his own crucial part in this triumph. Perhaps he did; perhaps this brief note was a tacit acknowledgment that Richard might want to know that Viola was well. Might care about her. But he didn't think so. He thought Edward was writing such triumphant letters to almost everyone he'd ever met in his life. In other circumstances, he'd have found the older man's hubris pardonable, even endearing, after so many anxious, disappointed years. Now he didn't.

At any rate, he had used it as an excuse. He had not been invited this time, but he had come. He needed to see her for himself. And see the boys, just once.

He didn't require anyone to show him into the great house, since he'd been a regular and welcome visitor here once. He made his way through from the stables, and then stood, hesitating, in the shadowy, marble hall. It was late and very quiet – he'd timed his arrival so that he didn't precipitate a dinner-table scene that would be awkward and unpleasant for Viola. At this time of the evening, he was almost positive that she wouldn't be downstairs, sitting chatting cosily with Edward. They were not that sort of couple, and she'd just recently given birth. And he didn't want to see his cousin at all, but he supposed he must speak to him, however briefly, not sneak about like a thief.

He headed for the library. Winterflood was there alone, in his accustomed chair by the fire. He looked ten years younger than he had in February, but the complex mixture of emotions that raced across his face when he saw Richard did him no favours. Panic left the most abiding impression – that, and self-interest.

'I haven't come to see you,' Mr Armstrong told him. 'And don't worry, I haven't come to take her away either – not that you'd care for that – nor take the boys from you. You have everything you want, and much that you don't deserve or appreciate. But you owe me this one brief visit. After this, I promise you I won't trouble you again.'

Edward had risen to his feet. 'Richard, my dear boy…' he murmured helplessly, as if anything he could say could mend matters at this late date.

'I don't have anything else to say to you, and I don't want to hear anything you might have to say to me. You cannot possibly apologise, because you would not mean a word of it. And I certainly won't discuss Viola with you. I'm going up to see her now. Then I'll leave. If I thought it would do any good, I'd tell you that you should treat her better. But I tried that before and it was to no avail, so wrapped up as you were in your own concerns. I grew up thinking you were a good man, and perhaps you were once, but your grief has made you selfish and cruel. People aren't pawns, Edward. Even a duke should know that.'

Richard shut the door behind him with a solid clunk and made his way slowly up the staircase. He'd never been to Viola's bedchamber, but he knew where it was. It had been his cousin Elizabeth's room once.

It occurred to him belatedly now that her mother was probably staying at Winterflood and could easily be with her, or some other female relative, and that she might be surrounded by nursemaids too, and therefore his sudden abrupt appearance at this hour could cause a fearful bustle and – when they thought about its implications – a scandal. He should have been much more careful, rather than creeping in at night. His own feelings had made him inconsiderate, reckless, which was ironic after his self-righteous accusation to Edward.

But she was alone.

25

Viola lay drowsing in her bed with a flickering candle beside her, knowing she should be sleeping while she had the chance but aware that at least one of the twins would surely be hungry soon and demanding food. She was exhausted, had no idea what day it was, and felt ridiculously happy. This was an unexpected gift, and she cherished it.

The arrival of the twins hadn't been a complete surprise – towards the end of her pregnancy, there'd been times when the number of limbs kicking and prodding her belly in a sort of vigorous internal country dance had definitely seemed more than the traditional four – but her child or children had always felt theoretical before they'd emerged after a long day of pain and fear. A son, a daughter – cut-out figures from a child's chapbook in frilled shirt or muslin gown. But these were *people*. Often angry, wailing little people, pink and furious, but people all the same. Robert – but she had already decided he was Robin – the younger boy, was easy enough to please. He would bellow lustily when he was hungry or wet, but he suckled with evident contentment, ceased crying as soon as he was made comfortable, and was already bigger than his brother. Edward – Ned, God knows he would never be Edward if she could help it – was more discontented, restless, his needs harder to fathom. But they both gazed up at her with such trusting dark-blue eyes, and she worshipped them from the top of their downy dark heads to their perfect toes. The Duke, of course, was besotted with them, as well he might be – but she didn't care about that very much.

When the door opened, she wriggled upright against the pillows, her breasts already leaking in anticipation – it would be her nursemaid, Sarah, bringing the insatiable monsters to be fed, though oddly, she couldn't hear any screaming. Perhaps they were just stirring and Sarah had decided to bring them quickly, before they woke the whole house.

But it wasn't her.

Richard strode across the room to her side and sank to his knees next to the bed. He was pale and travel-worn, and he didn't seem to know what to say. She reached out and stroked his dark head just for a moment – so like his sons', so very like.

'I didn't think I'd ever see you again,' she whispered.

He found her hand and pressed it to his cold lips. 'I had to come, Viola. I heard you were with child – it was quite the sensation in London, you can imagine. I wanted to see you then, I have never stopped wanting to see you, but I thought my coming here would be dangerous for you.'

New mothers were supposed to be a picture of milky contentment, but she was apparently the exception to that rule, now that she saw him at last. 'And now it isn't?'

'I know it is still. I know I could easily have found you surrounded by people – nursemaids, your family... But I needed to see you once, needed it too badly to be thinking straight. I hope you'll forgive me for the risks I took. It wasn't out of lack of love, I promise you. Are you well? You look well – you look wonderful. I'm so glad you did not come to any harm. I can't even imagine...'

Of course he couldn't; no man could. She knew she didn't look wonderful. She had huge, dark circles under her eyes, and spots, and her body was no longer her own, if indeed it ever had been. But let that pass for now.

'He wrote to you?'

'I think he wrote to everybody.'

She laughed, though she could have cried. 'He's very proud, considering he had nothing at all to do with any of it. But if you are worried that he will not love them just as if they were his own, you can banish that thought from your mind. He does. At first, when I saw him holding them, I wanted to yell at him, to say that he must put them down because he had no right. But I realised that would be wrong, and selfish. They deserve a father's love, and he will be their father. He *is* their father, as far as the world will ever know.' She saw the raw pain in his face and said with a little impatience, 'Richard, what other option is there? Once, I foolishly asked you to take me with you, but if I repeated that folly now, if I said, "Take me and our sons, so that we can be together as a family!", where would we go and what would we do? I don't blame you for it. It's just the truth. You were the sensible one once – well, now I must be.'

He said bleakly, 'I'll always love you.'

'I don't suppose you will, you know. You have your life to live. I don't ask it of you – I'm sure there will be other women. Perhaps there already are. What good is that kind of love to either of us? All it can do is hurt us terribly.' She became aware that she was weeping.

'Viola, I didn't come here to make things harder for you.'

She'd missed him so much, she'd lain awake for hours longing for the comfort of his embrace and the passion his lightest touch could evoke in her, she'd wept night after night at the thought that she would probably never see him again, but now that he was here, he brought her no comfort, only pain. He was a reminder of a world that lay outside Winterflood that she could never really be part of. Her life was here with Edward. Even if nothing else had tied her before, her unbreakable love for the boys did now. But that did not mean she had to be a helpless prisoner.

'I mean to speak to him, when I am steady on my feet again. I mean to tell him that he cannot keep me all but locked up here as he has done. My wishes must be considered in future. He has allowed my family to stay with me – because it suited his purposes, of course, while I was increasing – and that must continue even though there will never be another child for me. Perhaps Emily can come and live with me to keep me company. Once the boys are older, I would like to travel a little. London is not so far away.'

'You have it all worked out, it seems.'

Now she was growing angry. 'Should I not? You said to me once that I was only seventeen when I married Edward and didn't know what I was doing. It was true – but I did it, and I am obliged to live with the consequences. All of the consequences. Should I go into a decline because I cannot have what I want? Most people don't get what they want in life; it's childish to expect it.'

'I don't expect anything. You're right, I have nothing to offer you. Or any woman. Unless you think the boys might like a sister one day. I seem to have that ability…'

'That's a dreadful thing to say.'

'Is it?' He sighed. He was still crouching by the bed; it must be uncomfortable. 'I suppose it is. I'm sorry, Viola. I'm too weary to know what I am saying, and I should not make my pain your problem. I should go, perhaps.'

'Not before you've seen those you really came to see, surely? The nursemaid will bring them to me in a moment – you can hide in my dressing room until she is gone, and then come out.' She regretted the sharpness of her first words as soon as she had said them. It must sound to him as though she was jealous of her sons, their sons, resentful that he'd only come to her after she'd given birth, not before, when really, she wasn't. Of course he was allowed to care for the children he might never see again and she saw every day. In that respect, she was far more fortunate than he. It could break her heart afresh to think of all he had lost and all that he would miss. But it was all so hopeless. And the plain fact was that soon, he'd leave her once more. He was always leaving her and she was always being left behind. A few shopping trips to London next year, a week in Bath or Cheltenham Spa to take the waters, could not change that fact.

'I would like to see them just once. To hold them. I don't think that's unreasonable.' He saw the hurt and confusion on her face and said raggedly, 'This situation is broken beyond all mending, isn't it? If Edward were to die tomorrow, I could hardly marry you and live off his estate. What would that make me? And even setting aside my pride, as I might happily do if I could be with you, it's all too easy to imagine what the gossips would say, let alone my brother, the thwarted heir. What a gift that would be to him – one he'd be very quick to make use of. You'd still be in danger of ruin and disgrace if anyone realised the truth, and the boys too. It would not be at all hard for people to realise that truth, if you and I married. Tarquin would tell the whole world your sons were bastards. It's as I said, I have nothing to offer – all I can do is cause you more damage. I love you, Viola, but it's not enough, is it?'

'It doesn't seem to be.'

He rose to his feet and bent to kiss her – one last precious kiss, full of sadness and regret. She fought the urge to cling to him, and mastered it.

It was as well that they had not lost themselves in each other, for her sharp ears came to her rescue now. 'Richard, I can hear... Go and hide, quickly. That door – go!'

26

He stood in the darkness in a room that smelled of her perfume, of her, with the door open a crack, and heard low conversation, bustle, and unfamiliar little mewing cries that pierced his heart. After a while, he could not have said how long, Viola said softly, 'You can come out now, Richard. I've sent Sarah back to bed to get some sleep. She won't come here again unless I ring for her.'

He crept out, feeling ridiculously shy, and saw that she was already feeding one of the twins, his mouth sucking busily at her full breast, while the other lay swaddled in a tiny bundle on the pillow beside her.

'This is Robin, my greedy boy, and that is Ned. Why don't you hold him? He isn't as hungry, and Robin will take some time.'

Richard sat down beside her on the bed and very, very carefully picked up his oldest son. He was awkward, clumsy – he'd never held a child before, let alone his own. His throat closed up with tears and for a moment, he could not speak. The baby was so small that it was easy enough to manoeuvre him into the crook of his arm, as he'd seen people do, his head with its dark, downy covering resting against the rough sleeve. His dark-blue eyes were open and he looked up at his trembling father, his face crumpled as if in enquiry, though Richard could not have said what so small a child could actually see. Just shapes, perhaps, and light and shadow. Nothing he could ever remember.

When he was reasonably confident that he could get a word or two out, Richard croaked, 'Ned?'

'Edward had the naming of him, so he is Edward, officially. Lord Cluny, so very grand. An earl, by courtesy, while Winterflood lives, and then Duke. But he will never be Edward to me, you can be sure of that. I call him Ned.'

'He's so beautiful. They both are.' It was his turn to weep.

'We made them, Richard. Even if no one else ever knows it – even if they never do – you and I know it. I also know that's not enough for you, but it will have to be. I can't give you any more than that. Not even, as you said, if Edward died tomorrow.'

The room fell silent, save for the busy sucking of Lord Robin and the crackle of the fire that the maid must have built up before she left. Richard had so many things he wanted to say, but said none of them, holding the baby, who was barely any weight at all in his arms. How did people bear it? How did the world go on turning when this was all that mattered?

Lord Cluny gave a huge yawn, and Richard, his heart full, stroked his tiny hand, then bent to brush his forehead in a kiss. 'My son,' he whispered. 'My dear son. I am so sorry.'

After a while, Ned began to make restless movements with his head, and Viola, already experienced in his ways after so short a time, said, 'He's hungry too. If you place him here, I can try to feed him too. It's tempting to do one after the other, but if I do that, I will never sleep at all.'

Richard set him down as she directed, and Viola managed it so that he could latch on too, and began feeding, though less vigorously than his brother.

'You're very good at this,' he told her. It shook him, seeing her so assured and confident. He felt quite superfluous, which, of course, he was.

'There is a trick to it,' she murmured, looking down at them both, absorbed. 'There's a woman on the estate, a farmer's wife, who had twins a few months ago, and my mother found it out somehow and had her come and show me how best to do it. I don't know how I would have managed otherwise.'

'I'd like to hold Robin too before I go,' he said.

'You can help me change their napkins – both of them – before you leave. Let poor Sarah sleep.'

He watched her as she fed them, storing up the precious sight which he knew he'd never see again. It was impossible to deny the fact that he had no place in her life. He knew it; he'd said it himself. So why did it still hurt so much?

27

1813 – THE PRESENT

A few hours later, when she had breakfasted alone in her chamber, was dressed, and felt more fully in command of herself, Viola sought her husband out where he was walking in the gardens. She could see his tall figure pacing up and down through the window; perhaps he was waiting for her, or perhaps he had no idea where else he should go.

She wrapped herself in a favourite velvet pelisse and drew on her gloves; they would serve as a sort of armour, she hoped. Richard had wanted to talk – very well, they would. He could hardly complain if he did not like what he heard.

It was a sunny, blustery autumn day, but not cold, and Viola walked through the bright, whirling leaves towards the man she'd once adored beyond all reason. When she reached him, she continued fiercely, just as though there had been no break in the conversation, 'Your letter made me furious, and you cannot pretend not to know why. You insulted me when you spoke so lightly of my fertility, but perhaps you did not mean that, given what passed between us then and how much it hurt us both to be used as Edward used us. I can set that aside – I have done so.'

His expression seemed to lighten a little, since he could have no idea what she was about to say next, and she went on before she lost courage, 'I am angry, as I have every right to be and always will be, not because you left me, and not because you did not come back when Edward was dead. I never expected you to, because by then, I knew that you were not what you claimed to be. You were not a humble employee of some trading company, a gentleman with no means or expectations trying to make his way in the world in an honourable fashion. You were never that, and I was a naïve idiot to believe you were. You were, and I must suppose you still are, a suspected criminal. Lord Marchett made sure to tell me by letter that the Ton was whispering of nothing else. Shocking stories of theft and blackmail, and even rumours of murder. All the world seems to know as much, and yet you are still received – it's astonishing, really. But he told me more than that, things I have never spoken of to a soul before now, but cannot endure not to say to you, to seek your reaction.'

His face was unreadable to her now, and certainly, he uttered no word of protest or denial. The sun was still shining, the golden leaves still falling in the quiet garden, but now she felt cold.

'His Lordship thought I should be aware of secret matters that had come to his attention through his work at the Foreign Office, and gave him very grave concern. Perhaps he feared then that I might think to marry you, since Edward was dead, and wanted to do all he could to stop me. He told me that you were believed in government circles to be a very dangerous and skilful French spy, one they had long suspected but never been able to catch. One who had been put under surveillance, but had managed to evade it time and again, to go they did not know where, and meet people they could only guess at. It was feared, he said, that your position in the Ton and your wide trading contacts made you a central figure of some sort – one who had connections few could match, and channels of communication they had never been able to discover. Not just a criminal, though certainly that, but a traitor. So much more made sense when he told me that. No wonder you did not want me living with you and stumbling across your dirty secrets!'

His expression was grimmer than she had ever seen it now. 'I *was* an employee of a trading company, in fact – not a word of what I told you was untrue. I lived as I told you, and travelled to the places I described to you, and did the things there that I told you I did, and yes, I still despite that moved in polite society sometimes because of my family background. I never lied to you, Viola. Not once.'

'That's sophistry. If you worked as you described, even if I believe you when you say so, and there is no reason why I should, it was all just a cover for something else, something far more sinister. Wasn't it? *Wasn't it?*'

He took his time in answering her, but in the end, he said blankly, 'Yes. Yes, it was. I wonder greatly that you married me, knowing so much about my disreputable history.'

'Maybe I was mad, but I took a calculated risk. I'm aware it was a very rash one. I thought if all the power of the British government had not been able to catch you yet, perhaps they never would. And I assumed besides that a criminal whom everyone in England knows for one – including, as I have recently discovered, my mother and my entire family – cannot be very effective any longer. I wonder they do not point at you as you walk down the street and say, "Have a care, there is the man who cannot be trusted! Keep tight hold of your purses, and be sure you do not take your eyes off him for a second!"'

'Sometimes, they do,' he murmured, his mouth quirking wryly. He could never be entirely serious for very long; it was beyond infuriating.

'But you have not been arrested by the authorities, either as criminal or spy.'

'You are mistaken. I've been arrested more times than I can count, and released each time. It hasn't happened in a while, in fact, you will be happy to know. As you say, such notoriety as I now have would make my ability to carry out any dubious activities somewhat limited. It's my opinion that *the authorities* have given up on me, especially now I'm a peer and a man of property.'

'I'm glad to hear it, and I hope I may believe it. I will not ask you to stop your activities – at this point, I don't know if I'd trust you if you said you meant to, or even that you already had. But Richard, if you place my sons in any danger, I will kill you myself.'

'I would expect nothing less from you. But you do not think to give me a curtain lecture on honourable behaviour, or even on patriotism?'

'Would it do any good?'

He sighed. 'Probably not.'

'Then I won't. In the end, I'm not sure how much I care about men and their stupid wars. Unless you've done what you've done for money, and yet still claim you have none, I presume you did it out of conviction. So-called republican principles. Well, your precious Bonaparte has the blood of many thousands on his hands, but I'm not confident we are any better. Look at Badajoz, the British atrocities there. No woman or child who dies screaming in terror can be expected to care if a Frenchman or Englishman is responsible. I won't ask you for any sordid details. What I did think and still think was that you must have all sorts of low connections, and that you will be able to use them to make sure your brother comes nowhere near the boys. I'm not sure I care much about anything else.' This wasn't entirely true, but she had her pride.

'I've always done that,' he murmured very low. 'I've always looked out for them.' He must have seen the incredulity on her face, because he said then, with the first hint of heat that he had shown in all this extraordinary discussion, 'If you believe nothing else I tell you, Viola, believe that. You have guarded them sufficiently well at Winterflood, I know, surrounded by people who care for them, and whenever you have left there together, wherever you have gone with them, people of mine have been observing. Not to spy on you or on them, but to ensure their safety. And since they went to school, they have always had someone I can trust watching over them. They still do.'

'I should have known.' Despite her enduring anger that he'd never been the man she'd once thought he was, this revelation made her feel a little more kindly towards him. She had been right after all to trust him with her sons; they *were* his sons too.

'Yes, Viola, I really think you should.'

'Have you ever...?' She broke off, feeling almost as though it was not her business to ask the obvious question.

'Of course I have seen them. Following them out of Winterflood has always been easy enough for a person of average intelligence; that damn ostentatious coach of Edward's with the bloody great red crest on its door is impossible to miss. *Quod habeo teneo*, it says – how well we know the truth of that. And in London: two young boys of rank travelling to and from Armstrong House together, always in your company, who else could they be? But at school, with so many others... I had to be sure my men were watching the right ones. I had to go and see.'

'Was that the only reason?'

'You know damn well it was not! Good God, woman. Whatever you think of me, you shall never say that I do not care.' When she did not respond, he sighed and said in a gentler tone, 'I don't have words to say what they are and how much it meant to me to see them, strong and healthy and happy, and always together, friends as well as brothers. You've done a wonderful job as a parent, my dear. I knew you would, when I first saw you with them. I'm sure it hasn't always been easy.'

She had no answer to make to that; how could she even begin to describe what the last eleven years had been for her, the joy and the pain and always the loneliness? She wanted to scream at him, to send him away and never see him again; she wanted to hold him and never let him go. 'They look like you. You must have seen that. Ned, especially, has your quickness of movement. His smile, sometimes, is so like yours. And I see you in Robin too at odd moments.' It was true; she had cried over it a dozen times.

'Did you and Edward ever speak openly about them?'

'Just once. I told you, I think, that I meant to have a conversation with him, make it clear to him that we could not continue living as we had, in such solitude.'

'I was cruel to you when you said that, and knew it even as I uttered the unforgivable words. I was eaten up with jealousy of the life that you would have together.'

'It was only a life together because of the boys, and centred around them. If that topic ever was exhausted, we had nothing to say to each other and nothing in common. I went to see him as soon as I felt strong enough after they were born, and told him that I knew exactly what he had done – how he had manipulated us, and how I despised him for it. Told him in plain words that you were their true father, not him, in case he was deceiving himself with uncertainty. You'd spoken to him already, I know, so he cannot have been all that taken aback, but he was deeply ashamed when I confronted him, and had no answer to make me. He said he was sorry, but that was a lie and I challenged it. He was a weak and selfish man, I realised, and all he was sorry for was being found out. It is easy to be ruthless with other people's lives when you don't care about anyone much apart from yourself and your great inheritance. And his precious dead Elizabeth, of course. He loved the boys, was an excellent father to them both, and I was glad of that, but I could not respect him after what he did to us, and I told him so and never wavered.'

'Did he ever move that portrait of her from the dining room? It used to make me so angry on your behalf when I saw it there, and him glancing at it so often when he should have been looking at you.'

Perhaps he was striving for a lighter note now, and she did not resist. It could do no good to continue to upbraid him. She was as securely tied to him as she'd ever been to Edward, and only time would tell if that had been a terrible mistake.

'I did not ask him to – why would I? The damage was already done. I did not love him, so why should I care that he did not love me? I had no quarrel with her, poor lady. She is there still, and I often look at her and wonder. She must have been strong in herself, to refuse to pass another woman's child off as her own when he pressured her so and the stakes were so high. Later, he had me painted too, at great expense and by Mr Thomas Lawrence, which was a sort of apology, I suppose. I am up on the wall in the picture gallery now, in my best red silk, along with all those ancestors you showed me once. Future generations can marvel at my double chin.'

'But they will not be able to kiss it, as I have, and later will again, I hope. If you allow me that privilege. Painted with the boys?'

'Can you seriously doubt it? I always knew I had no value to Edward in myself.'

'Foolish of me even to ask. Where does all this leave us, Viola?'

'Apart from the fact that we have cleared the air between us a little, exactly where we were before,' she told him with a fair show of composure. But she wasn't sure it was true.

She realised now that she must have been hoping he would deny that he had ever been any kind of criminal, perhaps repudiate too the shocking idea that he had been a traitor with a vehemence and passion that might have gone some way towards convincing her – but he hadn't. He'd all but admitted it, every dirty part of it, and that must be a grievous blow. She could only hope the boys never came to hear of it – what could she tell them, if they did? It was yet another reason to take them out of school as soon as possible.

But he'd also admitted a deep-seated and long-enduring concern for his sons – not in mere words that could have been false but in practical actions that she must believe – that she had not previously suspected. She should have realised how deep his feelings for them ran – he'd been right when he told her that. Perhaps she hadn't wanted to accept it. The thought of him standing and watching them undetected, unable to speak to them, affected her very deeply. And she wasn't at all sure she wanted to be so touched, or to weaken towards him. Nothing had really changed, after all, just as she'd told him, except that she now knew for certain what he was, instead of just suspecting it. Speaking about the past did not alter it, or take away the hurt. Nothing could do that.

28

Eventually, the great party of Constantines left Winterflood, and peace was restored, but Viola and Richard did not move back into the big house. When they went over at her suggestion to look about them and consider whether they should, and which rooms they should take if they did, she was profoundly shaken by the memories of Edward, and most of all their younger selves, that lurked in every corner. It was almost as though out of the corner of her eye, she could see an eighteen-year-old Viola climbing the grand staircase, wrapped in the months-long frozen misery that she had managed by and large to put out of her mind till now. Or, in some dark corner, a much happier girl who'd been brought back to life by Richard's kisses, like Sleeping Beauty. His hand had caressed her face with a tenderness that had been entirely new to her, and she had melted into his arms with utter trust. They had both been so young, so innocent – but that wasn't true, she must remember, because even then, Richard had been lying to her. She had bared her soul to him all those years ago; he had not paid her the compliment of doing the same, and still hadn't. And therefore, she couldn't be sure she should trust him now. What did she really know of his life? Almost nothing, and all she knew was terrifying.

The second vision of her past unsettled her almost as much as the first; she did not want to remember how much she had loved him, and how little hope there had always been for them, for so many reasons. She didn't speak of it now, but she could see that Richard was aware of her unease; it might have pleased her to think that he was so attuned to her moods, just as he had been when they were young lovers, except that she supposed that spies must be trained to be observant – their lives might depend on it. So she should not flatter herself that it held any particular significance.

She was puzzled by her own distress when she contemplated her past life at Winterflood. Considering that she'd lived there for so many years – with Edward, in tolerable harmony once she had asserted herself, and happily with the children in the years after his death – and rarely been troubled in such a fashion, it was most odd. Such foolishness would have to be overcome, presumably, but not just now.

Lord and Lady Ventris stayed in the dower house for the rest of their honeymoon.

It was a strange time, or interval out of time. Viola was not sure she even liked her new husband, and his current feelings towards her were a complete mystery, but it could not be denied that they could not get enough of each other. The underlying reason for their intimacy, and the dire consequences if they failed, didn't seem to matter – they'd tacitly agreed not to discuss all that, at least for now. The lightest of touches, even a glance, could inflame them both. Whatever else they did not share, however much Viola feared that in certain ways, she could never depend on him or respect him, their mutual desire was overwhelming, even alarming in its intensity.

It was not just at night. Their passion was a compulsion that could overtake them at any time of day. If one of them came into a room and found the other there, it was more likely than not that in a heartbeat, they'd fall upon each other in mutual hunger. It was something quite outside her experience; their previous intimacy had been so brief and so constrained by secrecy that this mutual wild abandon came as a surprise to her, turning her into a person she barely recognised.

She entered the sitting room one rainy afternoon to find Ventris by the fire, reading; he rose politely at her arrival and set down his book, but she gestured impatiently for him to resume his seat. She did not speak, and nor did he, and in the absence of light words of conventional greeting, there was nothing to conceal the instant physical tension that stretched taut between them. He shifted a little in his chair, and she knew – because she felt the same – that it was arousal that made him suddenly uncomfortable. She crossed the carpet with swift, confident steps and sank to the floor at his feet, her dark-red gown pooling around her. Looking up at him, she saw that his grey eyes were black with desire. With fingers that trembled only a little, she reached out and began to unbutton him, and his fully erect member sprang into her waiting hand; he sighed, and jolted at the contact, skin to skin. Unsure whom she was tormenting, she bent her head and licked the slit with the tip of her tongue, and he leapt again at her touch.

'This will not put a child in your belly, madam,' he growled. She couldn't tell if he meant it seriously, or was playing with her, but still she gloried in the power she had over him.

'You don't want this, then?' She still held him, the skin hot and silky smooth under her caress, the blood throbbing so hard in him that she could feel it, and her mouth was so close to him that as she spoke, the breath feathered over his sensitive flesh and made him twitch once more. Her tongue-tip crept out and tasted the salty sweetness of him again, and now she allowed herself to draw him into her mouth and suck, just a little, before she pulled away. But not very far away.

'It must be obvious that I do,' he almost gasped.

She closed her eyes and moved her mouth upon him, and the feel of him against the tender skin inside her lower lip made her shiver, and draw him deeper in. She put her free hand on his hard thigh and pulled his legs tighter about her, enjoying the sensation of being encircled and held, and losing herself for a moment in mindless pleasure. Then she looked up, and the unguarded softness of his face affected her like a caress. Little tongues of flame spread through her limbs and kindled fire at her core. 'Indulge me in this for a little while,' she whispered between licks, 'and then take me. Throw me over the table and have me, if you will.'

'With so little ceremony? Are you ready for that, my lady?'

'I was ready when I walked into the room, Richard. You know I was.'

She slid her mouth down his length once more, and began sucking on him greedily, but after a moment, she heard him say raggedly, 'Stop, Viola!' and she instantly let him go. He pulled her effortlessly to her feet, rising with her, his hands hard about her waist. Her mouth felt bereft of him, and she moaned in frustration, but the last thing she would do would be to beg for his kiss. And then he lifted her up and laid her roughly down across the table that stood behind the sofa, and whatever objects stood upon it crashed unheeded to the floor as he dragged up her skirts and took her with a fierce, ruthless urgency that made them both gasp. He had always known how to hold her as she needed to be held, and she welcomed each powerful thrust, her feet seeking for purchase on the smooth tabletop, her legs spread wide to receive him. His hands were hard on her hips as he drove into her, holding nothing back – or nothing physical, at least. It was an animal connection that joined them, something savage and primitive and, always, dangerous. But she did not care, in the moment when he gave a great cry and spent himself in her, as waves of pleasure broke over her too and carried her away for a while.

When they came back to themselves, he helped her to her feet and smoothed down her ruined skirts around her shaking body. It was just a few steps to the sofa, and she lay down on it, her feet raised on a cushion. He looked at her intently for a moment, as if about to speak, and then apparently thought better of it, and resumed his seat by the fire, picking up his book with a fine show of unconcern. It struck her afresh, how little idea she had what he was thinking, and how strange this life was that they had both committed themselves to. What would become of them? Whether she had a child or not, what could possibly become of them?

29

Viola did not catch a glimpse of Ventris Castle when it appeared on the horizon; her view of it was blocked, as the carriage window was full of excited young limbs and craning heads. Richard had beguiled the latter part of their long journey by telling the boys stories of the ancient building and its unruly inhabitants, his mother's ancestors, and these stirring tales, well told, had inspired them with a great fascination with their destination, and a desire to catch sight of the romantic near-ruin as soon as possible. Though the border was almost a hundred miles away, the Castle's history, as he told it, was one of almost constant reiving, plenty of pitched battles with the Scots and almost as many with their equally warlike English neighbours, the Nevilles and the Percys. There had been trickery, bloodshed, betrayal and acts of almost insane daring on both sides. As befitted what she knew of the Ventris family, women were just as likely to have played a decisive part in all this mayhem as men. They'd defended the castle, raised warbands, and stabbed their enemies and friends in the back with as much gusto as their menfolk. The boys had, as far as they were aware, no personal investment in these matters, but listened to them raptly as they might to a Walter Scott poem read aloud; she could only guess how it felt for her husband, who knew differently.

Because he'd told them so, they knew that they were close now, as they crested a rise and descended towards the sea, and they jostled each other in brotherly rivalry to claim the prize of the first sight. But both called out in triumph at the same moment, and fell to laughing and squabbling amicably over who should carry off the honour.

'Perhaps you might let your mother see, you pair of savages, now that you have both done so to your fill,' Richard suggested drily, his face amused. They did not seem to resent the mild reprimand, if that was what it was, but apologised in haste, and returned, at least temporarily, to the rear-facing seat they shared.

It had been a day of fitful sunshine and sudden showers, and Viola had passed the time by listening idly to Richard – more his voice than his words, in truth – and watching the clouds and the sunbeams chase each other across the moors in an endless procession of light and shade that she found oddly soothing. The air was cold and fresh, and smelled clean. She'd never been so far north before – she could hardly call herself a well-travelled woman – but what she had seen till now she liked, as she watched the landscape grow harsher, revealing its strong bones, and the very stones with which the buildings were made changed colour on their days-long journey. They'd stopped last night at the Talbot Hotel in Malton, in the old coaching inn's finest newly refurbished rooms, and had come on in easy stages since they'd left the bustling town. Now they were here at last.

Viola seized her chance before the boys became restless again, leaning forward and peering out. She might have gasped at what she saw.

'It's not quite as bad as it looks,' Richard murmured. 'I swear there are actually several perfectly habitable rooms – if you aren't excessively particular – along with many that are, as you can see, open to the rain and the seabirds.'

It did appear to be a complete ruin, on first sight – jagged walls and broken towers reached up to the sky, in a dramatic manner that the boys, at least, found highly satisfactory. Robin had been most anxious to know if there were dungeons, and Richard had reassured him that there were indeed, down a spiral staircase that was as steep and perilous as anyone could wish for, though he was sorry to have to say that there were no chained skeletons to be found once you'd made your descent. 'Though perhaps I have not explored the subterranean regions fully, and you may make many gruesome discoveries when you do so – who knows?'

'I can well believe that there are dungeons, now that I see the place,' Viola murmured, surveying it. 'Having heard your family history, I can only hope you do not mean to lodge me in one of them.'

Richard's eyes gleamed wickedly, and she shot him a suppressing glance, but he said only, 'Of course not. The finest chamber shall be yours, my lady. Though it will not be anywhere near as comfortable as where you slept last night, I'm sorry to say. There will be a fire in the grate, on a hearth large enough to roast an ox, though I can't guarantee that the chimney won't smoke. It all depends upon the prevailing direction of the howling gale, I'm given to understand.'

'As long as there is a bed.'

'Oh, I promise you there is. Trust me for that.'

They'd picked up the boys from a school a week or so ago. Ventris had with rare delicacy encouraged her to go alone to greet them, so that they'd been able to see, as he'd put it, that their mother was unaltered, even if she was now married to a man they'd never met. They'd hugged her fiercely on seeing her, this time, and she knew they probably wouldn't have felt able to do so if their new stepfather had been present, so she could only be grateful for his tact. They'd needed that reassurance, she thought, and somehow, he'd known it.

It was idle to pretend that she hadn't wondered a thousand times over the past years how it would be when father and sons encountered each other at last, if indeed they ever did. But there was no great drama, and no tears except the ones she fought hard to hide; the meeting was quiet, restrained, if inevitably slightly awkward. Robin greeted Lord Ventris cheerfully, and Ned with a little more reserve, but both boys were polite, and shook his hand without any appearance of reluctance, calling him *sir* in a formal way that made her heart ache. It was still quite usual for men of an older generation, Edward's and Marchett's generation, to require that their children addressed them so; it was not quite so common amongst the young, and she believed Richard would never have insisted upon it, in ordinary circumstances. But he could hardly ask them to call him Father.

He was wise enough not to force the pace or assume an air of false bonhomie that must sit uncomfortably with them. It was possible to imagine the pompous fatherly speech that Lord Marchett, say, would have made in his position, and how it would have set their backs up and done lasting damage, but Richard made no speeches. He was frank, straightforward, his voice was level and controlled, and only Viola guessed how deeply he was affected. He certainly did not show it.

The initial meeting having gone well, matters proceeded smoothly afterwards. Richard was being careful – hard to say how much of it came naturally and how much it cost him effort. Perhaps no better training could be imagined for suddenly becoming step-parent to two sons rising twelve than that of a spy. He took no chances, asserted no authority, deferred to Viola, but at the same time somehow made it clear that he was not to be trifled with. She didn't think Ned and Robin were disposed to be scared of him, or even particularly on their guard after the very beginning, but she tried to look at him through their eyes and thought that though he was quiet, he was also formidable, and gave a sense of power held in reserve. They were taking his measure, and doing it cautiously.

The journey had in some respects been a godsend. They were all cooped up together for many hours, it was true, but this enabled them to talk in an unforced, desultory way, not least about the changing sights they saw from the carriage windows, and the places they stopped at night, lapsing into silence if they wished, with no pressure such as might arise in a more public setting.

Richard had taken them to explore some of these towns they spent the nights in, to run off their pent-up energy, and Viola sometimes let them go, and sometimes strolled with them, her arm in her husband's, their children running ahead and circling back breathlessly to share some quaint fact or sight they had discovered. They looked, she knew, just like any wealthy travelling family.

Last night, the talkative landlady at the inn had complimented Richard fulsomely on his fine sons. 'The spit and image of you, sir!' she'd gushed. After a tiny, almost imperceptible hesitation, as one who stood on the edge of a precipice and looked down into the yawning depths at his feet, Lord Ventris had thanked her gravely, saying nothing more. He had not replied that they were his stepsons only, and the boys, who'd both overheard – they could scarcely avoid it, since she was patting their blushing cheeks fondly as she spoke – did not correct her either.

Ned had said thoughtfully when he and Viola had a moment alone, taking the air after dinner, 'Do we look so much like Lord Ventris, Mama? That woman seemed to think so. It is odd to think she believed him truly to be our father.'

She had prepared herself for this, and did not mean to over-react. 'Well, she made a natural assumption, seeing us all together, but yes, I think you do,' she said calmly. 'You more than Robin, perhaps. It is not to be wondered at – you must see yourself how much Ventris resembles your father, and indeed many of the old portraits in the gallery at Winterflood. They are his ancestors too, of course, on his father's side.'

'Papa's face has faded a little in my memory,' the youthful Duke confessed, his tone suggesting that he was sorry. 'I was only eight years old… But I have seen the picture that was painted of him when he was young – he wears a powdered wig in it, like a regular old quiz; it must have been the fashion – and I suppose it does favour my stepfather a good deal.'

'The Angelica Kauffman portrait? It does, though I think Lord Ventris resembles your father more now that he is a little older than he did when first I knew him. Something to do with the bones of the face.' Viola had had to accustom herself to saying *your father* long ago, referring to Edward, and it had almost become natural to do so, but now she found it freshly harder. She looked forward to a day when she could use those words and mean Richard; she knew that many women who remarried came to refer to their new husbands in such a way, and the stepchildren the same, and nobody thought anything of it. But it was far too soon yet.

The coach had rumbled on while she had been lost in reflection, and now they were passing over an actual drawbridge into an inner courtyard, under the rusting remains of a portcullis. 'I had to have it replaced,' Ventris said; the boys were staring down at the bridge and could not fail to notice that the wood was new, and reassuringly – or perhaps from their point of view disappointingly – solid. 'My aunt neglected such essential repairs. In later years, she rarely left the Castle, and if the worm-eaten old planks had broken suddenly and some unfortunate soul had plunged to his death in the ravine below, I don't believe she would have cared overmuch. Especially not if it had been me. But I do care, and it was one of my first priorities on coming here. One can take a fondness for the Gothic altogether too far, I find.'

They hardly seemed to heed him; they had sought permission to alight and were tumbling eagerly out of the carriage almost before it had come to a stop. One could hardly blame them – it was a young boy's dream, a genuine ruined castle, and they were to make their home here, at least for now. What could be more delightful to a child of spirit?

The medieval fortress must have been close to impregnable once, Viola thought, with the wild sea surrounding it on three sides, but many of the walls had crumbled away with the effects of time and the elements, and at some stage, it was plain that the decision had been taken to let them go, and save only a part for human habitation. This section lay to her left, and was reached up a flight of worn stone steps. It was growing dark now, and the great door stood open in anticipation of their arrival, light spilling out, staff waiting to greet them. However primitive it might prove to be inside, the sight was pleasant after so long a journey.

'Welcome to Ventris Castle,' Richard said, leaning down to address them. 'Let's go inside and see if food has been prepared for us, as I'm sure it has. Boys, there is a great deal to explore, but the more ruinous parts are best seen in daylight, unless you wish to break your necks before you've been here five minutes. I assure you, there are enough passages and staircases and ancient chambers even in the more modern quarters – modern in the local sense of dating from the fifteenth century rather than the twelfth, you understand. Come and see! There is supposed to be a priest's hole, though I have never been able to find it.'

His invitation was well calculated to be irresistible, and they did not wait to be asked twice, but ran up the stairs to introduce themselves to the waiting butler. Richard jumped down lightly from the carriage and extended his hand to Viola. 'My lady…' he said, smiling. 'Your new home awaits you. And the bed, in due time, as promised.'

30

It wasn't the first time Viola had come into a great house as mistress in the place of a woman who was now dead. But this was different – worse in some ways, and better in others. Mostly, it was better. She wasn't replacing the beloved and much-missed Duchess Elizabeth at Edward's side, nobody was looking at her as though she was little better than an imposter, and above all, she wasn't a nervous seventeen-year-old with barely a clue of how she should go on and no one to help her find her feet. She might be a southerner, which she couldn't mend, and Richard might in some sense be an interloper too, but she was a grown woman now, and had run a household much larger than this one for many years. And as for her late predecessor being missed by her former employees, she soon discovered that this was only partly true. She'd been 'a rare character', with all that that implied. Viola knew all about rare characters – her mother was one. Living with them wasn't always easy or comfortable.

It quickly became clear that what she had first taken for unfriendliness, even disapproval, in the Castle's inhabitants' attitude towards her was, at least partly, sheer embarrassment. The rooms that were in use were spotlessly clean, and the food served to the family was hearty, well-cooked and decorously presented, but that was all that could be said. She found Ventris Castle to be barren of what most people would consider the necessities of existence, let alone the luxuries. Life there could only be described as primitive, for everyone, family and staff alike. The servants' quarters, when she saw them, took her breath away; they could have come straight from the Middle Ages, and presumably had. It might have been picturesque to see, in an antiquarian volume or portrayed upon the stage in a fairy tale – as a reality in the nineteenth century, in the home of a wealthy woman, it was shocking.

The building and repair work was under way, at least the most urgent parts of it, as Richard had told her, action that would make sure the Castle survived another winter without crumbling into utter ruin and sliding into the sea. But Richard and the boys seemed to think it was either a matter of indifference or a great adventure that there was not a piece of linen or a curtain anywhere in the house that was not practically in tatters, and that items of furniture – chairs, for example, or beds – were as likely to collapse into piles of firewood at moments of maximum inconvenience as to bear a person's weight in a reliable way. For her part, she would prefer less excitement and fewer splinters, though she was prepared to admit privately that she and Richard continued to make some heavy demands on the fixtures and fittings of their bedchamber.

Once the butler and housekeeper, a married couple named Codling, had realised that she did not blame them for the many deficiencies caused by their former mistress's miserly ways, and that furthermore, though the new Lady Ventris had once been a duchess, she was not at all high in the instep, they got on quite comfortably together. It was apparent that they'd feared for their position and their home – such as it was – under the new regime, and now could relax as it became clear that Viola had no intention of putting them out of doors in their late middle age and replacing them with smart London servants of her own. She meant instead to make their lives more comfortable along with her family's, and told them so.

Mrs Codling had been heard to comment that it was good to see children in the old place again – that they brought it to life after a-many years of sad emptiness – and Viola could see that this was a rare encomium, by Yorkshire standards. She could hardly hope for more. Her sons were boisterous, but the Codlings did not appear to mind the disruption they caused, but rather to see it as perfectly natural, and even, on occasion, entertaining. Mr Codling was largely silent unless circumstances absolutely required communication, as though somebody might be going to charge him a ha'penny a word, and he only had a shilling. But Mrs Codling had a wide repertoire of highly expressive sniffs, which could mean anything from extreme disapproval to grudging praise; there was even one that seemed to signify that she was highly if reluctantly amused, and Ned and Robin's antics often provoked her into deploying it. The boys had at first thought that she was suffering from a severe cold in the head, but had grown accustomed to her odd ways now, and showed alarming signs of wrapping her around their little fingers.

Viola was also aware that the woman – who was plainly nobody's fool – sometimes eyed her shrewdly up and down as they talked together, as if to ascertain whether her mistress's plumpness disguised the fact that a little Ventris might be expected to make an appearance in due course, to add even further to the bustle of the Castle. But she resolved to show no sign that she had noticed this scrutiny. Time would tell, and her body and its secrets were her own, for now.

And if the housekeeper or any of the other, junior staff thought that the young Armstrongs resembled their stepfather more closely than mere cousins should, they did not give the slightest hint of such a suspicion. They were sharp, she thought; if it were obvious, they'd have noticed it. Probably she was worrying too much about that particular matter, and could lay it to rest, if Tarquin Armstrong remained silent and inactive, as he appeared to have done so far. Maybe he was indeed intimidated by his half-brother's unsavoury reputation, as she had hoped. Or perhaps her fears, and Edward's on his deathbed, had always been fanciful and entirely without foundation.

It was easy to think cheerful thoughts here, so far away from all she'd known before, busy in her new life setting the Castle to rights, watching the boys and Richard learn about each other by slow degrees, learning about her new husband herself, and spending night after night in his arms. They'd not resumed their painful discussion about his past, and she did not mean to, since it did no good to dwell on what could not be mended. She'd ascertained that Tarquin had never been here, neither in his childhood nor more recently, because of course he was no Ventris, no relation at all, and had no business and no place here. Day by day, as they lived together undisturbed, she grew less anxious and more hopeful for the future.

31

Richard had taken the boys fishing while Viola had headed into York with a long list of items that might help in her continuing quest to make Ventris Castle vaguely habitable. He had suggested frivolously that the task was doomed to failure and that a substantial charge of gunpowder was what was really needed, but she was not a woman to be so easily discouraged, and was already making a perceptible difference, he would freely admit.

She'd left as soon as it was light, and would spend the night at an inn in the city if her errands took too long; he pushed away any notion of missing her, or wishing he had accompanied her. That would be the height of folly – York was a place best avoided by him, because of some passages in his recent history that he'd prefer not to dwell on.

He could only be grateful that she was allowing him to spend time alone with the boys, when many another woman might not have done. They had soon after their arrival engaged a tutor to make sure that their education was not entirely neglected – a young and energetic local curate who had the wit to keep them amused so that learning proceeded almost by stealth – but this was not one of his days, and Richard was making good use of it.

It wasn't the season for trout, for the gentlemanly sort of fly-casting in rivers that was so popular in the summer, but he had always found sea-fishing from this wild coast exhilarating, and he could see that Ned felt the same. Robin had been fascinated by the novelty at first, but had long since wandered off along the beach, looking for the curious stones and fossilised creatures that abounded there, leaving Lord Ventris and the young Duke perched on the rocks, wet with spray, faces flushed.

There was an icy wind blowing straight off the water. It was what made the season so perfect for the sport, forcing the waves up onto the rocky outcrops that stretched their fingers out into the stormy North Sea, and driving the cod along with them, but it would be all too easy for the lad to get chilled through, and Richard had no desire for illness to be the result of this first expedition; Viola would never forgive him, and he'd never forgive himself.

'I think it's time to stop,' he said firmly now. 'We've caught enough between us to make a fine dish or two for this evening's table, and my poor old bones are frozen through.' His own boyhood was recent enough for him to know that suggesting his companion might be cold was not the best way to put an end to the day's activity. A sturdy lad of eleven would allow himself to become a human icicle sooner than admit that he felt any physical discomfort or might need to seek out warmth. But he could raise no objection if his poor old stepfather admitted to such sad weakness.

'Of course, sir,' the boy said with alacrity. Richard couldn't be sure, not knowing his son well enough yet, if his ready acquiescence could be put down to good manners alone, or if he was relieved to be given the excuse to stop, to leave this exposed spot and regain feeling in his extremities – both, perhaps. It was a painful joy, this heaven-sent opportunity to be a part of their lives at last. Every moment spent in their company was more precious than anyone could know. But it was far from being a straightforward relationship, and he wondered if it ever would be.

They'd been wary of him – understandably – at their first meeting, when he and Viola had gone to fetch them away from school a few weeks ago in order to bring them north. But they seemed to have settled well enough in the Castle, and to have taken a great liking to the place and its people. They both seemed happy, at the moment – Viola, who knew them best, agreed that this was so. Yet he must be conscious that this, however much they seemed to relish it, was a substantial disruption to their lives. It was one that they would set entirely at his door, and rightly, if it ever occurred to them to resent it one day. Their existence had been ordered and predictable for years, they must think, till he had come along and upended it, pulling them away from their home and their friends, claiming his share of their mother's attention into the bargain, and threatening further upheavals in the future, with the likely arrival of new siblings.

Lord Marchett had been obliged to accede to his right to have the ordering of the boys' education himself now that Richard stood in the relation of a father to them; Richard had sought him out for a highly awkward face-to-face interview just before his marriage, and made certain of his capitulation by a little plain speaking.

Of course, he had not then known that Marchett had written to Viola some years before and warned her of his clandestine activities, but it was doubtful if the knowledge would have made any difference. If Marchett had risked speaking openly, *he* could not have done – not yet. The older man obviously thought no better of him in the role of Viola's new husband than he had as her clandestine lover twelve years ago, but he could do nothing in the world about it. Richard might easily have given him a dressing-down for the way he had so disregarded the Duchess and her wishes as a mother, but it had seemed pointless to pull caps with the old booby, who was not likely to develop more enlightened, modern views on the situation of women at this stage in his life. He was sixty, and no longer active in public life, suffering as he did from crippling gout. He'd aged a good deal since they'd last met, but then Richard often felt that he had too.

'You know as well as I do,' he had said bluntly to the Earl, 'that the boys are mine. Edward made you party to his deception, and you accepted that role, and will have to live with its consequences. I imagine that you greatly dislike my marriage – you make it plain by your stiff-rumped manner and your disapproving countenance. But you cannot say that it is anything but a belated step to set things right, and mend – insofar as such matters ever can be mended – the damage that my cousin did to all of us a dozen years ago.' He saw that the man's face was still frozen in aristocratic disdain, and said impatiently, 'What else would you have me do? I'd honestly love to know. You are a father. Do me the credit of admitting that my natural human feelings for my sons are as strong as any other man's. This situation is not of my making, nor of the Duchess's making. But we are obliged to do our best with it, and so must you.'

'You're all but blackmailing me, which I suppose should not surprise me,' Marchett said gruffly, shifting his bandaged leg restlessly on its footstool. It was unclear how much of his distress was physical and how much mental;

he'd never been a man who enjoyed being challenged, Richard recalled, and his pride was making him stupid now.

'Don't be ridiculous, man! Of course I'm not doing anything of the sort. I merely need your co-operation. You know I have not the least desire to bring disgrace on my sons, nor on their mother. It is not in my interests to expose their true parentage to the world – apart from anything else, that would risk making my dear brother Duke of Winterflood, which is the last thing I want.'

'And it would make you his heir, and him a libertine and wastrel who is not likely to reach a great age, so forgive me if I don't believe you, Ventris,' Marchett said querulously, as though the gout were in his grizzled head rather than his swollen extremities.

Ventris was silent for a moment, glad that he had long since been obliged to develop habits of rigid self-control. 'If you were a younger man, or at least one who could stand upright without a stick, I'd knock you down for that,' he said at last between gritted teeth. 'This isn't a damned melodrama or a three-volume novel; it's my life. My children's lives. Why in God's name would I marry a woman and then immediately plot to disinherit her sons and mire her in disgrace? If I wanted to cut them out because of some elaborate and fanciful scheme of my own, I could merely leave her be and spread the rumour that I'm their father without appearing in the matter at all. Not that such gossip would hold any water legally, after so long. What nonsense you talk. The plain truth is that I've never expected or wanted Winterflood to fall into my lap. I already have an estate that I never thought to gain possession of – I think one is enough. You'll be accusing me of murdering my poor cousin Simon next. Be sensible. You have no power to stop my marriage, whatever you think of me – all you can do is make Viola's life more difficult than it need be in your position as the boys' guardian. I repeat: you know perfectly well that I am their father, and how that came about. You have always known it. You're enmeshed as deep in this mess as we are.'

The old man had caved in, as Richard had always known he must, and in effect had resigned his charge, though he would still be guardian in name for the rest of the boys' minority, if he lived that long. And Viola had readily agreed to bring her sons to Ventris for the winter, though he knew that that was at least partly because she was still concerned for their safety.

He and Ned picked up their rods now, along with the basket holding the fish they had caught and all the rest of their paraphernalia, and headed back over the rocks, the boy running agilely ahead of him, but waiting for him once he reached the sand. He really did have excellent manners, but Richard would expect nothing less from Viola's son. Robin was a crouched figure in the distance, absorbed by some treasure he had found on the beach.

The young Duke said, in a tone that suggested this was something he had wished to get off his chest for some while, 'My mother told me that you were very close to my father, but you never came to Winterflood before he died, so I wondered if that was true, or if she was just saying it to reconcile us to your marriage.'

This was plain speaking. 'Your mother doesn't stoop to untruths, not even in a good cause. Edward and I were close when I was a boy, but it's true that we had grown somewhat distant by the time of his death. I think this was in part because my business carried me overseas a great deal, and it was difficult to maintain a steady correspondence, and therefore occasions for me to visit Winterflood became rarer, and then stopped altogether.' Viola might not lie, but Richard did – it could be said that he had made a career of it – and he had no intention of revealing any part of the complex truth to the boys. But he found he had an odd scruple about uttering blatant falsehoods to his son, so he was picking his way carefully through this thicket of difficulties.

Ned didn't seem to be satisfied by this bland response, and worried away at the matter like a terrier with a rat. 'Something I overheard one of my aunts say to my mama once made me think that my father did not always treat her well. And if you liked her even then, you might have felt angry with him...'

They were straying on to dangerous ground indeed. 'You know that your father had been married before, and that he loved his previous wife Elizabeth very deeply.'

The boy nodded; he too had seen the damn portrait a thousand times, no doubt, and heard Edward speak of her in his tactless way.

'They had many happy years together, though they were never blessed with children. When he married your mother, he was still grieving for his loss, and perhaps as a result, he was not as considerate of her feelings as he might have been. The age gap between them was very great, so they had less in common than a couple closer in age might have done, and it was harder, I believe, for the natural distance between them to be bridged. And you are right, I did mention it to my cousin when I saw how things stood. Perhaps that lay at the root of the separation that grew between us, yes. But it's also true that our lives were very different, so we might have drifted away from each other in any case.'

None of this was inaccurate, but it was as close as he wished to go to the perilous facts. If Ned and Robin were ever to be told the truth of their origins, it must be when they were fully grown and able to understand and not to judge. He was uncomfortably aware that many people, perhaps most, never reached such a happy state of maturity, however long they lived. For his own part, he knew little of the relationship between his own dead parents, and what little he knew, he did not care for much. He certainly had no desire to be acquainted with any more details of things that had happened years ago and were unalterable and far past crying over. So perhaps the day would never come when the boys could be told how it was that they existed in the world and passed as another man's children. And if that were so, he must accept it. Viola, he suspected, had perforce made her peace with this uncomfortable reality years ago.

'I don't like to think of my mama being unhappy,' Ned said baldly now. This was a boy who would not take the world or the persons in it at surface value, despite his youth; it gave Richard a pang to see in his son this awkward quality that he presumed must somehow have been inherited from himself, and which, as he already knew to his cost, did not tend to make one content in life. What would he have wanted someone to say to him on that awkward topic, at eleven? Not easy platitudes, such as little children were given to soothe them, certainly.

'I did not know your mother before she married, but I understand that she was very young, and conscious that her family circumstances required that she make a good match. But I know she was not forced by anyone to accept your father – do not be imagining anything so Gothic or dramatic. Many people – I do not say many women, for I do not think that distinction a fair one – might have been satisfied with the worldly advantages the marriage gave her, but she does not care greatly for such things, does she?' He stopped, and they faced each other across the sand. 'I do know that your happiness, both of you, has always been her greatest concern, from your birth and even before it, and that it was my cousin's chief preoccupation too.' In that moment, he could not quite bring himself to say *your father*. He was their father, in blood and flesh and bone, even if they never knew it.

He went on carefully, 'You have not seen a great deal of the world yet, but I daresay that you know already that marriages at every level of society, but perhaps particularly at the highest, are not always driven by love, or by free choice, and nor for that matter are children always cared for – in mansions as in cottages – as they should be. But you have been, and always will be. I think you should rest secure in that, and not dwell on past difficulties that cannot now be mended. Most people never concern themselves in the slightest about such matters, lucky devils, and are probably the happier for it.'

'That's what Robin says,' Ned replied with a slightly strained grin. 'He says I talk a deal of nonsense always, and perhaps he's right. He's always merry as a grig and never worries about such things. But I can't help being different. Are you that way too, sir? I thought from what you said that you might be.'

'I'm afraid I am. It can be both a blessing and a curse.' This was all he could manage, over some sudden obstruction in his throat. They had drawn close to Robin now, and found him still squatting upon his haunches, with a little pile of stones and shells beside him. But he didn't look up at their arrival, or even seem aware of it, being fully absorbed in gazing down in wonder at the miniature world of bustling life and colour in the rockpool by his toes. He didn't seem to want to interfere with it as many another child would have done – to catch one of the crabs or the tiny fish and transparent shrimps, to make himself a mighty and destructive god in their universe – but was content merely to observe. Richard wouldn't necessarily have expected such fierce concentration and forbearance from the livelier, more boisterous twin – but then, he was just learning to know them both after so many wasted years. He needed to remember that.

32

Viola sent off letters to her older sisters and to Emily, reassuring them that she and the boys were well and asking about their welfare and their families, and then set about her shopping with determination. By the time a couple of hours had passed, she had bought half the household goods in York, it seemed to her. She directed the slightly stunned shopkeepers to send the smaller parcels back to the rooms she had hired in the city's most notable inn; the larger items were to be delivered by carrier's cart as soon as possible, and she would pay for them herself, out of her own resources. All of the Castle's inhabitants deserved more comfort than they currently knew, especially since it would soon be winter, and she was glad to be able to give it to them and not count the cost too closely. She realised that Winterflood had never needed her, apart from impersonally, as mother to its longed-for heir – the house and the estate had run like a well-oiled machine before she'd ever set foot in the place, and still did now, whether she was present or not. But Ventris was different, Ventris desperately needed her care, and this gave her a warm feeling, over and above the heady pleasure of spending money in a good cause.

The staff at the Golden Fleece could hardly do enough for her. They didn't know or care that she had once been a duchess, as indeed why should they? What weighed with them was the Ventris name. Several of them spoke with easy familiarity of her late predecessor, who had been well known to everyone in the city before she'd retreated into a solitary existence towards the end of her life. Her blunt manners and many eccentricities, which had made her notorious in polite society, had apparently won their approval – since they didn't have to live under her leaky roof – or at least engaged their amused interest.

Viola could be blunt too, if it came to it. She had an odd desire that these people too should not think her a soft, southern fool – a fine lady who had come sweeping in on a high horse and was afraid to get her hands dirty.

'Well, I'm sure my husband's aunt was a most admirable person,' she said frankly, 'but if she had a bedsheet in the Castle without fifty holes in it, I've yet to come across it. Perhaps she was buried with her best ones, for spite.'

The landlady cackled at this, and admitted that the old baroness had been a rare caution, and that much of a nipcheese, she'd counted the pennies over and over and left the shillings to look after themselves. If she could have taken her fortune with her, she implied, the lady would have done so, never mind just sheets.

'With the result,' Viola said cordially, 'that I am obliged to remedy the deficit of years. But we are liberally provided with rags, I promise you, and may set up in business in that line to recoup some of our losses. Mice, also, we have in abundance, coming in from the abandoned parts of the building, though what they can have been eating all this time is a puzzle to me still.'

She decided to stay overnight, being by no means done with her shopping, slept well on sheets without great lumpy darns in them, and set out again in the morning after breakfast. She found it liberating to walk alone and unregarded along the narrow, medieval streets in the wintry sunshine, looking idly in shop windows at the wares displayed there, catching a glimpse of the great Minster every now and then when it appeared, framed by lesser but still ancient buildings over which it towered. Everyone was busy, or at any rate wrapped up in their own affairs, and nobody paid her any mind; she did not expect that they should, since she had no acquaintance in the city, and in truth wished for none. It was pleasant to be anonymous and unattended and to let her thoughts ramble where they would: the boys, who seemed to be happy in Yorkshire; Richard, who in many ways remained an enigma to her; their new life together, the possibility…

So she was surprised, and not entirely pleased, to hear herself addressed, hesitantly and by name, by a complete stranger. 'Your grace – I beg your pardon, Lady Ventris. Forgive me for approaching you like this. It is urgent that I have speech with you, even though we have not been introduced.'

Viola turned to see a woman standing at a little distance from her in the shadow of an overhanging upper storey, regarding her with anxious interest. She was perhaps fifty or a few years more – her own mother's age – and respectably though not fashionably dressed in good fabrics of sober, dark colours that looked like half-mourning. Her tones had been genteel, and she was a handsome woman, her dark hair sprinkled with grey, her face a little worn, as if by a life that had not been entirely untroubled by misfortune. It was impossible to imagine what in the world she might want.

The woman saw that Viola's face was not welcoming, and added hastily, 'I have been pondering whether I should write to you, since I had heard of your marriage and knew that you are in residence at Ventris Castle, but I could not see how to begin, it is so excessively delicate a matter. I am not importuning you, ma'am – I promise I am not. I require nothing from you but half an hour's attention. There is something I must tell you, something important that you need to know, for your benefit rather than mine.'

Viola feared she might be beginning to see some light. 'Is it about my husband?' she asked with a fair assumption of casualness, inwardly cringing. 'Because if it is, there is nothing you can tell me that—'

'It's not about your current husband,' the woman interrupted flatly. 'I know nothing of His Lordship beyond his name and title, though I suppose I may have met him briefly when he was a babe in arms and I a young bride, and I assure you that I have not the least interest in him. It's about your previous husband, in a way.'

'Really?' Viola raised her eyebrows. This was most unexpected. 'You do know that the previous Duke of Winterflood has been dead these three years or more?'

'I am aware. I was bound to take an interest in the matter, as you will see. My name is Lesmire, ma'am, Julia Lesmire. I have been living in York for some years with my family – my late husband and my grown children, and my little grandchildren now. But I was Julia Armstrong once, long ago, and Duchess of Winterflood, like you. I was Edward's first wife.'

33

A few minutes later, the two women sat together in the private parlour that Viola had hired for her stay at the inn. Tea had been brought, more for appearances' sake than anything else – as though this was a normal social call between acquaintances, when it most emphatically was not.

Madame Lesmire said earnestly, 'I'm glad I came across you, Lady Ventris, but it was not quite by chance. Our maid's sister is employed in this inn as an abigail, and is accustomed to talk idly of the visitors, particularly if they are ladies of quality. I heard last night that you were here, and was coming on purpose to seek you out this morning when we met. You were described to me; I could not fail to recognise you, and besides, I have seen your portrait in a print shop before now. Fashionable beauties, such as people of all ranks like to stare at – I was one myself once, long ago. How strange it seems.'

'I can't imagine that you have come merely to share impressions of Edward as a husband,' Viola said drily. 'In any case, I have absolutely no intention of doing anything of the kind, I promise you.' She could see that the woman had some distinct aim in mind, and wished that she might get to the point without further delay. She had some faint inkling that this point, when it came, would be nothing that she'd be glad to hear. Julia did not seem to be malicious in her intent – far from it – but she was highly agitated about something. It could hardly be anything good. Were dramatic and unexpected revelations about the past ever positive, in life or in fiction?

'No, I have not the least desire to discuss him in that manner, nor any expectation that you would wish to if I did. That would be most awkward, and in any case, my time with him was so long ago that my recollections of it are not strong, nor are they of such a nature that I wish to dwell upon them now. In brief, we found ourselves quite quickly to be ill-suited and unhappy; I ran away in 1781 with Philippe, who was my lover. He had his faults too, as I came to discover, but that is of no possible significance to you. All this would be before you were born, ma'am. Edward divorced me – but of course he did; he wanted a child, a son and heir more than anything in the world, and so remarried, to a lady named Elizabeth, whom I have heard he came to adore, as he never did me.'

'But Elizabeth did not give him a son, or a daughter,' Viola said quietly. 'I did, many years later. Two, in point of fact.'

'Did you?'

They regarded each other in silence. Julia said at last, her face serious, 'I won't ask you any questions; I make no accusations. I wish for no secret knowledge. God knows your life is none of my business, and though I daresay people have envied you, I am not one of them. I will merely share some facts about myself, and you can make of them what you will. Edward and I were married for five years. We were young. We did not love each other – love matches were not usual in those days, at our rank of society – but we found ways to please each other. We found them *frequently* – all the more often because we had so little else to say to each other. Even when he no longer pleased me in the least, even when we began to grow apart, I knew my duty, and Edward certainly knew his. I shudder to remember how well he knew it. And yet I never was with child, not the least suspicion of it. With Philippe... I carried his daughter in my belly before I married him, in the Catholic rite, in France. We went on to have four more children, in seven or eight years. There would have been more, had I not begun to be more careful, for the sake of my health and the infants I already had. Was Elizabeth ever in the family way, do you know, in all their long years together?'

Viola shook her head, trying to keep her face impassive. But she could not lie to this woman who was being so painfully frank with her. 'Not that I ever heard. I believe it was a great grief to her.'

'And to Edward, I am sure.'

'Certainly to Edward.'

Madame Lesmire went on, frowning, 'These matters I had not thought about for years are on my mind now, because a man came to see me a week or so ago, a stranger. He had gone to a great deal of trouble to find me, he told me, after a casual remark someone recently made to him that they had seen me in the street here and thought they recognised me after many years. And though I did not invite him into my house, he more or less forced his way in, and frightened me, though I admit he offered me no overt violence. He called me Duchess in a sneering sort of way – a title I have no right to. He made insinuations, on the matters I have just revealed to you. Whoever he was – he did not give me his name – he seemed to know somehow that I had never carried Edward's child, and nor had Elizabeth, and invited me to say that it was noteworthy, that I had proved so very fertile afterwards. With another man. And that you, by contrast, had provided Edward with his precious heir a mere year or two after your marriage, even though Edward was older then, and, he presumed, less *vigorous*.'

Viola shivered at the word, and at the echo of an unpleasant personality she heard in it, and Julia nodded. 'I liked nothing about the man, nor any of the things he said to me. His purpose was blackmail, it seemed to me, though he never clearly stated it. His insinuation was that Philippe and I were never truly married, or he would say we weren't, that my past is a scandalous secret, and that my children, who have good positions here in York as solid tradespeople, and are all of them respectably wed, are nothing more than bastards, and their mother a common... I'm sure you can imagine the words he used. If all this came out, I fear their business would be ruined, or at least badly damaged, and their lives too. They have already had trouble enough to rebuild everything after my husband let things slide before his death.'

'I am very sorry that this trouble has come to your door when you did nothing to invite it,' Viola said softly. 'What exactly did he want from you?'

The woman shrugged. 'Testimony, he said, and that was all. The truth, in a sworn and notarised document – that I had every reason to believe Edward sterile, from my own knowledge and experience. He did not ask me to tell any lies, he emphasised. There was no need. And the document need never be made public – I didn't believe that, by the way, not for a second. He made my skin crawl.'

He made Viola's skin crawl, too. 'I believe I could put a name to him.'

'I too. And that name is Armstrong. Your new husband's older brother –

Edward's heir, before you had your sons and forced him from his place. He looked like an Armstrong to me; he had a strong look of his dissolute father, whom I knew years ago and never liked or trusted.'

'Tarquin, his name is. Edward warned me against him on his deathbed. Said he would do anything to gain the dukedom he had expected for so long, and which I snatched from him. Did he give you any sort of ultimatum?'

'Yes. He told me he would come again to see me very soon. He seemed to enjoy the idea that I would be dreading his return, never knowing when it might happen. He has not been back yet, but I cannot doubt that he will, one day or another. And so I wanted to warn you – but I was not confident that a letter from me would even be read by you, or that you would believe it if you read it. You might so easily think that I was just a woman who has fallen from high rank in society to low, and wanted to make mischief. I thought it would be best if I could see you face to face and explain.'

'What do you mean to do, Madame Lesmire?'

'If he had offered me money, I would have thrown it back in his face. I don't need bribes; I am not so desperate. But I will write his paper – speaking merely of my own experience with Edward, and stating the undeniable fact of my children's birth. I don't have much choice, as I hope you can see. I don't trust him an inch, of course I don't, but I cannot jeopardise my family's situation. We are not wealthy people – not now. Philippe lost most of what he had when we fled France in 1792, in fear of our lives, and we were obliged to struggle to make a place for ourselves in a country that is not over-friendly to the French. It has not been easy, and my husband made it harder by his weaknesses. I cannot throw away what acceptance we have for the sake of principles.'

'And he is not asking you to lie, after all.'

'No. But I am sorry.'

'Don't be – you owe me nothing. We only met an hour ago. Indeed, I must thank you for your warning.' Viola discovered that she liked this woman – both her discretion and her directness. How odd, when they had something bizarre in common that might have been supposed to make them deeply awkward with each other, rather than comfortable.

'What will you do with the information I have given you, though? I meant to prepare you, and I have, but what can you do?'

'I have absolutely no idea.'

34

Viola hadn't felt like lingering in York buying bed linens and crockery after what Julia Lesmire had told her, and was soon on her way back to Ventris Castle – a journey of many hours even in the best of circumstances, since some of the roads were bad and the changes of horses numerous and time-consuming. She was uneasy as she sat idle in the carriage, and disposed to blame herself for carelessness. She had been lulled into a sense of false security lately, as though she and Richard and the boys were an ordinary family with an ordinary expectation of being happy together if no immediate ill health or mischance threatened their tranquillity. But it wasn't true – there was always a shadow hanging over them, the shadow of Tarquin Armstrong and his malice, the shadow of the past, and she had been foolish to allow herself to forget it. She told herself that falling prey to agitation would not help matters, but she was undeniably not in the calmest frame of mind when at last her chaise jolted across the uneven cobbles into the courtyard.

It was dark by now, since it was late autumn and even the sunny days were short, but there was moonlight, and she could not repress the feeling that the old building looked eerie in it, and somehow ominous, the empty windows gaping in a sinister fashion. *Bad things have happened here in the dark*, she thought with a shudder. It was a ridiculous fancy, and she shook it off as the huge door to the great hall opened and her sons came tumbling out to greet her, talking – at full volume and both at once – of all that they had been doing with Richard in her absence. He stood behind them, bathed in the warm light from inside, smiling a little – an undeniably reassuring presence, despite everything. She'd tell him, as soon as they were alone.

She had expected him to show some perturbation when he heard of his half-brother's recent presence in York, but he did not, to her surprise and irritation. When she accused him of not treating the matter seriously enough, he responded coolly, 'We knew his intentions towards you and the boys were not kindly – how could they be? This news is merely confirmation of that fact and nothing more.'

'I do not know how you can take it so lightly!' she said with some heat. They were in bed and both naked, the long, tattered velvet curtains at the mullioned windows closed against the evening chill, a fire of sea coal glowing in the imposing stone fireplace. There was little furniture in the room beside the big four-poster bed, and nothing that gave evidence of modern times; it would be easy enough to fall prey to Gothic fancies in such a setting.

'I don't take it lightly, Viola, I promise. But I think you overestimate what it is in Tarquin's power to do. As you said yourself, this woman can have no knowledge of your particular circumstances, and in fact claims none. She can only speak of her own situation, and the facts as they stood thirty years ago. That is not evidence in law of anything.'

'Of course it is not. But Madame Lesmire said—'

'Madame *what*?' His voice was suddenly sharp, a crack of raw emotion in the quiet room.

Her heart beat fast at the sound, the little hairs on her arms standing on end in some kind of primitive warning. 'Madame Lesmire. Julia Lesmire. Did I not tell you her current surname? Her husband was a French émigré, she said – a refugee from the Terror.' She was talking too much, too fast and high, as she often did when she was discomposed. Why had the woman's name affected him so? He could not possibly have heard it before.

'Ah,' he breathed, a wealth of meaning she could not hope to interpret in the single exhalation. And then, very low, 'I can never escape it, can I? Not even in bed with my wife, where I should be untroubled, if I can be untroubled anywhere.'

'You know her?'

'I've never met her. I am sure she cannot have claimed to have met me. If she did, she lied.' His voice was like a whip-lash.

'She did not say she had, unless she saw you when you were just an infant and she was married to Edward. What can she be to you, Richard?'

'Nothing. Less than nothing.' After a moment, he said bleakly, 'There is no point trying to conceal from you the fact that I knew her husband. But if she has ever heard of me from him, it would have been by another name, an alias I always used, and so she would not have made the connection. He might easily have known my true identity, indeed I expect he did, but I very much doubt he would have shared it with her. What a hellish coincidence.'

'I think she said, or implied, that he was a respectable tradesman in York, a living he took up after losing his position in society as a result of the revolution in France.' When Richard did not reply to this, she said heavily, 'Is that all he was? Or was he even that?'

'Would you believe me if I said so – that he sold me a pair of riding boots when last I was in the north, or some such tale?'

He had not reacted as he had because the man had engaged him in some casual transaction of business, she was sure. '*Should* I believe you?'

He laughed mirthlessly. 'It was not boots, at any event. He was a wine merchant, in fact, a very good one. I'd known him casually for years. He had all manner of connections across the Continent – Spain and Portugal, as well as France, with which country, of course, we do not legally trade at present. But if you wanted a fine French wine or brandy, even in these unsettled times, he would engage to obtain it for you, personally. He offered an excellent service to his customers. Nothing was too much trouble for Lesmire.'

'He was a smuggler.'

'Certainly.'

'A spy?'

He let out a great gust of breath. 'A very dangerous one. Whether his wife knows as much, I could not tell you, Viola. Such men are discouraged by their masters from idle domestic chatter, shall we say? But he's dead now, so any secret knowledge he may have had can no longer threaten… anyone.'

She could hardly believe that they were having this conversation, as the flames illuminated his disturbingly impassive face for a second and then it was concealed in the shadows when he turned away from her a little. Perhaps he could not meet her gaze, and no wonder. This man was supposed to keep her boys *safe*. This did not sound anything like safety. 'Unless he kept records.'

The response was terrifyingly swift and sure. 'He did, but there is no need to suffer the least anxiety over them. They have all been destroyed.'

'The only way you could be positive of that...'

'Is if I made certain of their destruction myself, yes. I did. I burned them, one by one; it took hours, and then I broke the ashes into pieces so no shred remained that could be read.'

She was silent for a moment. 'Julia did not tell me how he died. The topic did not arise.' She felt removed from herself, as if in some fever dream, and her voice echoed unpleasantly in her own ears.

'He suffered an unfortunate accident. He liked his own wares a little too much – and so he fell down the cellar steps on his premises and broke his neck. I do not think it came as a great surprise to anyone.'

'Not to you, at any rate, it seems.'

Again, the pregnant silence stretched. 'Viola, are you asking me if I killed him? Because before you do, you might wish to reflect upon whether you really want to hear the answer.'

'That sounds like answer enough to me. You did; you killed him.' She was unnaturally calm.

'Very well. Yes.'

The confession of murder dropped into the quiet room like a stone into a pool, and when she said nothing in immediate response – what was there to say? – he looked at her with what she began to recognise as desperation, which scared her more than all the rest. At last, he had been completely honest with her, and it was horrifying.

'Viola, I had my reasons for what I did, though I cannot share them yet. If you are disgusted at my actions, knowing just a tiny fraction of them, I cannot blame you. I am disgusted myself. I have done terrible things – as you once rightly said to me, I'd started doing them even before you and I first met. There are matters that lie far heavier on my conscience than sending Citizen Lesmire to his grave. But I will not ask you to accept any of this with complaisance. You should not. All I will ask is for you to be patient a little while longer. I need to tell you much more than I have – but I cannot yet. I am not deliberately being mysterious – I simply cannot. You heard me say that men such as Lesmire are not supposed to discuss their affairs, even with their loved ones. Especially with them, and on pain of death. The same applies to me – for now.'

'We've spoken of this before,' she said, suddenly bone-tired. 'You promised me you would not put the boys in any danger. That was all I asked of you, I think, and it does not seem like so very much.'

He was insistent; he took her hands and gripped them with painful intensity. 'And I won't. I haven't and I won't. Nor you. I'd sooner cut off my own right arm than harm any of you. I'm waiting for a letter that has been promised me, and when I have it, my situation will be different. As soon as it arrives, I will go and see my brother, and put a stop to his threats forever, so that you may be entirely easy in your mind.'

'Are you going to kill him too? Because Richard, if that is your scheme, I must think you have run mad.' She felt hysterical laughter bubbling up inside her, and only just managed to suppress it. 'There is no safety in that for any of us; you could hang. He is your own brother, whatever else he is. I suppose you have been lucky before, with Lesmire and perhaps with others of whom I know nothing, but you cannot count on that. You must surely be able to see as much, however far you have gone to dark places where I cannot follow.'

'It is true that I have been in dark places,' he said sombrely. 'But I hope to put all that behind me for good, and live in the light, with you. And I will make all sorts of threats to Tarquin, I am sure I will have to, just to get his attention, but I shall not kill him. I assure you I am not mad. I am saner than I have ever been in my life. I know exactly how much I have to lose now, when I had nothing before to live for.'

She could have told him that he had far more to lose than he knew. She wondered if he suspected it. But he had said nothing on the subject, and she did not. It was not the time. She snuffed out the candle at her bedside, and they spoke no more, though she did not sleep for hours and thought that he lay awake at her side too, with God knows what thoughts running through his mind.

35

A few days later, Lord Ventris's horse made his weary way up the drive that led to Mr Tarquin Armstrong's home in the Lincolnshire Wolds, Lindsey Manor. The poor beast had been plodding valiantly on for hours through the chill afternoon, but his pace increased a little now; perhaps he sensed that a warm stable was near, and a rest. He'd earned it.

Richard had not been here for years, and noticed signs of neglect even in the gathering dusk. Broken fences, overgrown rides, rank pasture. It was a rich, fertile hill-country, one from which it should be possible to make a good living, but that would require putting back more than one took out, at least at first – a concept which his late father had not understood, and Tarquin emphatically did not either. The Jacobean house had come into this branch of the Armstrong family through his late grandmother, his father's mother, and had been short-sightedly managed by men who did not appreciate it as it deserved for as long as anyone could remember, so that the damage ran deep. This had been his own home once, in his boyhood, but he would not think to call it that now; his home was where Viola was, or he hoped it would be. He'd never been particularly happy here, nor had his poor mother. He wished nothing more than to make his stay here now as brief as possible.

He still remembered his way about the old place, and half an hour later, after he'd taken good care of his footsore mount, he was making his way silently through the house to the library – a pretentious name for a room which had always been lined with crumbling books that nobody ever read. The estate was plainly not over-provided with servants; he'd met nobody since his arrival, which suited him perfectly. Despite what he'd said to Viola, he was quite prepared to kill Tarquin if he had to. But he hoped the necessity could be avoided; he needed no more deaths on his conscience. He had a thick letter in his pocket, heavy with official seals, and he had permission to show it to anyone who might need to see it. His brother was among that number, though he didn't know it yet.

If Tarquin's wife was here, she'd likely be in some comfortless private parlour, sitting sewing or reading, amusing herself as best she could. Mr Armstrong was not the sort of man who spent his evenings chatting sedately with a woman – certainly not his own wife. Richard expected to find his brother doing nothing at all, nodding over his cups just as their father had each night, and he was not disappointed. Tarquin was there alone, dozing, reminding him suddenly and unexpectedly of Edward doing the same at Winterflood so many years ago. They were all Armstrongs, after all. The squeak of the ill-oiled library door woke him, and he sat up startled in his shabby armchair, blinking owlishly at the unexpected sight of his only sibling, the black sheep of the family. Richard closed the door behind him, and locked it with the key he'd taken from the other side of the lock, out in the hall. 'Brother,' he said coolly, pocketing it and advancing across the dusty chamber. 'I hear you've been busy.'

It seemed to take Mr Armstrong an inordinate amount of time to gather his wits, such as they were. 'In York,' Richard prompted, his lip curling. 'Bursting into people's homes, making all kinds of melodramatic threats, like some villain in a pantomime. Boo! I say. You do nothing but make yourself ridiculous.'

They glared at each other, with rancour vivid and alive on both sides. There was a certain resemblance between them, in the colour of hair and eyes rather than in any particular lineament of face, or mannerism. But Richard's skin was tanned from exposure to the elements, whereas his brother did not look like a sporting man, unless gaming and drinking and wenching should be considered sports.

'I am not the one who is ridiculous,' Tarquin sneered at last, recovering himself a little and sitting up straighter. 'So, you've married the widow. Felicitations! I daresay she is happy enough to have her bed warmed after all these years, and doesn't much care who by. But it won't do you any good, or her. I mean to expose her, and her bastard brats. Are they yours, I wonder? I've not seen them, but I hear they look like Armstrongs rather than mongrel scum, so I expect they are your get.'

'Shut up,' Richard said emotionlessly. 'Stop posturing before you say something that prompts me to knock your silly head off and use it as a football. There can be no legal proof that what you say is true, and you should know it. In law and custom, a man's children are those he accepts as his, even if all the world knows different. Edward lived with the boys for eight long years, and with their mother; he made wills in their favour to provide for their future. He stood in church at their side, before his God, Sunday after Sunday. The older boy bears his name. Your efforts are preposterous, and everyone will know that they come only from your pathetic jealousy. You thought the dukedom yours – it never will be now. Get over it, can't you, and live your own life with what you have?'

Tarquin's face, which had been pale, was unhealthily flushed now. 'I *know* those brats aren't Edward's. They can't be. The world should know it too!'

'You should have considered a career on the stage, really. Nobody gives a damn, can't you grasp that? Half the children in the polite world were sired by men not married to their mothers. I grant you that you might once have made trouble and advanced your cause, if Edward had died when they were in the womb, or newly born. *Then* you might have had a case. But he didn't. You're too late. Get a new hobby, a more wholesome one.'

'Even if I admit you're right, I can still spread damaging gossip,' Tarquin said, ill-advisedly. 'I can make the whore you married as notorious as Lady—'

He was not destined to finish his slanderous sentence. Richard was at his side in a flash and had him by the throat, so fast, he was almost a blur. 'Now we come to it,' Ventris said into his brother's face, still eerily calm, his breathing apparently unaffected as his prey gasped and choked for air. 'And this is what I rode all this tedious way to say to you. You won't bully me or mine, and I'm no longer five years old and scared of you. You should be scared of *me*. If you smear my wife's name, or my sons' – yes, they are my sons, and if you reflect for a moment, you'll see why that should worry you – I will kill you.' Each word of that final phrase was punctuated with a vigorous shake. 'Do you understand me? I will kill you. I told my wife I wouldn't, but I lied. It's a bad habit I have.'

He released his wheezing brother and stood looking down at him contemptuously as he collapsed back into the chair from which Richard had half-dragged him.

'I don't believe you,' Armstrong managed thickly at last, his voice hoarse. 'I know you're a disgrace to the name, but you can't go round murdering people and expect to get away with it. Not in England, dammit!'

'But you see, I do expect to get away with it,' said Ventris, almost pityingly. 'You're right, for once – if I were what you think me, and what the world thinks me, I'd be rash indeed to lay a finger on you. My position would be precarious, and I couldn't afford to jeopardise it by killing anyone. You're not important enough for anyone but me to want you dead – don't flatter yourself. Unless your unfortunate wife does already, of course. So if I killed you as you so richly deserve and I were indeed the notorious felon you think me, I'd be the obvious suspect and I'd have to flee, leave everything behind, expose myself irrevocably as a criminal – and here I am like you, just married, as you say. Oh, I'm thoroughly tired of your theatrical nonsense. Read this – I seem to recall you can read, can't you, if you put your mind to it? I know you must be sadly unaccustomed to the exercise.'

Richard pulled out a bulky document from his inner pocket, and handed it to his brother. It crackled portentously, and bore two large, impressive seals.

Armstrong stared as he saw the familiar design on them. 'But this is—'

'Read it, for God's sake. Stop flapping your gums for a second and just damn well read it.'

Tarquin's lips moved, and some phrases he spoke aloud, as his expression slowly changed to one of almost comic incredulity and his eyes bulged in their sockets. 'Lord Wellington informs me... Many years of peril and secret service... Damage to your reputation... Debt that can never be repaid... Overthrown the most dangerous enemy agent... Course of the war... Our great nation... In recognition... Ancient and illustrious name of Ventris restored to its former glory... Invest you with the title...'

The final sentence seemed to be too much for him at last, and Richard's lips twitched as he saw the impact it made on his brother. It was bitingly ironic, and one might almost pity him as he absorbed the news – almost.

'So you see,' he went on cordially, as Tarquin seemed to have lost the power of speech and movement, much like a clock that had wound down and could no longer do so much as tick, 'I am in rather good odour at the moment, with the government and with our glorious Regent, may his name be ever blessed. He writes that he has summoned to meet him for a private audience as a sign of his special favour – did you get that far? I could probably dump your butchered corpse on the steps of Carlton House with my signature writ large on your forehead – does it have steps, by the way? You know, I can't recall, but then I'll be there soon enough – and still get away with it scot-free. You've read the letter, and can read it again if you doubt the evidence of your eyes. I promise you, it's genuine; its contents will be made public within the next few days, at any rate. Do you care to risk it?'

'You... you...'

'I know,' Richard said, amusement in his voice now. 'Believe me, I know. You've always disliked and resented me, and now you will think you have even more reason, I expect. But you know I'm not a traitor or even a criminal – quite the reverse. So if we're to talk of *disgracing the name*... I think that's more likely to be you, judging by the state of this place, and what I saw as I rode in. And your recent reprehensible behaviour in York, of course, threatening innocent ladies in their own homes.'

An uneasy little silence fell between them.

Richard said at last, 'Did you know that Winterflood warned his wife against you on his deathbed? He always hated you beyond all reason – of course you were aware of that. So she's been suffering the gravest anxiety ever since – thinks you'd stop at nothing, not even murder, to get your hands on the dukedom. I haven't really done as much as I might have to discourage the idea yet – but he was a sick man with an obsession and he was wrong, wasn't he?'

'Of course he damn well was!' Armstrong blustered. 'My God... they're only children. Of course I wouldn't lay a hand on them!'

'Nor pay anyone else to do your dirty work for you? You can understand why I ask, I expect. We're going to settle this once and for all, here and now, so there can be no misunderstandings later.'

'Dammit, Richard, we're brothers – what do you take me for?'

'A bully and a drunkard and a fool who likes to talk big, but not a murderer. That's what I thought. If I'm wrong, though, brother dear, I promise I will kill you in the slowest, most exquisitely painful manner a man of my wide and unpleasant experience can devise, and I won't care if I hang for it after or not. They are my family – not you, God knows – and I will go to any lengths for their sake. Any lengths at all. Do you understand me yet?' His tone was silky, but also deadly serious, and his brother nodded, guilty-faced and shivering.

'Then I have nothing more to say to you, and I shall leave you to your peaceful evening.'

Tarquin watched him cross the room with wet eyes, and just before he reached the door, said unevenly, as though his words pained him, 'I'm sorry. I am. You have every right to hate me, I suppose. I never treated you well, I see that now, even when you were a brat at my heels. You make me ashamed.'

Ventris stopped for a moment, as if he was unsure whether he should make any response, and then said levelly, without turning to look at his brother's face to see if his words had any impact, 'I'm the last man in the world to go round preaching morality or virtue – that letter must have given you an idea of the sort of life I've led till now – but I think I have earned the right to say this: you're newly married, you may have children soon. Look about you at how you're living; be a better husband and father and landlord and master and man than our disgrace of a father was. Call me a sentimental fool for saying it, mock me and jeer at me as you did when we were boys – I won't give a damn because I won't know. I'm not talking about a tearful family reconciliation, or any sort of sickly sentiment. You'll do what you wish; I won't stop you, though I swear I will make you pay if you try to damage my family. But think about what I've said, for your own sake if no one else's.'

He did not wait for an answer, unlocking the door and passing out through it, closing it softly behind him.

His brother sat staring blankly at it, and did not move for a long time.

36

Viola spent the days of Richard's absence in a fever of anxiety, all the more painful because she was obliged to conceal her agitation from her sons – from the Codlings, from her maid, everyone. He was gone away on unimportant but necessary business, and would be back soon, she said easily. She could only hope that the latter statement was true.

It was late when Ventris reappeared in the Castle. He was plainly exhausted after many hours of hard riding, and she directed that a bath be readied for him before the fire in his bedchamber. But when it was ready at last and she made to withdraw, he said, 'Stay with me, Viola. I am not too tired to talk, we urgently need to, and I can see from your face that you too will not rest until we have spoken.'

She watched as he disrobed and let his travel-stained clothing fall to the floor. The firelight flickered over the hard planes of his body, shoulders, chest, taut buttocks and thighs, and even now, when she had so many questions, when his own words had so recently branded him a killer, she could not suppress the desire that instantly flared to life within her at the sight. She wanted to touch him – she always did. He was her addiction. But she had enough pride that she did not go to him, but stayed seated a little distance away, maintaining her outward composure with an effort.

He lowered himself into the steaming water with a sigh of relief and lay back, his eyes on her. 'Tarquin will no longer trouble you,' he said abruptly.

'He is a foolish, weak man, but not so foolish that he will dare to cross me. We understand each other better now, and I promise that you have nothing to fear from him. Indeed, I'm not sure you ever did. He swears that he would never have done anything to harm the boys, not physically, and if I am any judge of character, I believe him to be truthful in this. Spreading malicious gossip and menacing the vulnerable is more his mark – and he says he won't even do that now. Madame Lesmire will be left alone – you might write to tell her so, if you wish. So in that respect, my dear, your worries are over.'

'You threatened him,' she answered slowly. 'Did you hurt him?'

'I would not have hesitated to do so if it had been necessary, but there was no need,' Richard replied coolly, soaping his chest, wet skin glistening. She looked away; in other circumstances, she might have offered to help, and she was very aware that she was naked under her wrap, her body yearning for his as it always did. But there was more to be said, much more for him to reveal to her, and she must not soften.

He stilled his hands and said, 'I told you I was waiting for a letter, did I not? Well, it came at last, which was what prompted me to set off to see Tarquin without delay, and resolve matters with him once and for all. It's in the pocket of my coat – I hope you will pick it up and read it, Viola. It explains matters much better than I ever could. God knows it concerns you more nearly than anyone else in the world.'

She rose and crossed the room to where his clothes lay carelessly discarded, and picked up his heavy wool riding coat, still warm from his body. The package was stiff and heavy, and crackled – it was not hard to find, and she retired to her chair and pulled the candle closer so she could open it. Like Tarquin, though she did not know it, she stared at the broken seals and the superscription: Windsor Castle. A hundred questions quivered on her lips. But she read in silence, and he watched her as she did. She could feel his gaze intent upon her all the while.

At length, she raised her head and stared at him. 'I have read it three times and I can scarcely credit it. It says you have always been…' Words failed her for a moment.

'A thousand times, I have wanted to tell you,' he said, his voice more uncertain than she had heard it in twelve years. 'It was… a grief to me that you of all people should think badly of me, though I had learned not to give a fig what the rest of the world thought. But it was necessary, you see, that everyone should believe me a desperate criminal, and that some high-placed people like Marchett should also think me a traitor, though the people with real power always knew better. That my reputation should be destroyed beyond all hope of redemption, as it seemed. Only then, when they were utterly convinced, when they'd investigated me thoroughly, did the French agents in this country and elsewhere relax their guard with me and admit me into their secrets. Such people are always on the lookout for spies in their ranks, and none of them are stupid. It has taken years.'

And been very dangerous, she thought dazedly. *Hideously dangerous.* 'That was why you killed Lesmire.'

'I wish it had not been necessary. The goal was to turn him; to bring his entire network under our control and use it against Bonaparte's regime – feed them misinformation to help bring them down. I had been doing so secretly for years, piecemeal, to some effect. But in the end, it was thought necessary to put a stop to his perilous activities and shut down his operations forever. And it became clear to me and to those who directed my actions that he was a fanatic, entirely personally devoted to his emperor. He had to die, or I did. He could not be allowed to escape with all he knew – not least the fact that I had been playing a double game for so long and none of my information could be relied upon.'

Richard was gazing into the fire now. 'His ruin was my final mission. It has been sufficiently obvious for years that he was at the centre of everything, but it was impossible to know how far his clandestine contacts stretched until recently. Only when we could be sure we had laid hands on all of them could we act to put an end to their schemes.'

His lips quirked in self-mockery. 'If you can credit it, Viola, although we were aware that he claimed to be a minor member of the aristocracy before the Terror, we did not know until you told me so exactly who he had been once, and who his wife was. His name was not always Lesmire, and he had covered his tracks with a great deal of skill. Tarquin will be receiving some insistent official visitors who will be asking how he found *that* out. It's not exactly to our credit that we were in ignorance of such a matter, while a drunken fool and a rank amateur stumbled across the truth. It shows, I think, that insufficient attention is still paid to women by the authorities. Once we were entirely satisfied that Madame Lesmire knew nothing, and that her children were equally ignorant, we paid her little mind, and certainly did not spend any time investigating her past or worrying about who she might be, even though it was obvious that she was English, and a lady of quality. And yet she had been my own cousin's wife... It's more than a little embarrassing. Thank God I never saw a portrait of her – you know that Winterflood kept none – or met her, being too young, though some of my superiors must have done, years ago. Danced with her at balls and saw her presented at Court at Edward's side, no doubt. Flirted with her. But all that is out of my hands now. It's a dirty business and I am very happy to put it behind me.'

'Are you really entirely free of it, as the letter says?'

'I promise you I am, my dear.'

'I see that your grateful country means to reward you very richly.' She had risen and come to stand at his side.

'None of that means anything to me. I don't need rewards. I just want my life back. I entangled myself in such matters through misplaced patriotic enthusiasm when I was too young to understand what I was doing, and by the time I met you, it was far too late to extricate myself. I couldn't tell you what I was about when we met – in 1801, I'd been working in America to set seeds that, it was hoped, might bring them in against the French on our side, though the whole project was misconceived, as hindsight shows, and ended in abject failure.'

'I never suspected a thing at the time.'

Richard shrugged, water streaming from his shoulders, candlelight gleaming on his sculpted muscles. 'You were not meant to. It was about that date that it was decided to use me in a more complex and risky way – to begin to establish me as a dubious sort of fellow with revolutionary sympathies. As an admirer of Bonaparte, in fact – a rake, a libertine and an all-round dangerous man. And when I had lost you and the boys to Edward – not that I ever had you – I saw no reason to object to any of it.'

He caught sight of her face and said urgently, 'I'm not blaming you, or our relationship, for anything. Please believe that. I was already set firmly on a spy's path before I met you. But you see, I hope, why encouraging you to leave Edward was never an option for me, much as I might have wanted to. The last thing I desired was to put you in danger, and associating with me would have done that in an instant – made you a hostage to fortune, really risked your life. It was impossible. I told you nothing less than the truth when I told you that.'

She shook her head and undid the fastenings on her loose robe, then let it fall. 'It's ancient history. Let's not speak of it any more. Is there any warmth left in that bath?'

'Surprisingly, yes, and there is certainly heat in me, enough for both of us. Do you care to join me, madam?'

She stepped in, and lowered herself into the water, sinking down to straddle his body and taking the soap from him. 'You've been talking instead of washing yourself. Clearly, you need me to do it for you.'

'Now, that's the sort of reward that interests me, not empty titles. I hope you'll be very thorough.'

'I always am,' she said, her hands on his chest, his heart thudding beneath her caress. 'Am I to understand that a great deal of your reputation as a rake was a fiction too?' She began diligently to soap him, biting her lip in concentration.

'Most of it, in truth, if not quite all. I've been careful, Viola, but not celibate. I won't deny there've been times when I've been lonely, and taken comfort where I might. There seemed no hope... but let us not speak of that now.'

He went on, as if to skate over the raw emotion he had shown for a moment, 'It's useful, to have an excuse to be in one house or another, supposedly with dishonourable intentions, at odd hours of the day and night. Ladies too have been known to have revolutionary sympathies; some of them do in truth, some of them don't, but quite the opposite. It was all in the cause of becoming a notorious reprobate and public scandal, you understand, and passing information in secret without being suspected. Making connections that nobody suspected. If I'd really been what everyone thought me, a government man like Lord Granville would never have allowed me across his threshold, you can be sure. He knows the truth, even if his wife doesn't.'

He went on wryly, 'Viola, some people will always be ready to say that there is no smoke without fire, both in terms of my personal life and politically. Oh, that's so good, don't stop... just there. Despite the letter, and despite the public recognition that you've seen is coming, I don't suppose my reputation will ever be spotless. You should know that.'

'But you will be,' she said, her busy hands moving lower on his slippery skin. 'Spotless.'

He gasped at what she was doing, and she smiled wickedly at him. At last, she judged that he must be clean enough by anyone's standards, and for her own part, she could wait no longer. With a great surge of water, she moved over him, and they slid together in delicious union. His hands grasped and held her, and the time for talking was over; they couldn't speak now, in any case, because his mouth was hungry on her breasts, and hers was on his neck, kissing him there, biting him, as they whipped up a storm to rival anything that might rage outside in the autumn night.

37

Much later, they lay damp and sated in each other's arms in the big four-poster bed. She murmured, 'Your timing is excellent.'

'It's been mentioned occasionally before, in a different context,' he replied lazily. 'But it's always pleasant to receive unsolicited compliments from a lady.'

'That's not what I mean and you know it, Richard. I have news for you, which I am happier to tell you now than I could have been last week, when I thought I had married a traitor and a murderer.' She sat up so that she could see his face.

'You're with child,' he said, smiling up at her and taking her hand, holding it against his heart. 'I suspected that you might be, but I was waiting for you to tell me.'

'And in the end, you did not let me do so,' she replied in mock-indignation, unable to keep a smile from curling her own lips. It was a momentous thing that she was sharing with him, and they both knew it.

'I'm sorry. I don't always get things right with you, Viola. It's not that I care too little, but that I care too much. I have been used to being so guarded always, so watchful and so careful… It's not easy to let that go. To take time, to behave naturally as anyone else would. How do you feel, my dear?'

'We are both learning about each other still, are we not? But to answer your question, I am well. Very well – no sickness yet. Last time, I was dreadfully sick at first. But yes, I am with child, I have no doubt of it, though a few weeks only. The baby should be due in July, or thereabouts. Well within your deadline. Naturally, there can be no guarantees...'

He was suddenly and surprisingly agitated. 'It doesn't matter. All that matters is your health. Of course I would be devastated if you lost our precious child, and I devoutly hope that you do not, but it's you I'm concerned for. Put the damn deadline entirely from your mind, I beg you, Viola.'

She stared at him. 'I appreciate your concern for me, and it is good of you to reassure me of it, but it is not like you to utter empty words. The deadline is crucial, surely. I am excessively glad that your reputation is to be rehabilitated, but your aunt's will still stands, and we are in desperate need of money to continue with the refurbishment of the Castle. How shall we manage without it, when there is still so much to be done, and the costs so high?'

And now it seemed he could not meet her eyes. 'Ah... that. Well, the plain fact is...' He did not seem able to continue.

'The plain fact is...?'

'I lied.'

'You lied about what?' She was cold all at once, shivering, the lingering heat of their lovemaking leaving her in an instant. 'I thought that all that lay between us now was the truth. I have had more than enough of lies.'

'I know, Viola, but... I have to tell you. I lied about my aunt's will. The need to have a child, the deadline. All of it. I made it up. My aunt, despite her grave reservations about my character, left me everything unreservedly. I have her fortune in my hands, to use as I please.'

'You...' She was speechless for a moment, and not angry yet, though she could feel anger building within her as the shock subsided. 'For what possible purpose?'

He sat up and dragged the coverlet across the bed to wrap it around her trembling body. 'I must go back a little to explain, I think. As soon as I heard Edward was dead, I knew that there was a chance you and I could be together at last. If I had ever concerned myself with the prospect of gossip about the boys' legitimacy, I was confident that that danger was long done with; Edward had accepted them unreservedly as his sons in the intervening years, though I knew Tarquin might yet try to make mischief. I was confident I could deal with him. But I still was not free to be with you, because of the path in life that I had chosen. I could not think of approaching you. God knows I wanted to.'

Her voice was high and indignant. 'This was three years ago. More. You wrote to condole with me, in conventional words anyone might have penned – of course I knew that you were bound to be cautious in what you wrote, for my sake if not your own, but I still did not trust myself to reply to you; I made Emily do it for me. And after that, nothing. Three whole years, Richard, without so much as a word!'

His tone was bleak. 'I know it; I counted every wasted day. But I could not risk entering into communication with you when my life was still so precarious. The last thing in the world I wanted was to put you or the boys in danger because you had begun to associate with me. I arranged a meeting with my masters – it is unnecessary and still unsafe to name them, though you would recognise their titles if I did – and made it clear that I had had enough. They had had ten years of my life by that point, and I could do no more. I wished to make an end of it. But they are hard, ruthless men, my dear, though if they ever spoke of it, they would tell you glibly that it is all in a good cause. They would not let me go.'

He sighed. 'Harsh words were uttered on both sides – that damn grandiose letter does not go anywhere near conveying the dirty truth of it, I assure you. I said they could not force me to continue; they told me I was mistaken, and had the gall to speak to me of patriotism and my duty. "Shoot me, then," I said. "Shoot me or hang me as the thief and traitor half the world thinks me. You might as well, for I want no more of this life." In the end, we came to an agreement – I would be free and publicly exonerated once I made sure that the serious matter of Lesmire was resolved. It's no exaggeration to say that his continuing operations threatened the progress of the war, and they would be satisfied if he were put down – neutralised, by any means available. They knew it gave me a great incentive for my labours, you can be sure. And I did resolve it, in such a way that scandal was avoided. Their gratitude was not unbounded, for that is never their way – they tried very hard to persuade me I had more to do, just one more important task, or maybe two, the merest nothings – but I was resolute in holding them to their word.'

'I understand all this.' That wasn't quite true – Viola's mind was still reeling from Richard's admission that he'd been determined to win her from the moment of Edward's death – but that was not her chief concern just now. 'None of it explains why you felt it necessary to lie to me and trick me in such an elaborate and pointless fashion.'

'Lying and trickery have become my way of life, perhaps,' he said with a trace of lingering bitterness. 'That's no sort of excuse, but... When it came to it, I did not have the courage to come to you and say openly, *I have always loved you, Viola, a day has not gone by when I have not longed for you, for the chance to be with you and with our children.* My reputation was so bad, and matters were moving so confoundedly slowly to set it right, and all at once, I could not wait. I dared not wait. I feared losing you to another man. I thought it was inevitable, if I delayed any longer, that you would be wooed and won by some smooth fellow with a past that would bear scrutiny in every particular, as mine would not. It seemed to me incredible as the months passed that you had remained unmarried as long as you had. The truth is, I panicked and concocted a ploy to win you without telling you the truth. And when I saw you laughing and flirting with Brummell, I was all the surer that I was right to do so. You wouldn't marry him – but you were bound to marry someone. And I was so close...'

Her voice was raised now, almost shouting. 'Why did you think up such a preposterous scheme? What could you possibly hope to achieve by it?'

'You. Secure in my arms and in my bed and in my life. Hope for the future.'

She glared at him, unappeased. 'Why could you not simply be honest with me about your feelings?'

'Because I knew that months might go by before I could tell you the whole truth, as indeed they have, and because I also knew that, remaining in ignorance as you did, you could not fail to be angry with me. You must still believe I was a criminal and always had been, as all the world did – and there was nothing I could do to change that yet. You might even have heard that I was a spy. And I gambled. I thought it safer to have you in my life angry, furious, hurt, than not at all.'

They fell silent. Then he whispered raggedly, 'I dared not make it a test. It looked too much like a test to me, and I have not been so loved in my life that would ever feel confident testing anyone. I dared not come to you and tell you of my enduring love and hope that you would say you felt the same, and that you did not care a damn what the world said of me. I dreamed a thousand times of you saying such wonderful words – but I could not quite believe in it. I did not know if you felt that – I still don't. So many years had passed since we had declared our sentiments towards each other that I was terrified. I had so little reason to be secure in your feelings for me, and yet I simply could not contemplate for a moment the prospect of losing you.

'I know now that in my failure to be truthful, I may have done the very thing I wished above all things not to do, and driven you away. In my unpardonably selfish desperation to win you, it did not occur to me until it was too late – until we were already married – that there can be no love without openness. I was naïve – I of all people, the great deceiver, it is laughable. I have lost the habit of trust, I fear, if indeed I ever had it in my life, but these weeks with you and the boys have scraped me raw and left me utterly exposed. Naked and defenceless. Have I ruined everything?'

Viola's head was whirling. 'You were so determined to have me that you did it by deception? You feared losing me so much that you did not stop to consider whether I might actually not still love you and want to marry you at all, and capturing me would therefore be worth nothing?'

He shook his head. 'You are only partly right. I would have done anything to win you, even though I see now that you are right, it means nothing unless you come to me willingly. The second – no. Of course I stopped to consider that you might not want me any more. I stopped there and could not get past it. I was quite confident you didn't. Why should you? And I saw that I was correct as soon as we met – there was so much pain lying between us that no simple declaration could ever have bridged the gap and rekindled your love for me. I still do not know what I could have done – waited, I suppose. Trusted. Hoped. I know I have wronged you; I know I made a terrible mistake. It's too much to ask, for you to forgive me. I can see that.'

He took a deep breath. 'Despite everything, having you and the boys in my life has made me happier than I have ever been. Only when I experienced that did I realise how much more we could have, if I could just tell you the truth. I knew I would have to in the end, all of my shameful secrets, and now I have. Whatever comes of it.'

38

Viola stood alone on the cliff by the castle and looked out at the stormy sea, her hair coming loose and whipping about her. It was morning now – a new day had started, full of possibilities both good and bad, but she had no idea how it might end.

She had called a halt to their painful discussion late last night and banished Richard from her bed, telling him that she was exhausted by emotion and needed to think, needed time away from him. Just then, she could not find it in her to care what corner he might find to lay his weary head for the rest of the night, or if it would be cold, draughty and uncomfortable, as seemed likely. That would do no more than serve him right, in fact. The castle need not be such a ruin as it still was; it could all have been put right by now, if he'd been honest with her in the first place. Had his world truly become such a convoluted mess that he could no longer distinguish between necessary and unnecessary deception?

She'd done this sort of thing once before, of course, a few weeks back – sent him away and then a short while later, fallen back into his arms all the same, despite all her doubts – but she was not sure if she would do so again. If she should. They'd been so close to something that had felt precious and real, for a tantalisingly brief moment; normal happiness such as she'd never known in her life had almost been within reach, and now this fresh revelation had come crashing down upon her, casting everything she'd thought she'd been building into question.

Viola had never imagined that the revelation of her pregnancy, which should have been a joyful moment they would both remember forever – so unlike the last time she had had cause to pass on such news – would lead to such a conversation, and to the pouring out of so many confidences, both welcome and unwelcome. It was a great deal to take in all at once, and hard for her to know what she should feel about it. It would be all too easy to let the knowledge that Richard had never forgotten her, and worked so diligently and for so long to win her, to sweep everything else away. But should she?

She stood, and watched the sea crash onto the rocks in relentless motion, and the clouds moved across the big Yorkshire sky, and still she did not know.

She'd breakfasted in bed, and the boys had come in to see her, bringing gusts of bracing air, chattering excitedly about their plans for the day. Richard was taking them to Whitby, they told her, and they'd been sent to ask if she wanted to come too; of course she would be very welcome. If they considered it at all odd that her new husband had not thought to ask her himself, they made no mention of it. She'd smiled with only a little effort and told them that she was rather tired, Lord Ventris having got back so late the night before. She thought she would prefer to have a lazy day here instead, and rise later than they would like, and so they should go without her and be sure to enjoy themselves. They'd run off without questioning her further, and their cheerful shouts had echoed up the stone stair for a while, until at last, the place had fallen silent and she must presume they'd gone, and their father along with them. She wasn't alone here, but in the oppressive silence, it felt as though she were the only person in the huge building. At least she had a little precious space to think.

He *was* their father. He had fought for them and for her, risked his life, even, and won them at last, or so he'd thought. He had always loved them even when he'd been deprived of the chance of knowing them, and they were coming to care for him, partly at least because he was being so careful and respectful of them. Certainly, they enjoyed his company and were beginning slowly to trust him and value his opinions. It was too soon to say that they needed him, but if they stayed much longer in his company, they soon would. If she intended to leave him – and of course, she'd take them with her if she did, she couldn't contemplate anything else – it had better be soon. Long before this child in her belly stirred, long before he or she knew what it meant to have a father, or to be deprived of one.

It was all too easy to say that she could not do this cruel thing to Richard – but she should forget him for a moment if she could; he was a grown man and had made his own bed – or to any of her children, born and unborn. Ned and Robin had lost one father already – must they lose another? Must her third child never know one at all?

Yes, he was their father and yes, she could not doubt that he loved his little family, including her, as fiercely as one might hope to be loved. But he wasn't perfect, far from it – he had behaved recklessly, even thoughtlessly, and allowed the ruthlessness with which he'd had to conduct his dangerous daily existence for so many years to seep into his emotional life when, from her perspective, it hadn't been necessary. Of course she had been waiting for him all this time, though she'd never admitted as much to herself, let alone to anyone else. But it wasn't reasonable to expect him to know that – he could not. Was she really going to throw everything that they were building together away because he'd cherished a wild, desperate hope about her underlying feelings for him that was, in fact, fully justified?

That was all very well, very feminine and noble, very much the way that women were expected to behave, always to forgive the transgressions of their men, always to put their children first above themselves, but of what of her in all this? What did *she* need and want and deserve? It was very difficult to say, hurt and confused as she was just now. Perhaps it was after all impossible to lose something you had never truly had. Nobody could be expected to enjoy being manipulated, and she with all her painful history with Edward least of all. And *that* he should have known. If in the end, she could not find it in herself to absolve him for what he had done, that would be why.

And so if she stayed for the children's sakes, and only for them, without ever being able to trust him fully, would it be a sacrifice of herself, a compromise too far, and one that she would later bitterly regret?

39

Richard had left her alone all day, exactly as she had wished, and when he'd returned home, they'd dined with the boys, which had made serious conversation impossible; it had been difficult enough to retain her composure and speak normally as they all sat together, as if nothing at all was wrong. But now the twins were in bed, she was alone with Richard, and she could avoid him no longer.

He looked exhausted, now that he too was no longer maintaining a cheerful facade for his sons' benefit. They sat at table and confronted each other. It was very quiet; the wind had dropped and the only sounds were the shifting of the coals in the grate, the soft hissing of the flames.

'What do you have to say to me, Viola?' he asked her very softly.

'I'm still not sure I know,' she answered wearily. 'What if I said that I could not find it in me to forgive you? What if I said that you had shown yourself no better than Edward in your manipulation of me, and that I must after all leave you, and take the boys? It could be no surprise to you if I did so. Good God, Richard, what were you thinking?'

It was almost as though that was exactly what he'd expected her to say, what he'd been anticipating through the lonely night and this long day. He let out an inarticulate sound of distress. 'Oh, Viola, my heart... I could not think to blame you, or try to persuade you, or, God forbid, trick you further if you decide you cannot bear this. I am done with all that. We are married, but if you do not love me and cannot get past this, our union is nothing more than a piece of paper. I was a damn fool ever to think otherwise. The direction of your life, and the boys', is yours entirely. It must be. You will go where you wish to go, and spend your time in the manner you wish to spend it, and share your existence with whomever you wish. I hope it will be me, but I can make no demands on you. I have not earned that right, if indeed any man ever has it over another free being, but forfeited it by my folly. I will not try to sway you now by speaking of my feelings. You would be right to say that they are no concern of yours.'

'Despite the fact that I am carrying your child?'

He had not touched her since she had told him, but he did now, very gently, and after a second's indecision, she did not push him away. He had moved his chair closer to hers, his hand lay lightly on her belly and there were tears in his eyes, she saw. 'Despite that, my love. You have no reason to trust me, I am aware, but please know that the last thing I will ever do is to exert the rights the law gives me over you. I did not do this bloody stupid thing in order to get you in my power, though I know it must seem that I did. You are nobody's possession. Nor are your children.'

'Our children,' she corrected him, and now she saw a fragile hope flicker in his bleak face.

It was time she made her feelings clear to him. 'When I considered whether I should marry you from my own point of view – because after all, your aunt's will was your problem, not mine – the reasons I could raise against it were two: your reputation, and the loss of my independence.'

'Only two, when there could be so many more?' he asked, with some return to his old sardonic manner. It was a fragile cloak he wore, she realised, to protect himself from hurt. 'Well, that's encouraging.'

'Just those two, and you have answered both of them now, it seems. I did not ever think that I could not marry you because I did not love you, Richard. I always loved you. I never stopped. I loved you even as I stood at the altar half-hating you.'

He was hesitant, torn as she could see between hope and disbelief. His life so far had given him little reason to believe himself loveable, and it might take years to put that right. She had been luckier in that respect – at least she had her sisters, and the boys, and Emily, even if her relationship with her mother would always be prickly. 'And my actions have not killed your love for me?'

She shook her head, and put her warm hand over his, where it still rested. 'Love is not so easily snuffed out, even if reason tells me it should be. I seem to have a gift for constancy. If years spent thinking you were a rake, a libertine, a murderer and even a traitor did not destroy my love, your recent actions could not. And I think – I should not say this, for it will give you a dreadful conceit of yourself – I think that in some respects, you were right.'

His smile was rueful, incredulous, as if he could not begin to understand his luck. 'How could that be, love? I came perilously close to ruining everything.'

'Your ridiculous scheme gave me an excuse to marry you. And I needed an excuse. However much I have pined for you for all this time, I am not sure how I would have come to that point by myself, if you had made me a more conventional offer. I have my pride, and Edward, as you know well, crushed it utterly. I had enough with him, more than enough, of sitting at home waiting for a husband to notice me, to treat me decently and give me permission to have any sort of life of my own. The hurt runs deep – it would always have been hard for me to trust you unless you had found a way of showing me I could, beyond mere words of wooing. Before yesterday, you have not been the most open and communicative of men, have you? And more than that, no man had touched me, from the moment you left me till you came back. How could I set all that wasted devotion, as I saw it, aside, thinking as I did that you had lain with half the women in London in the years between, when I had been so lonely? And yet I wanted to, with all my heart.'

'But in my clumsy desperation, I made flippant reference to your fertility, and I should have known that that would wound you,' he said soberly, clearly determined to have everything out in the open at last. 'I thought you'd realise that of course I meant both of us – the way Edward tried to use us both as little more than breeding livestock, the hope that we could somehow set it right. But I could not expect you to know how I had never stopped thinking of you, day after day after day, months, and weary years, wondering what you were doing, if you were happy, aware that I was missing so much, aware of the years with you and Ned and Robin that Edward and circumstance had cheated me of. I knew that I had no place in your lives – that one or all of you could be gravely ill or die, and nobody would think to tell me, for weeks, forever. It drove me a little mad at times. I could not dare to hope that you were feeling anything similar. Indeed, I should be generous enough to hope you weren't. I hate to think of you in such pain.'

'But I was, my dearest love,' she told him unsteadily. 'I have been happy with the boys, and shared moments with them that can never be restored to you, both while Edward was alive and after he died. Their first steps, their first words – I will not torture you with the recitation of it all. They have been the joy of my life. But always the shadow has been there – that it was wrong, what he did to us, and no less wrong because we lay down together with our eyes open, as we thought. I was eighteen and you were one and twenty – what did we know of what we were losing, of what he was taking from us permanently because of his own selfish obsession? He could easily have lived another twenty years, at your expense, and mine. I could have died, as you said, without ever seeing you again, or you could have, and yes, nobody would even have told me of it, because he had made sure we could be nothing to each other when we should have been everything.'

'Can it ever be mended?' he asked her unsteadily. 'When you describe it like that – and justly – it makes me doubt that it ever can. And I have done nothing but make matters worse, in my desperation and folly.'

'We can try to mend it,' she said firmly. 'We can spend the rest of our lives together trying to mend it, every precious day that we are granted, whether our time is long or short.' And then she rose, and came to him, and kissed him.

It was the first kiss they had shared in almost twelve years, and after a second of surprise, his lips opened under hers, and their eager mouths explored each other, memories flooding back of how they had loved to do this once, of how natural and perfect it had once been, and could be again. It was a closer union that the joining of their bodies had yet been, and said far more than all their words. It was everything.

In a moment, it was too much, too piercingly sweet, and they broke apart, overwhelmed, and held each other tightly, bodies pressed together, faces close but lips not quite touching. It was impossible to live at this pitch for long.

'Just one stipulation you had, madam, in our marriage settlement, and you have broken it after a mere month or two,' he teased her with mock-sternness, his voice unsteady but his hands warm and sure on her body. 'It is written in legal ink for all to see that I should never kiss you. I did not break it; I will always remind you – you did.'

'I did,' she agreed readily, 'and I mean to do it again. And again and again.' She suited her actions to her words, pressing little kisses to his lips, his cheeks and eyes. She could not easily have said if she or he was laughing or crying as she did so.

'You told me – in church, my wicked lady! – that I could fuck you but not kiss you. It must have been obvious, I suppose, that I was perfectly ready to do either or both on the spot.'

'I lied,' she said, smiling. 'You *can* do both. Indeed, I hope you will. I insist.'

'I'm always eager to fulfil your expectations,' he said as she moved to straddle him, and they came together in naked honesty at last.

40

Since Richard was obliged to go to London at the Regent's summons, and they were reluctant to be separated so soon after they had found each other again, Viola and the boys accompanied him, taking the long journey in easy stages that would not be too tiring for her. She was in excellent health, suffering no ill effects of pregnancy this time, but it could not be guaranteed that she would always feel so, and winter was coming on fast; wise people on the Ventris estate had looked at the signs in nature, and now shook their grizzled heads and said that it was going to be an uncommonly bad one this year. Thank God that the manifold improvements Lord and Lady Ventris had already set in train had made life more bearable there already.

It was decided that Ventris Castle could be left behind for a while by the family and occupation resumed in spring, when much of the interior work would, they hoped, have been completed. They'd stay at Armstrong House for a few weeks now, and then perhaps go down to Winterflood for Christmas with as many Constantines as cared to come. Richard had agreed to this scheme with the alacrity of a man in love who had absolutely no idea what he was letting himself in for.

This meant, of course, that Viola could spend time in Town with her sisters, and with her mother – an unalloyed pleasure, where the girls were concerned, but a mixed blessing, perhaps, in the case of Mrs Constantine. Lady Ventris saw her alone first, which seemed wise, as she was not entirely sure that Richard was quite prepared yet for his mother-in-law's devastating frankness and clear-eyed judgement. He still had a lot to learn about her family; she could only hope that since he had very little kin of his own, save for his unpleasant brother, he might be disposed to think them normal, even if they weren't. They were hers, and she loved them. Even Leontina.

Nothing had changed in Great Russell Street since she had last visited. Her mother looked her up and down in her usual penetrating manner and said flatly, 'I see that meeting your husband's ridiculous deadline will not be a problem for you, if all goes well.'

She was annoyed to feel herself blushing hotly. 'It is astonishing to me that you can tell merely from looking at me. In earlier ages, you would have been burned at the stake, Mama. But yes, you are correct, I am with child, though only a few weeks gone. And well, as you can see. We are all well, in fact.'

'That is satisfactory. You will be able to be comfortable together soon enough, without the incessant anxiety over money hanging over you, which counts for a great deal in life.'

'I know,' she said quietly. 'Believe me, I do know.'

'And how are the boys liking their new father?'

Viola thought it wise not to quibble with her mother's choice of words and say *stepfather*. 'Very well, I believe. There have been moments of awkwardness, but few of them. It would have been harder if Ned and Robin were older, I imagine. But no, they have accepted him better than I could have hoped. They have spent a great deal of time together over the past few weeks in the country – he takes them fishing, and is teaching them to shoot at targets, which is something I try hard not to think too much about. They go riding together, exploring the Ventris estate, and all enjoy themselves enormously. It is excellent for Ned and Robin to have a masculine influence in their lives again, and he's very good with them.'

'It is hardly to be wondered at,' her mother responded drily. 'He is their true father, after all.'

This was beyond uncanny. Viola's heart lurched, and then settled; she took a calming breath, and released it slowly. She was a grown woman, and had been for years. She should not be intimidated by her mother any longer. Nor would she lie – though in all honesty, that would probably be nothing more than a waste of time anyway, given Leontina's unnatural powers of perception. 'I do not know how you can possibly be so confident of that. I have told nobody, and you can be sure Richard has not either, except his brother, who was convinced of it already. I have not said a word to my sisters, or to Emily, even. I hope Tarquin Armstrong has not been spreading gossip abroad when Richard was so certain he would not!'

Mrs Constantine shrugged, apparently unconcerned. 'As to that, I do not know – I have not heard any rumours to that effect. I doubt there are any, and I doubt it would matter if there were, so long after the... event, and Edward safely dead these many years. I speak merely from my own observation. I suspected something of the sort when you first fell pregnant, given your husband's history, but there was no profit in talking of it while he was alive. I could see that you had no wish to tell me your secrets, which was probably wise, and he was plainly more than content with matters as they stood. But when I saw Ventris at your wedding, how much he resembles them both, and saw into the bargain the way he looked at you, and you at him, as if you claimed each other, despite grave doubts, after hurtful years apart, I was certain of it. Edward always knew, I suppose?'

Viola snorted derisively. 'Knew? He engineered the whole situation, I promise you. He did everything but lock us in a bedchamber together and feed us oysters. I promise you, Mother, I am not exaggerating. It was exactly what he wanted.'

She had rarely seen her mother taken aback, but she did now, albeit briefly, before the mask of composure – if it was a mask, Viola had never been certain – was resumed. 'Good heavens,' Leontina said mildly after a moment. 'Well, it is for the best you did not tell me this at the time. I was under the impression that you had taken matters into your own hands, realising that Edward was incapable in some fashion I don't propose to enquire into more closely, and I would not have criticised you or any child of mine for showing such good sense, however unconventional it might be. But I certainly did not realise your husband had forced you into another man's bed. I would have had strong words with him if I had known, I assure you.'

'Not forced,' said Viola resolutely. 'He was not quite that bad. And in all honesty, there was no need, in the end, so drawn to each other as we were. But he manipulated us both; invited Richard to stay for that purpose, then left us alone together deliberately for days at a time. I was so lonely and unhappy – he had made me so; perhaps even that was a part of his wicked plan, I have since thought – that falling in love with Richard was all but inevitable. And

Edward did not care about my feelings, not one jot, nor his cousin's, as long as he got the son he wanted. Richard has said that he tried to breed us like so much livestock, and with as little compunction, and it is true. He was a weak and selfish man, Mama, and used us like merest pawns. I could have no esteem for him after I knew that, and I told him so. In all respects but our shared love for the boys, our marriage was a sham for years.'

'I am sorry,' Mrs Constantine said slowly. Viola wasn't sure she'd ever heard her mother apologise before, if that was what this was. 'I deeply regret that I ever considered him a suitable husband for you. I always knew he was too old, of course – but I saw that as a positive, since I judged him not strong, perhaps suffering pains and telling nobody, and I thought that very likely he would die soon enough – especially if he over-exerted himself in the bedroom – and leave you an independent widow.'

The ruthlessness of it left Viola a little breathless, and she found herself laughing, somewhat against her will. 'Well, you were right in that, Mama, and must congratulate yourself on your prescience. He did not live ten years after our marriage, though not, I assure you, because of any exertions in my bed. I realised in the end that my maid Jennings was his mistress, and had been for years – but by that point, I didn't care. He had that comfort; I did not.'

Leontina accepted this further revelation with equanimity, which was perhaps why Viola had told her now, and never anyone else, not even Richard. 'No wonder you pensioned the creature off as soon as Edward was in his grave – I should have realised why, if I had thought. But ten years is a long, long time if you are unhappy. I do know that. Really, Viola, I *am* sorry. I have always been aware that picking men for you girls was a desperate sort of lottery, with similarly poor odds of success. I could justify my actions by saying that I had little option; it does not alter the fact that I choose wrongly for you. I allowed myself to be blinded to his poor character by his wealth and status, but a duke is a man like any other, and I should have looked deeper than I did.'

Viola shrugged. It had mattered so much once, and it still did, but it was far too late to change things now. 'I know you had little choice, and nor did we. How many women have the strength of mind to turn away a gentleman who has such a position in society, and is handsome and amiable besides? I have never claimed, even in my darkest times, that I was forced to marry him. He was a good man in many ways – you could have chosen much worse. If he had only treated me a little better... But it all came from his obsession with getting an heir. You must have known *that* when he offered for me. Dukes do not generally marry women of much lower social standing without an excellent reason for it. He knew that Sabrina had just had a son, did he not? That prompted his offer to me. Let us be frank at last, Mama, now that we are talking – I am sure you told him so yourself, so there could be no mistake.'

Mrs Constantine was long past the age of blushing, if indeed she ever had shown signs of normal human embarrassment or shame in all her life, but she had the grace to look a little uneasy now, which was a notable event in itself. 'I might say I don't recall after so long – yes, of course I told him with sufficient plainness, but subtly, as though it were a mere piece of happy family news. I knew we had no rank or connections to tempt him, and he could have looked much higher for a bride. I knew he was marrying you in a last gamble that he might get a son from you. Of course, I stressed your advantages of youth and beauty and a fertile line. You may say that makes me no better than he was. You may justly remind me that you were only seventeen and deserved better. It's true. I have no defence I can make to you for dealing so cavalierly with your future happiness.'

Viola had not expected such honesty from her mother, and was touched by it. 'You know better now, though, don't you, ma'am? I think you do. It has not escaped my attention, or Sabrina's, that all our youngest sisters are past the age at which we older ones went to the altar. Beatrice is almost four and twenty, Cecilia is turned twenty, and even Bianca is rising eighteen. I cannot believe that you have lost your touch in husband-hunting, that could never be, so I must hope that you have realised that there is no desperate urge to find them matches to avert destitution. We will always take care of you all and make sure you want for nothing. *I* will.'

'I know you will,' Mrs Constantine said, her voice as close to unsteady as her daughter had ever heard it. 'I have been luckier than I deserve, I think. As for the girls, Beatrice says she will never marry, that she has no interest in men, whether they be rich or poor – I do not know if this is true, but it is what she says at present, and Cecilia and Bianca are young yet. You and your sisters have bought them precious time, and I am aware that in your case at least, it was at no little cost to yourself.'

Viola made some incoherent noise of agreement, tears pricking at her eyes, and then, since so much unaccustomed emotion made them both uncomfortable, she turned the topic, and began to speak more lightly of her pregnancy, of life at Ventris with her sons, and Richard's visit to the Regent, and the grand title he was to be honoured with. Mrs Constantine took the news that her new son-in-law had never been a criminal but instead a trusted government agent with equanimity, just as she had originally taken the tidings that Viola was to marry him despite his sullied reputation. She had the enviable facility of worrying little about matters that she had no power to change; Viola would have said before today that the experience of regret was entirely foreign to her, in which regard, she was scarcely human in her coolness, but she knew better now, and felt happier somehow for knowing it.

41

Richard was received by his grateful Regent in the Crimson Drawing Room at Carlton House one foggy winter afternoon. He did not consider himself a person easily impressed by gilded splendour or exalted persons, but afterwards, he was surprised how jumbled his reflections were, when he attempted to describe the interview to his wife in detail.

He'd known he would be kept waiting, perhaps for hours; one did not walk in off the common street and find oneself ushered straight into the presence of the country's ruler. There was a certain etiquette to be observed. But his stay in the grand antechamber with its huge chandelier did not seem long, and other unlucky persons who had been in attendance before him were still there when his name was called, and watched him gloomily as he made his way across the ornate carpet. They must have been wondering why he was so favoured.

Viola had not been summoned to attend with him, and neither of them was sorry that she was so excluded. The Regent had been a notorious philanderer since his youth, and was known by all to favour more mature ladies with statuesque figures, a fact which was confirmed soon enough when he and Lord Ventris were left alone together by the laced and powdered flunkies who had shown the Baron in. Richard bowed deeply, and the magnificent royal head was inclined towards him with great affability. The Prince then gestured him to a seat, and took a thronelike chair opposite him. He found himself scrutinised intently by those famously prominent, pale-blue, Hanoverian eyes, and the first thing Prince George said was, 'I hear you are just married, Ventris, and that your wife is a great beauty. A damn fine figure of a woman, everyone tells me. You must bring her to meet me, by God you must!'

This statement was made in what Richard could only describe later as an oily, insinuating tone, which underlined the tasteless nature of the remark. He could not doubt that if he had felt like describing his wife's appearance and attributes in extraordinary and even indecent detail, which he emphatically did not, the Regent would have been very happy to hear it, and perhaps even forgotten the ostensible purpose of his visit. Instead, he murmured some banal response, and tried to turn the subject, which was no easy task.

He was very smartly dressed for his royal audience, in black, satin knee breeches and swallowtail coat, his dark locks brushed more neatly than was usual for him, and an old-fashioned bicorn hat, specially purchased for the occasion, under one arm. The boys had laughed at him when they had seen it, and clamoured to try the ridiculous thing on. But now he was sweating into his snowy white linen, and felt not the slightest inclination towards mirth. Apart from anything else, the apartment was hideously warm; he wondered if any of the windows in this palace had even been made to open.

The Prince was eager enough, when finally distracted from the contemplation of Viola's charms, to hear of Richard's unconventional career, on which he had obviously been briefed in advance. It was plain that he considered it all damnably exciting, especially the saltier aspects involving clandestine visits to ladies' bedchambers, and would have been prepared to listen to details all day long, as many as Richard cared to provide.

This was a problem in itself, as his masters had not failed to point out to him with awful threats and menaces. Nobody suspected the Regent of disloyalty to his nation – the very idea was preposterous, naturally – but clearly, nobody suspected him of possessing a particle of discretion either. There was simply no knowing what he might do with any confidential information Richard carelessly let fall, or whom he might tell, in his cups or in his bed. Much as Britain's spymasters might hope that they had rooted out all of Bonaparte's agents by now, they could not be completely sure of it, even at the so-called highest levels of society. And in this crucial time, when Wellington's army was about to cross the Pyrenees at last, and men would soon be fighting and dying on French territory, the need for intelligence was even more vital, on both sides. No wonder Richard perspired, and was obliged to use all his ingenuity to find things that he might safely say that would still satisfy his royal interrogator.

The man should have been ridiculous, even despicable, but somehow, he wasn't. He was a good listener, which was a surprise – it was obvious now why Richard had been warned in no uncertain terms to be careful what he told him. He was even charming, and Lord Ventris began to detect in himself a tendency to like him, which he could only quash by remembering that this was the man who had taken friends of his – and fine friends they must have been – into his poor mad father's chambers, to laugh at him and mock him, half-blind and confused as he was. That unpleasant thought did the trick, and kept him on his guard.

It was a curious interview from start to finish. He had understood already from those who knew the Regent that the Prince had the uncommon ability to absorb information about martial deeds and then genuinely convince himself that he had taken a prominent role in the events just described to him. In an ordinary man, you'd call it lying. He was known to be quite shameless in describing battles at which he was, naturally, not present, to people who were there, took part, and might be presumed to know about them much better than he. Richard now saw that this was all too true, as George – a man who had never known a moment's real danger and been safe in his bed in England when the event took place – evoked the recent siege of Pamplona in such vivid terms that it was hard indeed to believe it all came second-hand.

One of the distinguished men who'd once controlled Richard's fate had told him wryly the day before, 'If we win this war, Ventris, as surely we will if we don't bitch it up at this late stage, Prinny will be convinced in his own mind that he carried it all off himself. Wellington and all the other commanders will have had precious little to do with it. Let alone us poor bastards.'

Lord Ventris, recollecting this frank comment now, was hard put not to smile as he listened with feigned attentiveness to his Regent's flights of fancy and wondered when he would be free to go home to his wife and his dinner. It was all very well to be honoured, and he was grateful for it after all these years of danger and anxiety, but it wouldn't feel real till he had Viola in his arms again.

42

'And to think you once tempted me to lecture you about patriotism,' Viola said ruefully when she had heard all her husband could think of to tell her. She had been worried by his unexpectedly long absence, and greatly relieved to see him back, albeit exhausted and hungry.

'But you refused to be drawn,' he replied with a smile. 'You said with some truth that there is little to choose between one side and another. I was grateful for your cynical attitude at the time, of course, since you thought me a French spy and were still prepared to take me as your husband.'

Viola had been musing on this subject, and was glad to have an opportunity to discuss it. 'You don't believe that, though, Richard – that the French and the Allies are as bad as each other. I can't credit that you think so, even if others do. You've given your youth to your side, and it's not even as though you were a soldier and were paid to do it, and received honour and praise and a fine gold-laced uniform. Nobody's been throwing flowers at you in the streets, or giving you parades and prizes. Indeed, you've had nothing but scorn and opprobrium from almost everyone till now. You must have had strong private reasons for your actions, though you have never told me them. Can you really say that the Regent is more worthy of respect than Bonaparte? You've just described him as a buffoon, a man without shame or conscience, hanging on the coat-tails of better men, and men who have risked their lives while he's sat safe at home, bankrupting with his extravagance a country in which poor people are still going hungry.'

'It's perfectly true, my love. His private life bears no examination, he has let down everyone who has ever trusted him, has treated his wives and parents abominably, and is a spendthrift on a hideous scale, with no thought for the sufferings of others. I fully admit that he is a fool and worse, but he's not a tyrant. His father, when he was in his right mind, was a good man and a conscientious king, and both of them, for all their varying faults, are checked in their behaviour by Parliament, our true rulers. Rulers who can be replaced, at the will of the people.'

What he said was true – as far as it went. 'Yes, in theory, but Parliament is not fairly elected, since most men – and all women – have no say in the matter. You could not vote, could you, before you inherited your aunt's estate? And so you had no voice at all in how the country is run, just as I don't, just as almost no one does. The will of the people counts for very little, you must allow.'

'I do allow it, though with pain. We must hope that change is coming, as I believe it is. I am no advocate of our current corrupt way of managing things, and I will work for reform in the new situation I have been given.'

He broke off, as if searching for words to explain what he believed.

'Viola, Bonaparte has ravaged a whole continent in pursuit of his own deranged personal ambition. It is impossible even to begin to count the millions who have died directly because of him. I know many people of my age have grown up with revolutionary sympathies – but if *he* ever held them, which I doubt, he betrayed them years ago, and thinks only of his own advantage, and that of his damn bloodsucking family. Slavery was outlawed – he brought it back. Women gained some freedom, which they themselves had fought and died for – he took it away.'

Richard smiled rather wryly. 'The last person I debated such matters with was Lesmire. The man was a pure fanatic. He would have sacrificed his own wife and children without blinking for his idol – clamoured to do it, lit a fire at their feet and thrown kindling onto it with enthusiasm, crying, "*Vive l'empereur*" all the while. Such people are dangerous, and those who encourage them for their own profit are more dangerous still. George is a perfumed, coddled booby, no doubt, but we have some freedom to say so. Nobody is trying to make a god of him. Nobody will worship him when he is dead, and use him to justify yet more unspeakable crimes.'

She was astonished to see him so passionate. 'Well, I'm not disagreeing with you. I daresay Julius Caesar was a monster too, in much the same mould, and yet he is still revered and emulated, as you say. It is also true that war is a dirty business, and unleashes the worst in men on both sides, and it will always be the innocent and the weak who suffer for it. I had no idea that you felt so strongly, though I should have realised that something powerful motivated you to make the choices you have made. I see now that I have married a politician and a philosopher.'

He took her in his arms. 'I cannot make such grand claims. I was a rootless boy with no prospects and I found myself in humble employment in order to live – but then after a little while, I was approached to engage in clandestine work, in America at first and then France later, and undertook it for the excitement as much as anything else. I found I was good at it, and any hopes I might have had for another sort of life were lost when I lost you. My convictions, if they are convictions, were developed later, when I saw with my own eyes the ruin that the glorious French empire has brought with it. And sometimes, I wonder if my hopes will stand up to scrutiny when we see what victory looks like, and when thousands and thousands of hardened fighting men are told we have no use for their services any more, but no jobs to give them either, and they must steal or starve. But that is a worry for the future.'

She looked up at him, frowning, and he said, with his usual quick understanding of what she was thinking even though she hadn't spoken of it, 'Don't be worrying that I am sacrificing my principles for you and for the boys because I went to see the old fool and listened to his ramblings with patience. I am not. I am done with my previous manner of existence, and need a new one. It's true that my new life would be meaningless if it did not have you in it, but I would be doing this even without you. Our system is bad, and its figurehead a disgrace, but others I have seen are worse. I will sit in the House of Lords and do what good I can there – and for that to happen to any purpose, for me to make allies as I must, my reputation has to be restored.'

He pulled her down onto the sofa and kissed her till she was breathless. But after a while, he lay back and said teasingly, 'Kissing is all very well, of course, but I shall require you – and the boys, rascals that they are – to treat me with a great deal of respect and deference now that I am a duke, you know.'

'You can't be a duke yet,' she replied, beginning to unfasten his cravat and unwind it from about his neck. 'The Regent can't just have said, "You're a duke now, Ventris, what d'you think of that, eh?" and so you are. There must be some sort of ceremony, which I note you have not mentioned.'

'I don't know – there wasn't when I became Baron Ventris, but then that was by inheritance, which I suppose is different. I was half-expecting him to get out some great sword of state and invest me with it on the spot, and likely cut off my head in the process, since he can hardly be used to wielding weapons.'

'Save his own famous sword of state, I suppose,' she said outrageously.

'I believe that Lady Hertford handles that, minx,' he replied in the same tone. 'But no swords were unsheathed on this occasion, to my relief, and I didn't think to ask if there must be some ceremonial event at a later date. I was just grateful to escape and come home to you.'

'How remiss of you, your grace,' she murmured, moving to straddle his lap so that she could the better undo his shirt and slip her hands inside it.

'Well, I am still learning how to go on, you know, in my new exalted position. You will have to teach me. How does it feel to be a duchess again, Viola?' he asked her, setting his hands firmly about her waist, which seemed a good idea to her, while she still had one.

'Better,' she said. 'Much better this time.'

'Good.' He traced his lips down her throat, just brushing her skin and making her shiver. And then he nipped it with his teeth, where her neck met her shoulder, and she arched her back in anticipation of the pleasure to come, delighting in the feeling of his hard thighs under hers. 'You will go down in history as a rare phenomenon – one of those few women who has married two dukes.'

'I am a rare phenomenon,' she told him seriously, unbuttoning his black silk breeches as he freed her breasts from her low-cut gown and bent his head to kiss them with rapt attention as she pressed herself against him. 'And I might have married two dukes, but I only ever loved one.'

'And I always loved you, when you were a duchess, when you were not, and now that you are again. It makes no difference to me.'

'I think it should,' she told him, her hands upon his sword of state, which was a weapon that might make any woman lose her head when she saw it. 'Because I am *your* duchess.'

'But you always were.'

EPILOGUE
SUMMER 1814

'It's hard to believe that it's all over,' Viola said as she gazed out into the dusk. 'We have been at war for most of my life, it seems. During the brief peace, I remember wondering where you were and what you were doing, and fearing I would never see you again. I know now, as I did not then, that you could easily have been killed on many different occasions. It hurts my heart to think of it even though it's past and gone. And so many people *were* killed or horribly wounded. So much loss, death and suffering all over Europe and far beyond – I suppose it is understandable that everyone should want to run wild and celebrate the fact that it has finally ended.'

Armstrong House was quiet and almost deserted, all of the servants who cared to do so having been given leave to go and enjoy the enormous fete that was happening just a few yards away. She and Richard were standing looking out of the tall bedroom windows that gave on to Hyde Park; they had been watching casually to see if they could observe any of the fireworks or perhaps the balloon ascension. Laurence Da Costa had kindly taken Ned and Robin with him and his older children to see the mock naval battle and all the other amusements of this jubilee holiday.

But Viola had only given birth to her daughter Leonie Emily a couple of weeks ago, and had no desire whatsoever to go out among the vast assembly of people and be jostled and shoved about. She'd told Richard to leave her and join them, thinking it selfish to deny him sight of the spectacles, extraordinary things which might never be witnessed again, but he had refused. 'I have an odd dislike of crowds, my love,' he'd told her ruefully, 'especially in the dark. I cannot help but think that the place will be swarming with pickpockets and all manner of other criminals. A habit of vigilance in such matters has been so trained into me that I would never be able to relax and take any pleasure – particularly not if there are sudden loud noises, which there are bound to be, to set me on even higher alert. If Laurence loses his watch tonight, or the whole thing ends with a frightened child in tears, at least I have warned him. And you would not be there to see it with me, so there is little point in it, to my mind. Why should you sit abandoned and alone while everyone else celebrates?'

And so he was here with her, and kissed her hair now, his hands gentle and careful about her still tender body. 'I used to think of you when I was in danger, and my only regret was just the same as yours – that we had been separated so cruelly when we had had so little time together. All I wanted, all I want, is to be with you and our children, to make a life. No doubt there will be other victories to celebrate, and we will all enjoy them together.'

'More victories mean more war,' she said, leaning back against him. 'We have all had enough of war, surely. There is no appetite for fighting to be found anywhere.'

The Duke of Ventris shook his head, his silky locks tickling her neck and making her shiver pleasurably. 'I will believe that Bonaparte is done with France and with the rest of us when I hear from trustworthy sources that he is secure in his coffin. As long as that man draws breath, he will have an appetite for fighting and an unshakeable belief in his power to prevail against all odds. God knows he cares nothing for the deaths of others; all the thousands who worship him are merely so many chess pieces in his mind. And Elba is a few short miles from the Italian mainland: a curious choice of prison for such a man. A rowing boat with a determined crew could do it, or a fishing boat in no time at all. I fear these celebrations are somewhat premature – which is another reason I have no interest in joining in them.'

'I hope you're wrong. Otherwise we are all deluding ourselves, and have a rude awakening coming, and more tears to shed.' His words troubled her, and she had no desire to be troubled in this precious little moment together – but she knew he would not conceal his misgivings, nor tell her less than what he truly believed just because she was a woman, and his wife. She would not wish him to. They were partners, and owed each other the truth. She could not countenance any other kind of marriage now.

'I hope I am wrong too. But whatever happens, you need have no fear that I will be drawn back into my old occupation. I have done with that – apart from anything else, I am far too grand these days to get my hands dirty as I used to.'

This was nonsense, since he proved daily with his children that he was not grand at all, but she did not dispute it. 'And far too well known, I am glad to say, your grace. If there is trouble in Europe again and your invaluable assistance is needed, as I well believe it might be since they scarcely could have won the war without you, I hope it will be given from behind a desk.'

She felt his lips curve into a smile against her skin. 'Who am I to tell my clever wife she is wrong? But I have no objection to stepping back and letting others play their part. I am a family man at last, after all. What an enormous contrast in my life, love, from a year ago till now. I still can hardly credit how fortunate I have been. Then I was my family's disgrace, as far as anyone knew, living hand to mouth, facing danger and pretending I did not care, and now I am a wealthy and respected duke with a beautiful wife whom I adore, and a growing brood of children. It could almost be a dream – I had many such dreams, alone and sometimes frightened – but then I put my hands on you, warm and alive, and know that it is all real, thank God.'

His words were heartfelt, but he spoke them quietly. The little scrap of humanity who might one day be Lady Ventris in her own right was sleeping peacefully in her crib beside the bed, and must not be disturbed by loud voices. Viola had feared that the fireworks and all the other noises from the park and the streets would distress her, but she slumbered on still. Perhaps it was too soon to say, but so far, she seemed of a placid disposition, which was just as well, because it was a noisy, boisterous household that she had been born into.

Her brothers had greeted her arrival with as much enthusiasm as could have been expected. Ned had dropped a shy kiss on her dark head and looked at her miniature fingers in wonder as she clutched his hand, but Robin had shown scant interest in holding her and had said resignedly that he had known how it would be from the start, when he'd suggested puppies instead and nobody had listened.

But boys of their age could not be expected to show enormous interest in a bundle in a basket, and besides, they had been excited to fever pitch by the unprecedented preparations for the celebrations this week, with all London in an uproar. This was all the more the case because they had missed the Great Frost Fair on the Thames this past winter, as they had all been effectively snowed in at Winterflood for months, and the pair had not ceased complaining about the unfairness of it ever since. They were determined not to be cheated of any further pleasures, and had insisted on joining the crowds that gathered in public places to see the visiting dignitaries. Viola suspected that this new fervour sprang chiefly from a misunderstanding of the nature of the Russian delegation, and an unfounded expectation that they would bring bears with them. Gigantic bears of great and pleasing ferocity had apparently been a notable feature of the vast fair on the frozen river, or so the Da Costa children bragged, which was a particular cause of grievance for Ned and Robin, and would be for some time, no doubt. So far this summer, they had not seen even the smallest, meekest bear, for which she could only be grateful. But she knew they lived in hope.

It had been a busy summer, after the harshest and longest of winters, which had seemed as though it might never end. Viola had made her formal curtsey to Queen Charlotte as Duchess of Ventris once it had been possible to travel safely to London – and a very ungainly curtsey it was, perhaps understandably for a lady who had been well advanced in pregnancy by this date. The Queen had not remarked on that, if she had noticed it, but had commented that the last time she had seen Viola, she had also been a duchess, but a different one. Viola had acknowledged that this was true, but reassured her monarch that she was content with her present title, two dukes being enough for anyone. Charlotte appeared to stifle a smile, and gravely agreed that she saw it might be so. 'Your husbands are getting younger, too, and more handsome,' she'd added, looking thoughtfully at Richard with her customary intimidating stare. It was impossible to doubt that she knew a great deal more than she chose to say. 'You are to be congratulated on your enterprise, Duchess, and any further alteration could scarcely be an improvement.'

'That's what I think,' said Viola, smiling at her husband as he stood at her side, handsome in dark-grey velvet. 'I am more than content, I assure you, your majesty.'

The Queen had smiled with perhaps a touch of pensiveness, and Viola had removed herself from the royal presence as clumsily as she had arrived. In a huge hooped, high-waisted gown and tall feather headdress, it was hard for anyone to be graceful, she consoled herself. At least she hadn't fallen over, and her waters had not broken in the grand salon of Buckingham House and caused a great bustle there. Going into labour – even giving birth – in the palace had been horribly possible, and more embarrassing than could be contemplated. The long, boring day, with so much waiting about, just to speak with the Queen for a brief moment and receive her nod of approval, must be counted a success.

'It's good to have this time alone,' she said now. 'Well, not alone, but Leonie is quiet, and the house so peaceful for a change. Richard, will we ever be able to tell the boys the truth, do you think? It's been preying on my mind, since their sister's birth. It seems wrong that they should think her only their half-sister, when she is so much more. But they wouldn't understand it all now, I know that. It would be selfish and wrong to expect it of them – to burden them with the knowledge too soon. I must not be impatient.'

'Few people would accuse you of impatience,' he answered gently. 'I've thought about it too, of course. And I believe that it is up to us to make sure that there is no distinction between half-siblings, as the world will see them, and full siblings. I don't know when they will be old enough to hear the story of how they came to be born. Older than you and I were when we created them, perhaps, since I hope their young lives will be easier than ours were, with fewer pressures and responsibilities to age them prematurely. I can only hope they will be ready to hear it one day. There is no doubt that in the end, they deserve to know the truth, for their sakes as well as ours.'

She sighed. 'I must put it from my mind. It is a small worry, after all, when we have so much happiness in our lives. Who would have thought twelve years ago that we would ever manage this, to be here together, married, with our newest child, when our love seemed so hopeless for so long?'

It seemed they were both in a reflective mood tonight, as half of London ate and drank and laughed and danced and kissed a short distance away, and they stood apart from it in the shadowy room, wrapped up in each other.

'It's nothing less than a miracle,' he agreed softly. 'I hope I never grow so complacent that I take any of it, and most of all you, for granted. I do not mean to, I promise you, my dearest love.'

'Be sure that you do not,' she said, her voice catching a little with emotion, 'and I will not either.' Then she turned into his arms and kissed him. If they were missing fireworks and all manner of excitements outside, they did not care. They had each other at last.

* * *

MORE FROM EMMA ORCHARD

Another book from Emma Orchard is available to order now here: https://mybook.to/EmmaOrchardBackAd

ACKNOWLEDGEMENTS

I wrote my first novel in lockdown, over five years ago now. I would never have developed the confidence to do it without the encouragement of all the complete strangers who commented so positively on my Heyer fanfic on AO3 (and still do). But the main inspiration came from my good friends in the Georgette Heyer Readalong on Twitter/X. I'm particularly grateful to Bea Dutton, who spent so much of her precious time setting up and running the readalongs when they were very badly needed to keep us sane. The group has become much more than an informal book club, and though I can't name everyone – there are too many of us – we talk every day, on every topic you could imagine and some you luckily can't, and support each other through tough times and celebrate good ones. Thank you, magnificent Dowagers!

Thanks also to my family, Luigi, Jamie and Anna, for your invaluable support, understanding and patience.

I am very lucky to have a superb agent in Diana Beaumont of DHH. She has believed in my writing ever since she first read it in 2021, and I couldn't have a better champion. Thanks too to Guy Herbert and to everyone on the teams at Marjacq and DHH; I know better than most people how important the whole behind-the-scenes teams at agencies are.

Many thanks to everyone at Boldwood, including Emily Reader for the fantastic copyediting, and for stopping me from making a fool of myself. To Team Boldwood as a whole for your unflagging enthusiasm and constant professionalism – Amanda, Wendy, Claire, Niamh, Ben, everyone, all the time. And of course most of all grateful thanks to my enormously talented editor, Rachel Faulkner-Willcocks, to whom this book is dedicated, for very good reason. Rachel Lawston is responsible for my gorgeous, striking covers, and I can't thank her enough; and lastly (fittingly) Gary Jukes, who means I actually look forward to doing proofs, because he makes it fun.

One of the many things that makes Boldwood special as a publisher is the extraordinary spirit of mutual support that the authors share, so I'd like to thank you all, especially Sarah Bennett, Jenni Keer and Jane Dunn, for your generosity, wisdom and friendship.

Finally, if you're reading this because you've reviewed, bought or borrowed this book, THANK YOU!

ABOUT THE AUTHOR

Emma Orchard was born in Salford and studied English Literature at the universities of Edinburgh and York. She was a copy editor at Mills & Boon, where she met her husband in a classic enemies-to-lovers romance. Emma has worked in television and as a Literary Agent, and started writing in 2020.

Sign up to Emma Orchard's newsletter to read her exclusive short story "The Lost Jewel of Mayfair"!

Follow Emma on social media here:

𝕏 x.com/EmmaOrchardB
📷 instagram.com/emmaorchardbooks
📌 pinterest.com/EmmaOrchardRegency

ALSO BY EMMA ORCHARD

A Duke of One's Own

What the Lady Wants

For the Viscount's Eyes Only

A Gentleman's Offer

To Catch a Lord

A Tale of Two Dukes

You're cordially invited to

The home of swoon-worthy historical romance from the Regency to the Victorian era!

Warning: may contain spice 🌶

Sign up to the newsletter
https://bit.ly/thescandalsheet

Boldwood

Boldwood Books is an award-winning fiction publishing company seeking out the best stories from around the world.

Find out more at www.boldwoodbooks.com

Join our reader community for brilliant books, competitions and offers!

Follow us
@BoldwoodBooks
@TheBoldBookClub

Sign up to our weekly deals newsletter

https://bit.ly/BoldwoodBNewsletter

www.ingramcontent.com/pod-product-compliance
Lightning Source LLC
Chambersburg PA
CBHW011404210526
45464CB00009B/3033